Books by Maisey Yates

The Carsons of Lone Rock

Rancher's Forgotten Rival
Best Man Rancher
One Night Rancher
Rancher's Snowed-In Reunion
A Forever Kind of Rancher

Gold Valley Vineyards

Rancher's Wild Secret
Claiming the Rancher's Heir
The Rancher's Wager
Rancher's Christmas Storm

Copper Ridge

Take Me, Cowboy
Hold Me, Cowboy
Seduce Me, Cowboy
Claim Me, Cowboy
Want Me, Cowboy
Need Me, Cowboy

For more books by Maisey Yates,
visit maiseyyates.com.

A FOREVER KIND OF RANCHER

—

MAISEY YATES

HARLEQUIN
SPECIAL
EDITION

HARLEQUIN®
SPECIAL EDITION™

Recycling programs
for this product may
not exist in your area.

ISBN-13: 978-1-335-59467-9

A Forever Kind of Rancher
Copyright © 2024 by Maisey Yates

Breaking All Her Rules
Copyright © 2014 by Maisey Yates

This is a work of fiction. Names, characters, places and incidents are either the product of the author's imagination or are used fictitiously. Any resemblance to actual persons, living or dead, businesses, companies, events or locales is entirely coincidental.

For questions and comments about the quality of this book, please contact us at CustomerService@Harlequin.com.

TM and ® are trademarks of Harlequin Enterprises ULC.

Harlequin Enterprises ULC
22 Adelaide St. West, 41st Floor
Toronto, Ontario M5H 4E3, Canada
www.Harlequin.com

Printed in Lithuania

MIX
Paper | Supporting
responsible forestry
FSC® C021394

CONTENTS

CONTENTS

A FOREVER KIND
OF RANCHER

Chapter One

She was the most beautiful woman he'd ever seen. A vision dressed in pink, and somehow it made him think of strawberries, which got him to wondering if her skin tasted like strawberries.

She wasn't dancing, and she should be. Hell, Boone was wearing a suit, and he didn't much care for that shit. He didn't much care for dancing either, but this was the kind of thing you wore suits to, and danced at, so it felt like a crime she wasn't dancing.

It was his brother's wedding after all.

And he was damned happy for Chance. Really. He'd fallen in love and all that. Boone was in love too.

Had been for years. In a way that had left him cut open, hollowed out and embittered.

He respected the hell out of love for that very reason. He knew how intense it could be. How long-lasting.

He decided to remedy the fact that she wasn't dancing, because hell, he was in a suit after all.

He knew better than this. He stayed clear of her, except when he couldn't. He knew better than to approach her. She was forbidden. Because of what he wanted to do with her. To her. If all he wanted was a chance to say hi, a chance to shoot the breeze, they could be friends.

But it wasn't what he wanted.

It never had been.

Tonight this place looked beautiful, and so did she, and she was standing there alone, and that was wrong.

He ignored the warning sounds going off in the back of his head and crossed the old barn that had been decorated with fairy lights and flowers for his brother's big day.

"Care to dance?"

She looked up at him, and he saw it. That little spark of awareness that always went off when they were near each other. They saw each other way too often for his taste, and hers, too, probably. He loved it, and he hated it. He had a feeling she only hated it.

It only ever ended one of two ways. With her turning red and running in the other direction or getting pissed off and getting right in his face. As if one or the other would hide the fact that she wanted him. She did. He knew that.

Not that either of them would ever do anything about it.

They were too good.

Boone hadn't often been accused of being too good. But when it came to her...

He was a damned saint.

She lifted her hand, and the diamond there sparkled beneath the light.

"If he's not going to dance with you," Boone said, "you might as well dance with me."

And he could see it. That it was a challenge he laid out before her, and she wouldn't back down.

Wendy never backed down from a challenge. It was one of the things he liked about her.

That diamond ring was the thing he didn't much like.

And the fact that it meant she'd made vows to his best friend. Wedding vows.

Boone wanted his best friend's wife. And it felt so good he couldn't even muster up the willpower to hate it.

He didn't wait for her to answer, instead, he reached out

and took her hand and pulled her up from her chair, led her to the dance floor, and tugged her against his body like they were friends, and it was fine. She looked over her shoulder, her expression worried. And that spoke volumes. Because they were friends, as far as anybody here was concerned. Because there was nothing between them, not outwardly.

But they both *felt* it. And that was what made dancing with her dangerous. He had known Daniel for a long time. He loved him like a brother. At least, he had. Before he'd married Wendy.

Daniel, as a husband, sucked. Witnessing that had started to damage their friendship. Boone had never been satisfied that Daniel valued that marriage.

He'd never witnessed anything concrete—if he did he'd be the first one to tell Wendy—but Boone had always had the feeling Daniel took his marriage vows as suggestions when he was on the road with the rodeo.

Not only that, Daniel missed a lot of his kids' milestones, not that Boone had any kids. Not that he was in a position to judge. It was only that he *did* judge.

Because he wanted what his friend had so very badly.

"What's wrong?" he asked.

He knew she wouldn't answer that. Because she wouldn't admit it.

Never.

And maybe they never danced. But they knew this particular dance well. They'd been doing it for fifteen years.

"Nothing is wrong," she said, linking her fingers behind his neck, and he wasn't sure if she was preparing to strangle him, or trying to keep herself from moving her hands over his body and exploring him.

"You look beautiful," he said.

She paused for a second. "Boone…"

"Where is Daniel?"

"Drinking," she said, looking up at him, her eyes defiant, as if she was daring him to comment.

He didn't have to. Instead, he moved his hand just a little bit lower on her back.

Her nostrils flared, and he even thought that was hot.

"If he's drinking, then he won't miss you."

And why the hell should Daniel have her anyway? He didn't fucking care about her. Boone was almost certain that every time he went out drinking with the guys, Daniel was screwing around with buckle bunnies. There was no way he was only dancing with them at the jukebox. Boone could never bear to stick around and find out, because he would have to tell Wendy, and his loyalty was supposed to be to Daniel, but he was at a point where he didn't feel like it could be. Not anymore. And he'd told himself he could not feel that way, and he couldn't act in the way he wanted to, because he had an ulterior motive. But now he didn't care. Right at this moment, none of it mattered.

"Come with me."

"Where?"

"Does it matter?"

Slowly, very slowly, she shook her head no. And he led her off the dance floor, out of the barn and into the night. And in one wild, feverish moment, he pushed his best friend's wife back against the side of the barn and pressed his mouth against hers.

Boone woke up with sweat drenching his body.

Dammit.

For a second, he let the dream play in his mind over and over again.

It was the sliding door. The other path.

The one he had decidedly *not* taken at his brother's wedding, when he had gazed across the barn and seen Wendy looking like a snack that night.

He hadn't even danced with her. Why? Because he'd known he was too close to losing control. But in his dreams…

In his dreams he held that pretty pink slice of glory in his hands. In his dreams, he had pushed her warm willing body up against that barn and tasted her mouth.

It was so real. It was so real he could scarcely believe it hadn't happened.

Damn it and him, to hell.

He was wrung out. It was all the sleeping in cheap-ass motels.

He missed home or so he told himself. Because it was better than missing a woman he'd never actually held in his arms.

He had bought himself a ranch, one that currently had no animals on it, with a damned comfortable bed in one of the rooms—a bed he hadn't brought a woman back to yet—in preparation for his life changing. He was on the verge of retirement, because… Hell. His brothers were all out of the rodeo, so he didn't understand why he was still in. He was the last one standing. The last one who hadn't left, who wasn't with the person that they…

Well. He had no idea what the hell Buck was doing. So maybe that wasn't fair.

Buck wasn't in the rodeo—he knew that much. But he knew nothing else since Buck had cut all ties with their family.

You have to face it, Buck. It happened. There's no use sitting down and crying about it, there's no use falling apart. You have to be realistic.

Not his favorite memory. The last time he'd seen his older brother. Eighteen months his senior and the heir apparent to the Carson Rodeo empire.

Not now, though. Now the heir was Boone.

Someone had to keep the legacy going. It was in his blood.

Because, after all, the Carsons were rodeo royalty.

He nearly laughed.

Rodeo royalty in a shitty motel. Oh well. That was the life. The royalty part came from the fact that they all had trust funds, something Boone had sat on until he got his ranch outright in Lone Rock, Oregon, where he would be near his parents and his brothers… Where he would finally settle… He supposed, because there was a point where the demands of the rodeo would get to be a little bit much, and he wasn't going to be bull riding past his fortieth birthday. He could, he supposed. He could keep going until he gave himself more of a trick back than he already had.

He could downgrade himself to calf roping, keep on keeping on, because he didn't know what the hell else to do, but he did feel like maybe there was a fine art to just quitting while he was ahead.

Except when his brothers had quit there had been a reason. There had been a woman.

He got out of bed and looked at the bottle of Jack Daniel's on his nightstand. Then he picked it up and took a swig. Better than coffee to get you going in the morning.

He grimaced, his breath hissing through his teeth, then he threw on his jeans and his shirt, his boots, and walked out of the hotel.

It was the third night of the championship, and he would be competing for the top spot tonight. Finally, for the first time in a long time, not competing against one of his brothers.

Not that he minded competing against them. It was all fine.

He wondered if Wendy would be there, or if she would have to be home with the girls.

And he had the feeling he had put more thought into Wendy's whereabouts than her husband probably had.

He spent the day doing not much. Had breakfast at a greasy

spoon diner near the rodeo venue and didn't socialize, stayed in his own head, like you had to do.

He got to the arena right on time and cursed a blue streak when he drew the particular bull that he drew, because that bull was an asshole, and it was going to make his ride tonight a whole thing.

And then he saw Daniel from across the way, his friend tipping his hat to him, the ring on his left finger bright.

That was when Boone decided he wasn't going to let Daniel have *two* things that he wanted. He couldn't do much of anything about Wendy, but he'd be damned if he wouldn't get this buckle. It was only when it was his turn to get in the shoot that everything felt clear. That everything felt right. The dream finally wasn't reverberating inside of him when he got on the back of the bull—the bull who was jumping, straining against the gate.

Eight seconds. That was all it took. He couldn't afford to blink. Couldn't even afford to breathe wrong. Couldn't afford to have his heart beat too fast. Adrenaline could take him after, but not before. Before was the time for clarity.

Before was when everything became still. It was when he was at peace. At least, the most that he ever was.

It was damned near transcendental meditation.

He didn't question it.

And when the gate opened, the animal burst forth in a pure display of rage and muscle and he clung to the back of him, finding a rhythm. Finding that perfect ride. Because it was there. In every decision he made, and the way he followed all the movements of the animal. In the way he made himself one with him.

And maybe no other cowboy would relate to that way of thinking about it. For sure his brother Flint would laugh his ass off. But Boone didn't care.

There was a reason he was the last one in the rodeo, and it

wasn't just because he hadn't gone and fallen in love. It was because no matter what he loved, part of him would always love the rodeo in a way he didn't think his brothers ever had.

Part of him would always know he found purpose there. And if he won tonight, he could leave being the best. And that was what he wanted more than anything. Quit while he was on top. Quit while he could still love the rodeo with all that he had, all that he was. To leave it wanting more. To leave himself wanting more. Because what the hell was worse than overstaying your welcome?

He couldn't think of much.

He'd set out to prove himself, and he was doing it.

So he rode, and he rode perfectly. And when that eight seconds was up, he jumped off the bull. He wasn't unseated.

And the roar of the crowd was everything he could have asked for. Except the one thing he really wanted. So he let it be everything. He let that moment be everything.

Nobody was going to outride him. Not tonight.

He was number one on the leaderboard and he stayed there, for the whole rest of the night, and damned if he didn't give the people kind of a boring show. Because nobody could touch his score, and he loved that.

In the rodeo, Daniel Stevens was second.

And hell, for Daniel that was probably enough. With the Carsons, all except Boone, moved out of the way, that was a damned high ranking for Daniel.

But Boone felt mean about it. Because he was number one, while Daniel was number two, and if Boone couldn't have the other man's wife, then it seemed like a pretty good alternative prize.

There was no question about going to the bar after, because the mood was celebratory, and the women were ready to party, and Boone figured it was just the right night to find himself a pretty blonde dressed in pink, one that would make the fantasy easy. He would lay her down in that bed he'd slept in last night, and he'd find himself back in that dream, make it feel real.

He didn't feel guilty about the fantasies anymore.

He'd been doing it for too long.

But when Daniel came up to him just outside the barn and clapped him on the back, he felt a little bit of guilt. Just a little.

"Hell of a ride," said Daniel. "You made that bull your bitch."

He frowned. "I don't work against him. I work with him."

"Whatever. Seems to work for you."

"It does."

One of the other riders, Hank Matthews, sidled up to both of them as they made their way into the bar. "Does that thing weigh you down?" Hank asked, pointing toward Daniel's ring.

"Oh, hell no," said Daniel, holding his hand up. "If anything, there's a certain kind of woman who likes it."

Boone let his lip curl when he looked at his friend. "Is that so?"

"Hey, don't worry about it," said Daniel. "Just having a little fun."

And after that, the intensity of the excited crowd broke up their group. Fans, male and female alike, were all over the place, and this was their moment of glory. There wasn't a medal ceremony, instead, they were showered with praise in the form of Jack Daniel's and Jesus. Free shots and a whole lot of glory to God.

It was normally the sort of thing he loved, but he was still distracted. That dream was in his head, and then what Daniel said about the wedding ring had gotten under his skin and stuck there.

He hadn't seen Wendy tonight, and it was kind of odd, because it was a championship ride, although they were pretty far off from their home base.

Still. He would've thought she might show up.

And there were women all over her husband.

Normally, Boone would be determinedly paying attention to his own prospects. Not tonight.

There were two women on either side of Daniel, both of them touching him far too intimately for Boone's liking. And then Daniel turned his head and kissed one of them, and Boone saw red. He was halfway across the bar, on his way to do God knows what, when a car alarm cut through the sound of the crowd and the music in the bar. The door opened and some guy came running in like the town crier. "Some bitch is going crazy out there on a pickup truck."

That was enough to send half the bar patrons pouring out into the night. And when a loud smashing sound transcended the noise of the alarm, Boone found himself moving out there as well.

He stood at the door, stopped dead in his tracks by what he saw. A black pickup truck seemed to be the source of the sound, the headlights on, casting a feminine figure into sharp relief. A slender silhouette with a blond halo all lit up by the lights. She was wearing a short, floaty-looking dress, and she was holding a baseball bat. Then she picked up the bat and swung it, and made the headlights go out, casting everything into darkness like a curtain had fallen over the star of this particular show.

"What the *fuck*?" It was Daniel, behind Boone, who shouted that. "That's my truck," he said.

"And I'm your *wife*," came the shouted replied, as the bat went swinging again, and dented the truck right in the hood. "I got you the deal that got you gifted this truck, by the way, so I think it's fair enough for me to vandalize my own property."

Wendy.

Somehow, he'd known it was Wendy. Or at least, his body had.

An avenging angel, looking beautiful and dangerous, and hell…he'd never wanted her more.

Daniel pushed past him, his jar of whiskey still in his hand. "You're being a fucking psycho," he said. "What the hell?"

Wendy advanced on him, her chin jutted out, fury radiating from her. "Tell me you weren't in there with another woman."

Daniel backed up, his face going bland. "I wasn't with another woman."

"I got the most interesting series of pictures texted to me today, Daniel. And it's definitely you, because I'm intimately familiar with your *shortcomings*."

"What the hell does—"

"Pictures. Of you. Screwing someone else."

"I never…"

"Save it. What's the point faking it? You don't have a reputation big enough to try and save it. Like I said. I know every detail of you just a little too well for you to try to tell me it's Photoshop."

And then Wendy stormed right up to Daniel, pulled her rings off and dropped them in his glass of whiskey. "Keep them."

"Baby," Daniel said, reaching out and wrapping his hand around her arm, and that was when Boone lost it.

He was right between them before he even realized he'd moved. "Get your hands off her."

"Boone?" Daniel asked, looking at him like he'd grown another head.

"I said," said Boone, reaching out and putting his hand around his friend's throat. "Get your fucking hands off her."

"She's my wife."

"And you put one hand on her while you're angry and I'll make her your widow. Step back."

"You should be defending *me*," Daniel said, as he moved away from Wendy. "You know I'd never—"

Boone growled. He couldn't help it. And it shut Daniel up good.

Wendy looked high on adrenaline, her eyes overly bright.

And Boone wanted to grab her and shield her from all of this. From the onlookers, from everything. From the truth of the fact that Daniel just wasn't the man that he should have been for her.

Like you are?

No. But he hadn't made vows to her. And if he had, he would never have…

"I can't defend you if there's nothing to defend," he said.

Wendy looked around, and it was as if the reality of everything crashed over her. As if she suddenly realized what she'd done, and how publicly she'd done it.

Yeah, this was the kind of thing that got you on the news. And it was likely she'd only just realized that. And he wondered if she had driven all the way from California to Arizona riding high on anguish and anger.

He wondered if she'd even given it a second thought.

And now she was giving it a second thought. And third. And probably fourth.

But for what it was worth…

He moved near her, and she looked at him like she wished he would disappear. He didn't take it personally. She kind of looked like she wanted the whole world to disappear.

"Whatever you do," he said. "Don't regret *that*. Because it was damned incredible."

And he meant it.

"I don't have anywhere to go now." She looked numb.

"Sure you do," he said. "You can always come to me."

Chapter Two

Three weeks later...

If there was one thing Wendy Stevens did not want to do, it was depend on another cowboy. She'd learned her lesson. Some fifteen years and two kids too late, but she'd learned it.

She tried not to think about that night. The one that hadn't exactly covered her in glory. But it had covered the ground in shattered glass, and for a moment, it had made her feel satisfied.

For a moment, the images of her husband with another woman had felt dimmed, dulled, because all she had seen was the destruction she had caused to his truck. Technically, her truck.

Except you bought it with his money...

Well. That was the problem. She had given up her life in service to that man. She had acted as his agent, essentially, getting him endorsement deals and other things. He was good-looking. It had been easy to do. He was charming, that had made it easier.

Both of those things had likely made it easy for him to get women into bed too.

She was still reeling from the truth.

For a few days, she'd clung to the belief that he'd only cheated on her the one time. The time that had come with photographic (emphasis on the *graphic*) evidence.

She knew it was naïve. But it was deliberate. A form of protecting herself.

It hadn't lasted long.

Because once the floodgates of truth had been opened up, more truth had kept on coming.

Fast and swift.

More women had stories. Texts. Photos.

He'd *never* been faithful to her. Never even once. Their entire marriage was a lie. Everything they'd ever built in their relationship was a lie. She supposed the one thing she had to be grateful for was that he had been judicious in his use of condoms. One of the first things she had been worried about was what hideous disease the man had given to her, but he had sworn up and down that he'd had protected sex with all those other women.

As if that earned him some sort of commendation.

I would never do that to you, he'd said.

She hadn't even known what to say to that.

But she hadn't known what to say for a good three weeks now. That was the amount of time she'd given herself to clear up her life and find another place to go.

She had given everything to that man. When his career in the rodeo had started to take off, she'd discovered she had skills she hadn't known she possessed. She'd brokered all the endorsement deals that he'd gotten over the years. Her reputation was tied to his. Her career had been all about making money for him, and they'd put it all in one pot rather than having an official split because why would they ever need that? They were in love. They were forever.

The phrase *all your eggs in one basket* was suddenly far too clear for her liking, and yet there was nothing she could do about it.

Her eggs were in Daniel's basket.

She made a face. She did not like that.

"Mom?"

She turned to look at her daughter. "What?"

Fifteen-year-old Sadie looked at her from the passenger seat, and then twelve-year-old Michaela—Mikey for short—leaned forward. "Are we going?"

Wendy was at the end of a long dirt driveway. The one she knew would take her to help. The one she didn't want to drive down.

"Yeah. In a second. I'm just sitting here thinking about how little I like any of my options."

"You have our support," said Sadie.

"Yes," said Mikey. "It isn't your fault that Dad's an untrustworthy blight on humanity."

"Your vocabulary," said Wendy, rolling her eyes, but she was actually very proud, and beamed a little every time Mikey opened her mouth.

"It's because I read," said Mikey. "And also, because I binge-watch TV shows that are probably above my age rating."

"Let's just leave it at reading," said Wendy.

"I thought Boone was Dad's friend," said Sadie.

"He is," Wendy said slowly.

And she left out all the complications that Boone made her feel. She made sure to keep the pronunciation of those words as simple as possible. She made sure to leave any kind of subtext out of what she said. Because she had to. She had no room in her life for subtext. Not right now. And never when it came to Boone.

"So, why are we going to stay with him?"

"Because he offered." And he'd offered her a job. It was humiliating. But she didn't really have another choice. The one thing she had any kind of experience with before marrying Daniel was housecleaning. Boone said now that he was back from the rodeo, he needed a cleaner, and he had more than one house on the property, and more than enough room for her and the girls. She was in no position to turn it down. She had to take the offer.

Anyway, that night…

She kept seeing it. Over and over again. She'd been unhinged. But brave. And she couldn't help but admire herself. But also, she kept seeing the way Boone had put his body between hers and Daniel's. The way he'd been. Like fire and rage, and completely on her side.

And then the way he told her…

Don't regret it.

So she hadn't. Because Boone had told her not to, and maybe that wasn't healthy, but dammit all, she didn't have a whole lot of healthy available to her right now. Mostly she had disillusioned and confused.

"He didn't take Dad's side on this."

"Good for him."

"I admire his willingness to break with traditional toxic masculinity," said Sadie.

"Well, don't go giving that much credit," Wendy said. "He *is* still a rodeo cowboy. He just happened to…bear witness to some things."

The brief text conversation she'd had with Boone after her grand performance in the parking lot had confirmed that Daniel had been well on the way to cheating on her that night too.

At that point, she had known it was a routine thing.

Any guilt she might have felt eventually over smashing up the truck had been effectively squashed at that point.

There was no room for regret in the well of rage created by Daniel's own actions. If he didn't like the way she behaved, he should have been different. From the very beginning.

"I need something to get back on my feet. And I think we all need a fresh start. This isn't where we're going to stay forever but…"

"It's pretty," said Sadie.

She had expected her daughters to be a little bit angrier about leaving California than they were.

They'd lived in Bakersfield, and it didn't often feel like there was a lot happening there but heat and drought. They complained about both, often. And they seemed to be in places with friends where they were glad for a fresh start and a change of scenery. She couldn't help but wonder if some of it was the pain of having Daniel break up their family. And maybe leaving rather than having to tell everyone about it was easier. At least, that's how it was for her.

Their life had been quiet and stable. He might've been out chasing glory, but she hadn't been. To her, their life had been glory.

But it hadn't been enough for him.

She should've known.

He wasn't home all that much. When he was, they'd had a healthy sex life, but she had honestly just imagined that he was like her. That he turned it off when she wasn't there, like she did with him.

That's oversimplifying things, isn't it?

She gritted her teeth.

Maybe.

Maybe it was.

But she was happy for oversimplification right now. She needed it.

As if simplification didn't cause some of this mess in the first place.

So she started up the car engine and continued down the road that would take her to Boone's house.

When the house came into view, her stomach twisted. It was weird, because it was Boone. And she didn't need to go getting wound up about her own inferiority complexes, or her memories of growing up poor. Her memories of being a have-not in a sea of haves. Of her mother being the one who cleaned and now she was...

It wasn't the same.

Not because she was ashamed of her mother. She wasn't. She never had been. The difference wasn't in the work, it was in the person needing the work done.

Those people had all fancied themselves better than her mother. And that wasn't Boone. And it never would be. It wasn't why he had asked her to come.

He felt guilty, she knew that.

She also wondered how much he had known for all those years...

Well. You have plenty of time to talk.

Seeing as she would be living on his property and cleaning his house.

"Wow," said Sadie.

The house was beautiful. Even more beautiful than the one they had left behind in Bakersfield.

Their house had been elaborate. Because it was the kind of fancy Daniel liked. It had been positioned across from a field that was just empty.

And now she kind of felt like it was a metaphor. A dream house surrounded by a whole lot of nothing.

Empty. Like his promises.

She ached, and she couldn't quite work out exactly what she was feeling. If it was heartbreak or the sting of having been tricked. If it was betrayal or the loss of her marriage. Or simply the loss of her life.

She didn't know. Maybe it was all those things. It seemed like each moment one of those things felt more prominent than another. And then it would shift.

She didn't have time to think about anything shifting at the moment. What she needed to do was get her game face on.

She pulled the truck up to the front of the house and turned the engine off.

Okay. It was just Boone.

And something about that made her feel every inch a liar.

There was no *just Boone*. There never had been.

He'd been a particularly problematic thorn in her side for years.

Mostly because...

Of one moment. A very clear and terrifying moment—the minute she had first seen him.

She and Daniel had only been married for two weeks. It had been a whirlwind romance, and she'd been head over heels, and pregnant far too quickly, so they'd had a shotgun wedding, though Wendy had never felt forced.

She'd wanted it. She'd wanted to secure that life. She hadn't wanted to be a single mother. She'd found an easy man. A fun man. A happy man.

Her life had felt lacking in those things, growing up with scarcity was a feeling Wendy was very sensitive to.

Daniel had felt like excess. Excessive joy, excessive drinking, eating, happiness. She'd loved it. And when their love affair had had consequences...he'd been kind and he'd done the right thing.

He'd told her he loved her.

She'd said she loved him, because it was best if they did, and eventually she was sure she'd meant it.

And then she'd gone to the very first cowboy thing she'd ever done with him, and Boone had walked in, and it was like everything in the world had fallen away. Like something inside of her had whispered, *This is him*.

She had never in her life believed in the concept of the one. Ever. But right when Boone had come in, it was like the universe had whispered across her soul. That it was *him*.

She had never been so completely devastated by the impact of another person in all her life. He was ruinous. And glorious.

And the moment she had first seen him, she had wanted to *not* see him just as quickly.

Had wanted to go back to living a life where she had no idea Boone Carson existed in the world.

It was just easier if she didn't know.

When she was married to another man. Pregnant with that man's child.

She had told herself that all of it was silly. Boone was handsome, that was all. And she'd been surprised by the impact of him.

You didn't expect to see a normal man like that just…out and about in the world. That was all.

She was very, very good at telling herself that story.

She loved Daniel.

She had loved Daniel.

Did she still love Daniel?

Right now, she felt hollow.

She loved her daughters. She knew that much.

She let out a long, slow breath.

That was going to have to be enough, because it was going to be the thing that was driving her now.

She missed her anger.

It had been so bright and glorious and wonderful. And far too fleeting.

But it had fueled her for a while there and now she was just…

Well, she was at Boone's house.

She sucked in a sharp breath and killed the engine on the truck. She got out and the girls followed suit. Then she went around to the bed of the truck to start gathering their bags.

Boone walked out the front door.

"You made it," he said.

She stopped, and she wished she didn't feel like she'd been hit by a train, because she did. Just looking at him. She'd known him now going on fifteen years, and she couldn't understand how or why the man still did this to her.

"Yes," she said. "We did. Kind of a long drive."

"Not as far as Arizona." The corner of his mouth lifted.

She didn't smile back. "Yes." She moved to the bed of the truck to grab her bag, but he started moving toward her purposefully.

"You don't need to get anything," he said, and then he reached into the back of the truck and plucked up her bag, her daughters' bags and a suitcase, which he lifted up over his shoulder. "Your place is just a walk out back here," he said, gesturing behind his grand house.

She stared at him. At the way he held all her baggage so easily.

It was a very weird metaphor to be confronted with right in this moment, and was it bad that she wanted him to carry it all? Was it bad that she was tired? That she wanted him to carry her worldly possessions in his strong arms and over his shoulders because she was just so damned tired of…everything?

Yes, it's bad. You need to figure out how to stand on your own. That's your problem. You let a man carry you for too long.

Well, that wasn't fair. Daniel hadn't carried her, but she'd wound herself around him so tightly that cutting ties was painful.

Difficult.

But it wasn't the same as being carried.

But she figured she could also chill out and not see her literal baggage as a metaphor. Because physically Boone was stronger than her and he knew where the house was, so why not follow him?

"How was the drive, girls?"

"Good," said Mikey, "we played the alphabet game and also discussed elaborate ways men should die."

"We didn't do that," said Wendy quickly.

"Wouldn't blame you if you did," said Boone.

"Not *you*, of course," Sadie said.

"Appreciate it, Sadie," Boone responded.

Boone had always had a decent rapport with the girls. It was weird that right now it made her feel…lightheaded.

But Boone had been that fun uncle figure when he'd been around, which had been often enough, and of course the girls enjoyed him.

It turned out their dad also thought of himself as a fun uncle. Which really didn't work when you were supposed to be a husband and father.

The path behind the house led to a cottage. It was small, with freshly planted flowers all around the front, and two hanging baskets with flowers on the porch.

It was beautiful. Small, she wondered if the girls would see it as a major downgrade. But right then…she saw it as salvation.

It was hers.

Theirs.

For now.

"Thank you," she whispered, her throat going tight.

She looked up at him, and her breath caught. His blue eyes were startling, arresting, there in the sunlight, and the way the gold played against the whiskers on his face did something to her stomach, low and intimate. His face was just…perfect. As if an artist had lovingly sculpted him by hand with the intent of making him the perfect masculine figure.

His jaw was square, his nose straight, his cheekbones so sharp she could cut herself on them. And then there was his body, which she'd spent a lot of time not contemplating and she surely wasn't doing it now, with her daughters present.

She freed the breath from the little knot in her throat and got herself together. She didn't need this kind of drama. Not now.

"This is so cute!" said Sadie, her voice going high, and the delight in her tone shocked and pleased Wendy.

"It's like a fairy house," said Mikey.

Wendy had to wonder if her daughters were being overly happy for her benefit, but then she decided she didn't care.

They'd been so supportive of her through everything.

If they'd been younger, she'd have tried to shield them. But the thing was, she'd sort of made the news.

"Scorned Wife Goes Full Carrie Underwood Song on Cheating Husband."

It was all over the country music news sites, given the rodeo circuit was sort of adjacent when it came to industry interest crossover, and also because, indeed, she had *sort of* had a certain set of song lyrics in her head when she'd driven across state lines.

Lucky for him it was more "Before He Cheats" and less "Two Black Cadillacs."

The article had actually made that point.

But because of that there had been no shielding the girls from the truth. She could have handled herself better, though she had a feeling there would have been some news about it anyway since Daniel was a minor—very minor—celebrity who both rode rodeo and had done some reality TV, so the breakup would never have stayed entirely between them.

"I'm glad you like it," Boone said.

He walked up the steps and pushed open the door and revealed a house that was immaculately put together. Everything in it was new. And she had to wonder if it had been furnished like this when he bought the place or…

She decided to stop wondering.

And just enjoy the experience.

Tomorrow she was going to get the girls off to school,

and she was going to start work. She would give herself four weeks of this. Of taking Boone's help, and then she was going to need a plan. A real plan.

She was resourceful, and she was a hard worker, so she knew she would be able to come up with something. But it was hard to do when you also had deep wounds that needed a little healing.

And also had to be an adult and a mother when you just wanted to keep on being subject to the whims of your emotions. Being that woman, the one with the baseball bat, had been easier than being this woman. The one making plans and trying to hold it together.

But that was what she needed to do; it was who she needed to be.

For her girls if nothing else.

"I'll leave you to get settled," he said. "If you need anything, just give me a holler."

And then he put their things down and left them, shut in the little house that felt somehow indescribably safe, secure and...wonderful.

Like shelter from a storm she hadn't realized she'd been in.

Right now, she could rest.

Even cleaning his house for a few weeks would feel like rest.

And then she would have to figure out what to do with her life.

But until then, she was going to take the shelter he was offering. Since the man she'd made vows to had kicked her out into the elements.

So why not have this? Even just for a time.

"Why don't we get our things put away and then explore town?" she asked.

She knew Lone Rock was small, and the exploration wouldn't take long, but they needed to find some food, and a distraction would be good for everyone.

Her daughters smiled at her a little too bravely, and right then she hated Daniel. Because he'd done this to them.

"Great," she said. "This will be great."

"You did *what*?"

"I gave her a place to stay," said Boone, looking down the bar at his brother Jace, who was staring at him incredulously. His sister-in-law Cara leaned over the bar and stared at him as if she was waiting for more details.

"What, Cara?" he asked. "There's nothing to say."

"I don't believe that," she said. "The whole breakup was headline news, and he's your best friend."

"He is *not* my best friend," said Boone. "I *was* friends with him. More importantly, I was friends with the man I *thought* he was. But I didn't think he was out there betraying his wife every week out on the road."

"You really didn't know?" Chance, his other brother, who was seated next to his wife, Juniper, asked.

"No," he said.

And he left off the part about how he'd never *wanted* to know because it wasn't simple and never could be.

"Sounds unlikely," said Shelby, his other sister-in-law, from beside her husband.

Shelby and Kit had recently had a baby, but Boone's mother was always so happy to babysit that the happy couple could go out whenever they wanted. And were practically forced out by the well-meaning grandma even when they didn't want to go.

All his siblings—except Buck, as far as he knew—were coupled up now. And the only couples *not* present were his younger sister Callie and her husband, Jake, who lived out of town, and his brother Flint and his wife, Tansey, who was a famous country singer currently on tour. Flint was with her.

Talk about revenge songs, Tansey had written a hell of a song about her and Flint's first go-round that had made him infamous. Flint would probably have measured words for the whole situation since he knew how the media could whip up personal issues.

But Flint wasn't here, so no one was being measured.

"Good for her, I say," Shelby said to her husband. "But I'd leave your truck intact and take it. Your dick on the other hand…"

"Same," said Juniper.

It served his brothers right for marrying sisters who were as pretty as they were badass. Boone loved them. He loved it even more when they gave his brothers hell. His brothers seemed to get something out of it too.

His brothers had all married pretty badass women.

Bar owner Cara was no shrinking violet. And Tansey, well she'd gotten rich with her revenge, and made his brother infamous in the process.

He thought of Wendy and how fragile she'd looked today. He'd wanted to tell her he'd done all that for her. The flowers, the new paint, the new furniture. He also hadn't wanted to say a damned thing because he didn't want her to think she owed him, and he didn't want her to thank him for something a man ought to just do for her because she was there and breathing and *her*.

He didn't want to do anything to crack her open when she was working so hard at holding it all together.

She was badass too. Hell yeah, she was.

She'd smashed the hell out of Daniel's truck.

But she was also wounded. And she needed to be taken care of.

He couldn't say he'd ever had experience with that, but if he was going to push the boat out on caregiving it was going to be now and it was going to be her.

"Did it really go down like they said?" Jace asked.

"It did," he confirmed. "But if you see her around, don't ask her about it."

Cara snorted. "We aren't feral."

Jace gave her a long look. "Well…"

"Okay, but we do know how to behave and not hurt people's feelings," Cara said.

"I know," Boone said. "But she's not going to be here forever. I'll talk to her more tomorrow about her plans."

Because if there was one thing Boone was certain of, it was that no matter how much he might want it to be, this couldn't be forever.

He might love her. He did love her.

But she was still married, and he didn't have the first clue how to…

He'd never had a real relationship, and there was no way this would ever be what she needed.

She had kids.

He had a ranch, which was a step into adulthood, but he didn't know how to do feelings and all that. It was one thing to carry a torch for a woman he couldn't have.

He was good with not having her.

One thing he wouldn't do was leave her uncared for.

He would make sure everything in her life was set to go just as she needed it to be, and then he'd let her go, because it would be the kindest thing.

She didn't need another project.

He wouldn't be the cause of any more pain for her.

If he was certain of anything in this world, it was that.

"She's with you?"

He regretted answering his phone as he walked out of the bar.

"Yes," said Boone. "And if I see you, I'll run you right off my property."

"What the hell, Boone? I thought we were friends."

"And I thought you were a husband, but it turns out you're just a little boy who can't control his dick."

"Boone… I'm sorry, I have to get her back. I royally screwed this up. I can't live without her and the kids."

The change in tone did nothing to sway Boone. Because he just didn't care. He wondered if Wendy would, though. Daniel was the father of her kids and all that. Boone didn't have kids, and the thought didn't sway or soften him at all. But he figured that could be because it was a connection he didn't especially get.

It maybe wasn't up to him to decide that Daniel should never speak to Wendy again. But he wasn't going to facilitate it, that was for damned sure.

"You should have thought of that before you cheated. Extensively, from what I understand."

"It was separate to me," he said. "I never thought of it interfering with what we had as long as she never knew. When I was home, I was always with her."

And I'm with her every time I'm with anyone.

I'm with her when I'm home. When I'm on the road.

Always.

He didn't say any of that. But he wanted to jump through the phone and strangle Daniel.

"She deserves better than you," Boone said, his voice rough.

"What? She deserves you?"

And that cut him deep because right then he knew Daniel wasn't as oblivious as he pretended to be. He only played like it when it suited him.

But of course he couldn't be as dumb as he played. He was a pretty big success and that didn't come on accident.

"No," Boone said. "But she does deserve someone who's honest with her."

"Is that why you brought her out to your place? Have you been screwing my wife, Boone?"

"When the hell would your wife have time to screw around on you, Daniel? She's busy raising your kids and holding your life together. Say what you want about me, slander me all you want, but don't project your bullshit onto her."

Boone hung up then.

He shouldn't have, maybe.

Because if Daniel was going to make up a story about him and Wendy it would probably only be reinforced by him hanging up like that.

But he just didn't care to speak to that asshole for another second.

He couldn't bear it.

Instead, he drove home, and when the phone rang again, he ignored it.

Chapter Three

The alarm went off too early and Wendy wondered at the wisdom of making the girls start school right away. Or at all.

If they were only going to be here a month…

But maybe they'd stay in Lone Rock for longer. Or maybe not. But it would be normal for them to have a school day and ultimately, that was what she wanted. For them to have something that felt normal.

She couldn't promise them a long time here, or forever or anything close to that, but she could give them something that felt like childhood.

She'd discovered last night that the fridge was fully stocked, and she wondered who had done all this. Boone? It didn't seem likely since he'd said he needed a house cleaner and had acted like he couldn't perform basic tasks without help because he was so slammed with setting up the new ranch.

Maybe one of his sisters-in-law had helped.

She'd have to thank someone for it. For the miracle of waking up to having coffee in the house and having bacon and eggs to fix the girls.

And she really didn't count on Boone showing up right when they were about to walk out the door.

"I thought, if you'd like, I could drive you because I know the way to both schools."

And she could have figured it out with GPS, she knew, but she very dangerously wanted to take this easier option.

Couldn't she? For just right now?

"Okay, if…if the girls don't mind."

"Sure," said Sadie, casually.

Because why would she care? This was definitely Wendy's issue, not her kids'.

"Yeah," Mikey said, reinforcing that thought.

The girls climbed into the back seats of the crew cab pickup, and Wendy got into the passenger seat. Suddenly, when he closed the door, the cab felt tiny, and she tried to remember if she'd ever been in such close proximity to Boone before.

She hadn't. She'd remember.

She did remember being at Juniper and Chance's wedding, because Daniel knew Chance from the rodeo and they'd been invited, and it had an open bar, he'd joked. She'd been sure then that he really wanted to support his friend's love and happiness. Now she thought it might have really been about the bar.

She remembered Daniel being out drinking and being alone at the big wedding reception.

She remembered looking up and seeing Boone. Looking at her.

Not just looking at her, though, it had been something hotter. Something deeper.

It had stolen her breath and made it impossible to breathe.

It had made her feel…

She had to stop thinking about that now.

She had to.

She kept her eyes fixed on the two-lane road and tried not to let the silence in the truck swallow her whole.

"Well, if you need anything or you need me to come get you, you can text me," she said, addressing both her daughters with an edgy desperation because she needed something to take over her awkwardness, even if it was a random comment she hadn't needed to make.

"Thanks, Mom. I'm sure we'll be fine," said Sadie.

"Or we won't be," Mikey said. "And it will either be a story of great triumph of the human spirit, or our villain origin story."

"I think we know which one it would be for you, Mikey," Boone said.

"Villain, for sure," Mikey said, happily.

The middle school came first.

As they drove away after Mikey got out, Wendy was struck by a feeling of loss and a sense of weird wrongness. She always felt that after summer break, and apparently a new school did that to her too. This weird feeling that she was leaving her kids with strangers. They weren't strangers. She'd had video meetings with the teachers before they'd come here, and the kids had had a chance to meet them too. But it didn't make it feel less weird.

She had the same feeling after dropping Sadie off.

But it was replaced instantly by the electric shock of realizing she was alone with Boone.

Alone with Boone, without her wedding rings. Without her kids.

Without anything keeping her from…

"So, what do you need done today?" she asked, because filling the horrible silence with words, any words, was all she knew to do.

"Oh, I'm easy," he said, slow and lazy and she felt it between her legs.

What was wrong with her?

Was this a trauma response to discovering her husband was a ho?

She would be able to write it off as that much more easily if Boone wasn't a preexisting condition.

Something that made her feel, deep down, like maybe she'd deserved for Daniel to betray her.

The thought made her feel like she'd been stabbed.

She hadn't realized she'd been holding on to that feeling. But she had been. Deep down.

She'd been attracted to Boone for years, and she'd done her best to avoid him. Not that avoidance had done anything to make the feelings go away.

She'd done her best to keep it hidden.

Maybe Daniel had known, though, that part of her had always been tangled up in Boone.

She needed to stop thinking about that.

Why did you come to him, then? Knowing it was this complicated, why did you choose this?

Because he'd offered.

That was all.

It was never all. It was never that simple with him.

She took a sharp breath. "I just want to make sure that I'm paying you back, because you're being so kind to me and..."

Tears welled up in her eyes and she hated that. Now she was crying? What was happening to her?

Why couldn't she just take what he'd offered, which had been work. And she'd been grateful he'd done it that way because if he'd just given her a place to stay it would have felt loaded, and like charity she couldn't afford to take, and he hadn't done that because he'd known. She knew he had known. That she couldn't take his charity, that she had to earn this fresh start.

That she couldn't feel like she owed him.

So why was she now falling into crying like it was a favor? Like it was personal.

They were both trying so hard to not make it that and now she'd gone and made it very, very weird, and she couldn't stop her throat from tightening, couldn't stop a tear from falling.

She hadn't cried.

Not once.

She'd gone from rage to determination and she didn't want to weep now. But it was the kindness of it all.

From a man she'd love to call just another rodeo cowboy.

A man she'd love to lump in with her husband.

But she just couldn't do that.

"I need to know what you want," she said, trying to get a handle on her emotions. Her breath. Everything. "Because you offered me work, and I do know how to keep house. Do you need a meal? Do you need something organized?"

"I just moved in, and there are a lot of things yet to unpack."

But the little cottage was perfectly set up.

"I can do that if you don't mind me deciding where things go."

"As long as you tell me where they end up, I don't mind."

"Okay, so what do you like to eat?"

"If you want to make me dinner I won't complain but do something you and the girls like and just make an extra portion."

She almost wished he was being high-handed. So she could get ahold of herself.

The kindness was almost too much.

You really can't be pleased.

Well, maybe in her position that was fair?

They pulled up to the house, and she realized she hadn't been conscious of where they were at all.

He killed the engine, but didn't get out of the car, and she did something foolish. Very foolish.

She turned her head and looked at him.

And it was like all the space around them became less. Like it contracted and sank beneath her skin. Shrinking around her lungs, her heart, her stomach. She couldn't breathe. She couldn't think.

She could only see Boone.

His blue eyes.

That moment at his brother's wedding when they'd seen each other across the room was suddenly alive again in her memory. Because they'd seen each other that night. They hadn't simply looked at each other for a moment across a crowded space.

The two things were different.

They were so different.

She hadn't truly realized it until now.

She tried to breathe, but she couldn't. Because everything in her was too tight. Too bound up in him.

Bound up in him…

And that did it. Like scissors cutting a string. Everything in her released.

Because she'd thought about being tied up in someone just recently.

It was the very way she'd thought about her relationship with Daniel.

She hadn't left to get tied up again.

She couldn't afford that, not ever.

She found herself practically dumping herself out of his truck, her boots connecting with the dirt and sending a cloud of dust up around her.

"I'll go get changed and then start work," she said, trying to sound bright, and like nothing had happened.

"Okay," he said. "Do you need me to show you the lay of things?"

"No. No you go ahead and get started on your day." She didn't want to wander around the house with him.

She wished she could pretend.

She wished she could pretend that her strange moments of attraction were indigestion. Or at the very least that they were infrequent, or one-sided.

But if she'd ever been able to trick herself into thinking her attraction to Boone wasn't mutual, he'd destroyed that with a glance the night of his brother's wedding.

Because that moment had contained so much deep truth, she'd had to turn away from it.

Because that moment had been filled with an acknowledgment they'd both spent fifteen years turning away from.

They'd been two seconds of prolonged eye contact away from admitting it, for all those years. Never speaking of it wasn't enough. Because their eyes were determined to give them away.

Then the hitch in their breath.

And Boone…

She remembered him looking like the big bad wolf and the savior of the universe all at once. She'd wanted him to take a step toward her, and she'd wanted him to turn away. She'd wanted him to come for her, and she'd wanted to pretend she'd never even met him.

He'd taken a step.

And she'd taken one back.

And he'd stopped.

He'd listened to her. To everything she couldn't say. To the single footstep that had been her begging him to stop. To not take them another step further because it would be too far to turn back, and she'd wanted—she'd needed—to be able to turn back.

Just like she'd needed to jump out of the truck now, and he'd let her. She appreciated that.

The way he listened, even when she didn't speak.

"I'll just… I'll just go change," she said again. "And then I'll get started."

His face was like granite. Like at the wedding. "Okay. See you later."

She couldn't have made it any clearer that she didn't want him in her space today. She also couldn't have made it any clearer that she was attracted to him.

Attracted was a crucial descriptor. Because it was different from wanting.

He wanted her.

He wanted to take her into his arms and kiss her. He wanted to take her to his room and strip her naked and have his way with her.

He wanted her.

Like breathing.

More of a need than anything else.

She was attracted to him, and she did not want it. Not at all.

And he…well, he knew his place here. He was helping her. He cared about her, dammit all. And he was far too familiar with the fallout that happened when people didn't fulfill their obligations to the ones they were supposed to love.

She'd trusted Daniel and he'd betrayed that trust. Boone would never do that. He would never put her in a position where she felt obligated to him.

That wasn't why he was helping her.

He never shirked his responsibilities. Not ever.

He didn't leave people to fend for themselves.

That might be his oldest brother's way, it might be Daniel's way. But it would never be Boone's.

Some people might live in a fantasy world, and others lived with their heads up their asses. Not Boone. He was a realist, and he handled things. He didn't need to lie to himself or anyone else to get through life.

He'd been like that once. Someone who couldn't face the hard truths. It caused more harm than good, that was for sure.

He thought about that, a whole lot. The lines between attraction, desire, want, need and feelings. Obligation. All while he worked. Mostly he thought about her. Because she was in that house behind his, and it was the kind of proximity he'd wanted with her for a long time.

His phone buzzed in his pocket.

He pulled it out and saw Daniel's name again. "What?" he growled.

"Can you just ask her what I can do?"

"If she isn't answering your calls then there's not shit I can do for you."

"We went through hell together, Boone. Who was there for you when you were crying drunk over your brother taking off, huh? When you were the one who had to deal with your mama's broken heart because her firstborn ran off, after all the pain she went through losing her baby girl…"

"Don't talk about my family," he said. "Yeah, you were there for me when Buck ran off, I'll give you that. You were there when I was feeling squeezed by the family obligation he left for me, but here's what you're missing, Dan. Buck and I will never have a relationship again because he had a duty to this family, and he chose himself instead. I don't like it when people misuse and mistreat people in their lives. When they fall down on their obligations. I can't respect weak men, and if you don't live up to your responsibilities, you're a weak man." He breathed out, hard, and his breath was visible in the early evening air. "You're a weak man, Daniel Stevens."

Then he hung up, because honestly.

He got into his truck and drove back toward the house. It had been a long day of chasing up permits at the county, making arrangements with contractors and going over the sections of land he could use for grazing, what he could irrigate and a host of other things.

Setting up the ranch wasn't going to be easy. But until his dad retired…

Well, he supposed he'd be taking over as rodeo commissioner in a few years. And he had to do something until then. Maybe after that he'd do what his dad had always done and hire out workers.

Buck had been the one who was supposed to do all this.

But Buck was gone.

Boone knew his brother had been through some shit, he did. But it was no excuse. At least not in his mind.

Even if you were going through something, you should be there for the people in your life. Your responsibilities didn't just…go away.

He'd told his brother that, the night before his brother had split town for good. Buck had been drinking, far too much. Like alcohol would erase the accident he'd been in. Like it might take away the horror of that night.

And Boone had snapped.

"You have a family, and you aren't dead. Stop acting like you're six feet in the ground with your friends. You aren't."

"It should have…"

"It wasn't! You're alive. Have some gratitude and get back to it. You have responsibilities."

And then he'd gone.

Boone had felt guilty about his brother leaving until he'd realized guilt was a waste of time. Time he didn't have to waste. It had been Buck's choice to leave. It was Boone's choice to deal with it.

There was no use getting lost in what-ifs.

Boone knew, from the outside looking in, people would probably think of him as a guy who didn't take much seriously.

They saw a cocky bull rider who could have a different buckle bunny every night when he was in the mood for that. They didn't see he was the one who held his mom while she wept on difficult anniversaries.

He was the one who took the brunt of their father's expectations onto his shoulders as the de facto oldest in the absence of the eldest son who had gone off to lick his wounds. A car accident the year Buck graduated high school had resulted in the loss of three of his friends, with Buck as the sole survivor.

It wasn't that Boone didn't get why that had fucked him up.

It was just…

They were all a little messed up. They'd watched their baby sister die when they were kids. So why not band together? Why not try to support each other?

That was what he'd never understood.

They'd been a support system, the Carson Clan, and never as close or as stable once Buck had taken his support away.

But his issues weren't the order of the day.

Today Boone wanted to make sure that Wendy was doing all right.

He pulled up to the front of the house and he smiled, just a little bit, when he saw the lights on in the kitchen. He wondered what it would be like to come home to her, and then he pushed that aside because it was a pointless little fantasy, and if he was going to have a fantasy it was going to be a big, dirty one, not a little domestic one about her in an apron holding a casserole pan.

Except he wouldn't even let himself have a dirty fantasy about her, not right now. She was too vulnerable, and he wasn't that guy. Not when her husband had proven to be such a horndog.

He wouldn't even go there in his head.

He walked up the front steps and into the warmth. This was his house. His home. He hadn't had one before, not really. It had been a place on his parents' property, and places on the road all these years, and it was all fine and good, but there was something surreal about walking into something permanent.

Nothing is permanent, Boone.

Yeah, he knew that. Not relationships with older brothers, or little sisters, or anything.

You couldn't trust a damned thing.

But when he walked in his house it smelled like heaven. And his kitchen was empty.

There was a plate sitting on the counter with foil over the

top, and he assumed she'd done the cooking here, but took the rest back to her place and then vacated before his return which…was about right.

Attracted. Not wanting.

He lifted the corner of the tin foil and his stomach growled when the smell of roast and vegetables hit him.

Wendy might not be here, but a home-cooked meal was a close second. And when it made his mouth water, he could have it. So, there was that.

He opened the drawer in the kitchen island and took out a fork, and hunched over the counter, taking bites of food. And then there was a knock at the door.

His stomach went tight, and his heart did something he couldn't recall it doing before except when he was about to ride a bull in competition. "It's open," he said, around a piece of roast, and without moving from his spot.

"I didn't know if you'd be here yet or not."

Wendy. And she was lying. Because she'd probably seen him come in and that was why she was here. Because she'd wanted to avoid him. Except she didn't really.

He could relate.

She came into the kitchen, and she was holding a plate with something on it, but he couldn't look away from her for long enough to take in what it was. She was wearing pink. The same shade as the dress she'd had on at the wedding.

Her blond hair was in a ponytail, and she had on just a little makeup. Her cheeks were the same color as her dress, and so were her lips. Like a strawberry fantasy just for him.

Even though she wasn't for him.

There was something about it that made him want her more, and he had to wonder if that was just his body pushing back at years of being good.

Very few people would characterize Boone Carson as good. He understood that and he understood why.

Again, it was the bull riding, drinking, carousing, and on and on. But they didn't see all the shit he did *not* do. Like turn away from hardship in his family. Like running away. Like kissing his best friend's wife at his brother's wedding.

He deserved a damned Boy Scout patch.

Did Not Fuck My Friend's Wife.

Also knot tying.

He was good at knot tying.

He didn't get credit for the things he deserved to.

"I baked a cake over at the cottage while the girls and I had dinner, so I figured I'd bring you some."

Oh. Cake. That's what it was. He could see it now, even if it was fuzzy at the edges because he'd rather look at her hands holding the platter than at what was on it. But she'd made it, so he would eat it.

"Are you really eating standing hunched over a counter like a rabid wolf?"

"I don't think rabid wolves eat pot roast, I think they eat pretty women carrying cake."

He shouldn't flirt with her. But her cheeks turned pinker. So he considered that a win.

"Maybe just a regular wolf, then."

He grinned, making sure to flash his teeth. "Hard to say."

"You should sit down. There are studies on how you shouldn't eat standing up."

"Are there?"

"I'm pretty sure. It's something I'd say to my kids, anyway."

"Oh, well, then, I guess I'll consider myself chastened."

She glared at him. "I don't think you are."

"No. You need shame to feel chastened, I think."

"And you don't have any shame?"

He made sure to grin even wider. "None whatsoever."

If only that were true.

If only he didn't care so damned much about doing the

right thing, and at this point it had nothing at all to do with Daniel. It was about her.

And that was immovable, as far as he was concerned.

"I really…" She closed her eyes for a moment, and he looked at how her lashes fanned out over her high cheekbones and felt a bit like his heart had lifted to the base of his throat, and his lungs right along with it. "I appreciate you doing this," she said, opening her eyes, letting out a breath.

It was like she released his breath along with it.

Then she walked over to the kitchen island and set the cake plate on it. There was nothing more than a slim length of counter between them now.

She put her hands on the counter and examined them.

He did too.

Her hands, not his.

"Why wouldn't I?"

"Daniel has been your friend for longer than you've known me," she said. "You didn't take his side."

"There's no side here," he said. "To be very clear, I was done with him the minute I…that night, before you got there, he kissed another woman. I had never seen that before, I swear to you. And I looked the other way, I'll admit that. There were things I didn't want to know, because…" This was dangerous ground. They both knew it. "You know why."

"Do I?" she asked.

The words were too loud in the silent kitchen, even though they were practically a whisper.

"Yes," he said. "You do."

He cleared his throat. And took another bite of roast. Then he looked at her again. "I tried to keep myself out of your marriage. But I wouldn't have after I saw that, okay? I want you to understand. I was outright done with him the minute I knew he wasn't faithful to you. I told him so today."

"You…talked to him?" Her blue eyes went round.

"Yeah. He called. He wants you back."

She laughed. "Of course he does. I cook, clean and manage his career. I am an idiot who devoted years of my life to him and gave him two kids and asked for very little and when he wasn't with me, he was able to pretend I didn't exist. Who wouldn't want that woman back?"

She shook her head. "I'm not going to be her anymore."

He didn't have any place in this. Didn't have the right to lecture her, but he was going to do it anyway.

"Don't blame yourself. I didn't see it either. Like I said, I had some suspicions I shouldn't hang around and watch to see what he did with his evenings, but that's different than actually believing someone is a serial cheater. It's about him, and what he thinks about the people around him. How much he values them. Not how much value they have."

"Thank you, Boone," she said, though she didn't look at him when she said his name.

How many times had they circled each other like this?

There were so many moments over the years.

So many barbecues where they talked with a table between them and very little eye contact. So many rodeo events where Daniel would leave to get a drink and they'd be standing there, and it was like electricity. But the thing was, they'd never moved toward it.

They both knew it was there.

And that was the most unfair thing of all.

Daniel was the kind of guy who'd hump a table leg. He strayed just because he could.

Boone wanted Wendy in a way that went beyond anything normal, average or everyday. What he felt for her had been instant. It had been ruinous.

It had destroyed something in him he'd never built back up.

Desire like that wasn't common. It wasn't typical.

And the man standing in their way, the man who was still

in their way because of the position he'd put Wendy in…didn't deserve the label of roadblock because he wasn't important enough. Because she hadn't meant enough to him.

What they'd resisted for the sake of responsibility was something you could write a song about.

And Daniel didn't resist a damned thing.

But even without any loyalty left to him, Wendy was facing starting over, with her girls. She was in Boone's care, and Boone would never take advantage of that.

"You're welcome. I promise when I eat the cake I'll sit down."

She did look at him then. "Good."

He started to move around the side of the island, he didn't even think about it, but then he watched her eyes get round, watched her posture go stiff, and he stopped.

If he got too close to her…

"Good night," he said, firmly.

"Good night."

Attraction wasn't the same as wanting.

He had to remember that.

Chapter Four

She felt breathless still the next morning, and all the way through taking the girls to school, and definitely when she walked cautiously into Boone's house to begin the day's chores.

There was quite a bit to do because the man wasn't settled into his house at all. There were boxes to unpack and things to organize and it was nice to lose herself in the satisfaction of a small task, easily completed in a short amount of time. Each little section—kitchen utensils, plates, cups, clothes, toiletries—was its own kind of satisfying.

It was also intimate, though, and she had to stop herself from running her fingers slowly over his T-shirts as she put them away.

Which was perverse behavior and she needed to quit.

She needed to focus on the fact that at least today, right now, there were small things she could make better.

Because Lord knew everything else felt like too big of a mess to even look at right now. So she closed the door on what she'd left behind, and what was up ahead, and she focused on folding Boone Carson's laundry.

That should demystify him.

He was the sexiest man she'd ever seen, and when he'd looked at her last night across the kitchen island and taken a step toward her, in the space of a breath she'd gone from being in that moment, to imagining what it would be like if he took her in his arms and...

Folding his socks should make that go away.

It was all fine and good to look at a man and think he was a sex god when you weren't handling his woolen boot socks.

Though here she was, socks in hand, still breathless.

This should be exposure therapy. She and Boone had had no choice but to try and avoid each other through the years. There were moments where she'd felt guilty for sharing a long look with him, because sometimes those looks were so sexually charged, they left her feeling more aroused than actual sex with Daniel.

It was a terrible thing to admit—or at least it had been.

And so she'd done her best to avoid ever acknowledging that sticky truth.

Part of her had wondered, though, if some of his appeal was that he was a fantasy. Daniel had always seemed affable and easy. She'd never thought of her husband as a bad boy— ironic—but Boone had seemed…edgy.

Raw.

There was something about him that called to unhealed places in her. To darkness she'd never felt like she could express with Daniel. He wanted his life to be easy. They had money and security in the grand scheme of things, so he didn't much want to hear about the way hunger pangs sometimes gave her flashbacks to a childhood of occasionally empty pantries.

How she'd had to mend the holes in her hand-me-down clothes.

How she'd spent her summer days alone in an overheated house because her mom had to work and there was nowhere else for her to go.

How, on those long hot days, she'd gotten good at hiding when the landlord came trying to chase down rent.

Daniel didn't like to hear about those things. They didn't matter. They were in the past.

She'd thought—more than once—that Daniel couldn't handle the idea that there were issues inside her that weren't solved by being married to him. He wanted to be everything to her. To have fixed everything.

It had never really occurred to her what narcissistic nonsense that was until that very moment, with Boone's wool socks in her hand.

She thought of Boone. The way he had looked last night. Intense and close. He was always intense. But there was usually something between them. Something other than a countertop. Her marriage. Her dedication to her vows. Her love for her husband. Because for all that she had wanted Boone from the first moment she had laid eyes on him, for all that it had felt significant and real and like something bigger than she was the first time she'd seen him, she had always loved Daniel.

She sat there, feeling the silence of the room pressing on her. Did she love Daniel?

No.

And it wasn't the infidelity that had done it.

Suddenly, it was like the truth was raining down on her, as if invisible clouds above had opened up and let it all come down.

They had been disconnected for a long time. She loved her life. She had loved their house in Bakersfield, even though it was hot there. Even though there was a big empty field across from them.

She had loved her routine of taking the girls to school. Of bringing them home. Cooking them dinner. She loved the freedom she had, the financial security that had come from his career as a bull rider and the way she had managed it. She had loved that her daughters didn't have empty pantries and long days at home by themselves. In that sense, she had been the happiest she'd ever been. But she didn't think she had been the happiest she'd ever been when he was home. It wasn't that she'd been unhappy when he was around, she just didn't think he was the main part of that happiness.

When he was away she could do whatever she wanted. She got to binge-watch TV shows and wear ratty pajamas. She had ice cream out of the carton and she took up the middle of the bed.

She was content with her fantasy life when he was away, and she didn't mind being by herself.

And none of those things were signs in and of themselves that she didn't love her husband. It was only that she could be a little bit more honest in this moment than she'd been able to in those first couple of days. She wasn't heartbroken. She had felt deeply wounded by the fact that she had lost her life. That she had lost these things she cared about so deeply. That her life had been compromised and shaken.

That she was thrown back into the space where she didn't know how she was going to survive. And she had never wanted her daughters to experience that.

She had never wanted them to feel any instability, and she was the most upset about that. And being betrayed. That had been a knife wound straight to her chest. That had been unconscionable. She really and truly hated it. She didn't like that she had been lying next to a man, making love to a man, telling a man she loved him, while he was able to take those hands, that mouth, that body and make love to another woman.

She would never have cheated on him. Not ever. She would've coasted along in this marriage that functioned primarily because…

Even though she had never betrayed him, she was in many ways functioning as a single woman when he was gone. And she had a feeling that was part of why their marriage had worked as well as it had.

He pretended she didn't exist when he was away, and she sort of did the same to him.

That didn't make her feel guilty, it just made her recognize that some fundamental things were missing from her marriage. And maybe that was why Boone had loomed so large in her fantasies.

She had done her best—her very best—to never fantasize about Boone.

She was *attracted* to him. But she didn't lie in bed when Daniel was away and think about Boone intentionally when she lay there and put her hands on her own body while imagining they were his.

Now sometimes he popped into her head, and she replaced him with Captain America because it was totally fine to fantasize about a man you weren't married to, but he really should be a man you also didn't know in real life. At least, that had been her arbitrary set of rules.

Every woman needed an arbitrary set of rules.

She did not need to follow those rules now.

Daniel had rendered them void.

That made her feel hot. She shifted, and she put Boone's socks down a little bit too quickly. Yes, she could fantasize about Boone now if she wanted to.

She didn't love her husband.

Suddenly, she felt dizzy. She didn't know if she was elated or if she was crushed by that realization. But she had been living a life she hadn't intended to find herself in. Daniel's betrayal was not the biggest issue with her marriage.

The problem was, they had met and they had fallen in love quickly. And Wendy had always been guarded. But he had gotten through her defenses with his charm. She hadn't been one for casual sex. She'd been waiting, and not because of any great moral reason, but because she was afraid.

He had gotten past all of that, and when he had asked her to marry him two months into their affair, she'd said yes. She didn't have anything else. Her mother had passed away the previous year, and she'd just felt so alone. So being with some-one... To make a family, she had loved that.

And she had to wonder how much of it had always been loving that. Loving that she had someone. Someone she was attracted to, someone she genuinely liked—most of the time—but perhaps someone she had never actually been head over heels in love with.

She didn't want him back. She wanted the stability back. She wanted to be comfortable. But...

But if she were being perfectly honest with herself, she was thinking about more than comfort. That moment with Boone in the kitchen last night had been so electrically charged. And the way he had responded to it was... It was unlike anything else she had ever experienced.

Because he had been watching her. And more than that, he had seen her. He had responded to the way she had stiffened up, the way she had resisted.

And it was only because she knew if he had gotten any closer she would've kissed him. And more than that, she knew the minute she and Boone touched it was never going to stop at a simple meeting of mouths. Their clothes would be off in-stantly, and...

That terrified her. Because she was trying to start over, and she was trying to find something new. Because once she had imagined herself in love with a man because she had been at a crossroads in her life, because she had been afraid and inse-cure. Because she had thought it would be preferable to grab hold of the first man she slept with rather than be by herself.

And she didn't want to go from one relationship straight into another.

It doesn't have to be a relationship...

Now she really was being an idiot. She had to stop think-ing about that. She had to.

She picked the socks back up and started folding again,

and then she heard a sound downstairs. She stood up from the bed, the socks still clutched in her hand, and went down the hall, looking over the rail of the staircase down to the front door below.

Boone was in the doorway. He looked up at her, a cowboy hat placed firmly on his head. And right now, at this point in her life, the sight of a cowboy certainly shouldn't make her tremble.

"Hi," she said.

"Hi, yourself."

"What are you doing here?"

"I decided to come back for lunch today."

"Oh. Let me… I'll make something for you."

"You don't have to do that."

"I'm not taking charity from you," she said.

"I didn't ask you to."

"All I'm doing is very slowly folding your laundry," she said, holding up his socks.

"All right. Well, I hate to interrupt the very serious business of sock folding. But if you really want to make me a sandwich…"

"I really do."

She went down the stairs, and every step she took closer to him made her heart start to beat just a little harder.

Damn that man.

And damn her for being so…thrilled by it. She felt like a teenager. The kind of teenager she had never been. Because she had never indulged in flirtations, and she had certainly never experienced that wild, reckless feeling she heard people describe when they were in situations where no one was there to stop them from doing something stupid.

She felt it now. There was nothing to stop her from closing the space between them and wrapping her arms around his neck. There was nothing to stop her from touching him.

Nothing. Except for good sense. And the fact that there was no way she could carry on a physical-only affair under the watchful eyes of her far-too-perceptive daughters.

And there was no way she was going to put them through something like that when their lives had just been upended.

So yeah. Nothing stopping her.

It made her want to laugh.

She had behaved for her mother, of course, who had been deeply afraid of her becoming a single mom and struggling the way she had.

And now she had to behave herself for her daughters. Caught in between a mother-daughter relationship always, she supposed.

It can be a secret.

No. They would figure it out. That was just asking for the kind of sitcom hijinks she did not want to be embroiled in anymore. She'd reached her limit. Dirty pictures being texted to her of her husband's affair, and her busting out his headlights, were either a police procedural or high comedy, depending on how you looked at it, and she wanted no part of either.

"What's for dinner tonight?" he asked.

"Spaghetti," she answered.

He grinned, and she felt like he'd touched her.

She looked away and beat a wide path around him to the kitchen.

"I could get used to this," he said.

"I probably shouldn't stay more than a month," she said, reiterating what she'd told him before. On the phone. Before she had agreed to come.

"The cottage is awfully nice, and it's there for you as long as you want. Don't feel the need to move on quickly."

"I don't think I can stay for too long. I don't want to get... dependent."

"Is that really why?"

"That is the only reason we should discuss."

He nodded slowly. And she could see he was holding back. It was a strange thing to say. Because Boone was strong, and he was fearless. Because she'd watched him ride in the rodeo before, and he wasn't a man who ever hesitated. But there he was, holding back. And she knew it wasn't because of him. It was because of her.

Because he cared about how what he might say affected her.

And that touched her deeper than just about anything. Because she'd been married to a man who hadn't given a second thought to how his actions would affect her.

To what she felt, to what she cared about.

Boone cared.

"There's not a *should* anymore," she said.

Except there were. So many. And they both knew it.

"What's that code for?"

"Say what you're thinking."

"Be very sure," he said.

"I'm sure."

"You don't want to stay because you're afraid of what will happen between us."

She felt like a layer of her skin had been peeled away, but she nodded slowly. "Maybe."

"I don't think there's any maybe about it. It's been two days, Wendy. Two days and I swear to God if I come too close to you…"

"I know." She was suddenly desperate for him to stop talking. And she realized now why he held back.

"I won't, though, is the thing. I need you to know that. I recognize that what he did to you is going to have you messed up for a while. I don't want to be part of that. I don't want to be part of this… Hurting you. I don't especially want to have anything to do with him. You understand that?"

"Yes," she said.

"I would never do anything to take advantage of you right now. Or ever."

His words were raw. And the most real thing she had heard in so long. After so much bullshit.

"I appreciate that."

It was such a weak statement. And it didn't tell the whole truth. Or even part of it. *Appreciate* wasn't the right word for him. It never could be. It was much, much too insipid.

She felt torn apart looking at him. And mostly, it was regret. Regret that she couldn't afford to feel. Because she had the life she had. And the truth was, without Daniel in it, it was so good. She had Sadie, and Mikey, and they were wonderful. She would figure out what to do, and it wouldn't always be a struggle. She had confidence in herself now, confidence she didn't have when she'd been younger, and it hadn't been given to her by Daniel, so it couldn't be taken away by him.

She couldn't regret those things. And yet, she looked back on that moment when she had first seen Boone, and she felt… pain. This deep wish that she could go back in time with two doors in front of her. Two men. That she could walk toward one and not the other. If only those moments had joined up. If only they had been side-by-side.

If only Daniel hadn't been first.

But then she might not have confidence because of him, but she had made the steps she'd made in life in part because of her relationship with him, and she could never take him away and expect that she could have been the same person she was now.

So regret was pointless. But appreciation wasn't the right word either.

Because Boone made her feel bruised. And swollen with need. All kinds of it. And she felt…tired. And where before that exhaustion had made her want to let Boone carry her bags, carry her burdens, now it made her want to let her guard down.

Because it just took so much strength to be near him and not get nearer. She hadn't realized how much strength it had taken all these years, but they were closer now. Closer than they'd ever allowed themselves to be, and that created a situation, or rather it exposed one she hadn't fully realized she'd been in.

She went to the fridge, and she got some mayonnaise. Some lunch meat. Then she got bread and tomatoes. And she began the very mundane work of making the man a sandwich. This was on the heels of having done the very mundane work of his laundry. She had none of the excitement with him. None of the electricity. And all of the chores.

And that should demystify him. It should make this feel as bland and dry as appreciation. As thanks for helping her out, and nothing more.

She got a knife out of the drawer and she began to spread mayonnaise on a piece of wheat bread. Truly, what could be more boring?

"I like a little mustard on that."

"Oh," she said.

She turned back to the fridge and opened it again, hunting around for the mustard.

"You said you wanted to make me a sandwich."

"I do."

"But you don't want me to tell you how I want a sandwich?"

"I didn't say that."

"But you're annoyed."

"I'm not annoyed."

Maybe she was. Maybe she had kind of wanted to intuitively guess exactly what he wanted on his sandwich. She blinked. That was a very odd thing to want. A strange thing to worry about.

"Listen," he said. "At the end of the day, I would probably like it however you wanted to make it. But if you want a little instruction…"

"Who says that I like to take instruction?"

"I'm sure you don't."

And here they were, standing in the man's kitchen in the middle of the day. The sunlight streaming in through the window. There was no sexy mysterious lighting. A broad shaft of light was going across his face. But it only made him look more handsome. He was the sort of man who could withstand being on a big screen with high-def. She was sure of it.

He didn't have a flaw in his features. He was perfect in every way.

And so even the broad light of day couldn't diminish it.

"Tell me, then. Tell me how you like it."

His smile shifted, turned wicked. And they might not be in a bedroom, but his eyes held the suggestion of it.

She took the mustard out of the fridge.

"Just make sure you've got a firm grip," he said.

"For God's sake, Boone."

"What? You wouldn't want to drop a bottle of mustard."

"I guess not."

"Give it a good squeeze."

"Boone," she said, not sure whether she wanted to laugh, or get irritated, or... If she was a little bit turned on. That was ridiculous.

"Just trying to help with best kitchen practices. You can lay it on a little thick."

She rolled her eyes because she decided faux irritation was better than melting into a puddle over this kind of thing.

She turned the bottle over and squeezed a generous helping onto the sandwich.

"Just like that, Wendy."

His voice was like silk, and the sensation it sent along her nerves was glorious.

"I don't need encouragement to make the sandwich."

"All right."

She got the tomato and sliced it, then laid it on along with some turkey. And then she handed him the sandwich with no ceremony. But when he took it from her, their fingertips brushed, and her breath was sucked straight from her lungs.

He looked at her. And he really looked. Saw her. Looked into her. He took a slow bite of the sandwich, and there was something about the way he did it, purposeful, and intense, that made the space between her thighs throb.

She shook her head and turned away from him.

"It's a good sandwich," he said.

"You're welcome," she said.

Doing housework for the man felt like sex. And that seemed unfair. Because it should defuse things. Everything. This reminder that he was normal. That he was a human. That he could never live up to whatever fantasy her body was convinced he would give. Because how could he? No man could. No man could live up to the ridiculous thing she had built up in her mind.

Or rather, tried not to build up.

"So you only want to stay here a month," he said.

"Yes. That was my thought."

"And what do you want to do after that?"

"I don't know."

He set his sandwich down on a paper towel on the counter. And then he grabbed hold of the loaf of bread and took two pieces out. "Do you like mustard, Wendy?"

"No," she said.

"Mayonnaise?"

"Yes."

"Okay."

And then, slowly and methodically, he began to make a sandwich. This one without mustard. And she could only stare at him because she didn't know why it made her want to cry. Because this was such a small thing. Because she was supposed to be working for him, and he was doing things for her, and she had made him a sandwich, and they could've easily made their own, but he was making one for her.

And it just seemed exceptional. Maybe it shouldn't. Maybe that was the biggest commentary on her marriage to Daniel so far.

That she wanted to weep as she watched strong, scarred masculine hands put turkey between two slices of bread.

He handed it to her, and she did her best to swallow the lump in her throat.

"Thank you."

"You're welcome."

She took a bite of the sandwich. "I don't know what I'm going to do," she said finally.

"But not this."

"No," she said. "Not this. My mother cleaned houses. It's a good job. It's a great job. I don't look down on anyone for any kind of work that they do."

"But you've been looked down on."

She nodded slowly. She felt exposed, and he could see that. Quite so easily.

"Yes. I have been. I grew up in a community where being the daughter of a cleaner made me a certain thing to other people. Mostly, the worst part about my mom's job was that sometimes the people she worked for tried not to pay her. And that would create gaps between paychecks. And she was never quite in a space where she could just walk away from that work, not while they were dangling money owed over her head. There was no protection. No rights. No power. It's the kind of thing you never forget. And I never wanted to be in that position. I never want my girls to be in that position. And here I am. We don't have a prenup or anything, and I know he's going to have to pay child support of some kind, but the truth is I earned so much of his money for him. Right now, I don't want it. I want to wash my hands of him and walk away. But I know that in the long run that isn't the best decision. I know it isn't going to serve me. It isn't going to serve my daughters, so it isn't the way I can treat this situation. But I want... I want to find myself. I want to *be* myself. Whatever that means."

"I know who you are," he said. "You're the woman that showed up with the baseball bat and smashed the hell out of that asshole's truck. Even though you could've gotten in trouble for it. Even though it destroyed a perfectly good vehicle. You've got a lot of passion. And you're right, you have a lot of what you have because of that passion. Because you got him all those deals, because you were so good at building him up. And what did he do with that? Tried to tear you down. If you need anger to motivate you, to kind of guide your way... why not use it?"

"Well, the problem is, I'm not all that angry right now. I'd like to be. But anger just implies a level of passion I'm not sure is there. I felt scorned. I felt tricked. And that made me mad. I felt disrupted. That made me mad. I'm not heartbroken, though."

Something in his eyes sharpened. "Really?"

"Really."

This was dangerous. She had tried to steer them back into something mundane. Tried to think about socks and turkey sandwiches, but he had gone and changed everything when he had made the sandwich for her.

Her husband had found it a turnoff for her to talk about her past. And yet here he was, listening to her, and he didn't seem turned off.

"No. Because I think that I love the life I had as a result of my marriage a lot more than I love my marriage. Or maybe seeing a picture of him quite literally sticking it in another woman did it for me. That could also be it."

"I'm sorry. It was a terrible thing."

"It was. But you know the truth… There have been very few moments in my marriage when I haven't wanted another man. You know that."

She was being so dangerous right now. So very dangerous. "And I might not have acted on it… But the truth remains… I was with Daniel and the whole time I wanted someone else."

"Yeah," he said, his voice suddenly gruff and strangled.

"I was poor," she said. "And I've been shaped by that. The way you saw me react to my divorce, it was all the anger that had built up inside me all those years. All that hunger. Because I know what it's like to have an empty pantry and I never wanted that for my girls. Because I didn't have a father growing up and I didn't want that for them either. So I clung to the shape of my life because it was the shape I wanted, even if the content was never quite what I had fantasized about it being. It didn't matter. I found a man, and I thought that was going to keep me safe, so I clung to it. And even though I know better, I've seen better—in all these years I've learned I don't need him to keep me safe, I don't need him to make me money— I was afraid that by walking away from the marriage I was walking away from security. And so, when he ripped it out from under me, I was furious. Because I felt like he was taking from me the one thing I cared about the most. My security. That was why I was so angry."

"As you should be," he said.

"Does it bother you? To think of me that way."

"In what way?"

"Does it bother you to know that the woman you met, the woman who was dressed nicely, who looks like she's never known a struggle, isn't real?"

"Why the hell would that bother me? You're strong. And I like that about you. I always have. Did you really think I was responding to a certain brand of cowgirl boots? Did you think I was responding to the rhinestones on your jeans? I don't give a shit about that. It's your backbone. There are a lot of beautiful women, Wendy, but I haven't spent fifteen years fantasizing about what it would be like to get them naked. It isn't just how pretty your eyes are, or the shape of your mouth, though I think it's beautiful. It isn't just the way your tits look in what I assume is a pretty expensive bra. Though I like that too. It's not your ass. Though again, I like it."

His words were the single most erotic thing she'd ever heard in her life, and maybe that made her simple, but she didn't care. She just did not care.

"It was always the spark in your eyes. It was always that little bit of wicked in your smile. The way your ass moves because of the way you walk, which has nothing to do with the shoes or how expensive they are, but with the way you carry yourself. You're strong. And he never gave you any of that. And he does not have the right to take any of it away. No. Finding out that you were broke when you were young doesn't turn me off. It just explains what I saw in you already."

"He didn't like to hear about it," she whispered.

"He's a weak man," he said, restating it.

"And you're not."

"I'm just a man," he said. "I'm a man who wouldn't dream of turning away from my responsibilities, not on the level he has. But also, I don't take on shit I can't hang on to. I don't try to carry something I can't hold."

That felt like a warning more than a promise. And she should be grateful. Because she knew it was foolish to go straight from a marriage into another relationship. Hell, it was foolish to go straight from a marriage into Boone's arms, but suddenly it seemed like maybe it was a stupid thing *not* to do.

"Fifteen years," she said. "That's how long it's been since I walked into that bar and saw you," she said. "That's how long it's been since I…since I looked down at my wedding ring and wanted to take it off. I didn't want to do that all the time. Not for the whole fifteen years. But pretty much every time I was with you. I wanted to break my vows for the chance to know what it was like to have your hands on my skin, Boone Carson. Do you know what kind of insanity that is?"

He moved closer to her, his blue eyes blazing. And there was no counter between them.

"Yes. Because it's the same kind of insanity I felt since the moment I saw you. Forget friendship and all of that. Because I just wanted you."

"I had kids with him," she said.

"I know," he growled. "Do you have any idea how much I hated that? Knowing... Knowing just how tied to him you were. Your girls are great, don't mistake me. And I'm not saying that I should've been a husband or father or anything like that. But I am saying... Damn, honey, I wasn't gonna go here. I wasn't gonna touch you."

"You still haven't."

"I'm going to, though, you know that."

"It was inevitable. From the beginning."

"Maybe I should thank him. For being the one to blow it up. Because we don't have to."

She shook her head. "We wouldn't have."

"Are you sure? Because I'm not. You've been here two days. And here we are. Being just a little too honest."

"You made me a sandwich."

"So?"

"Yeah, I asked myself that same question. Why should that matter so much? Why is it so damned impactful that a man is showing me basic concern? Because it's what I've been without. Because I had a marriage, but just the framework of one. We were business partners, and sometimes I think we liked each other. We had sex, and it was fine. I gave myself to him when I was nineteen, and that was just that. I thought I had to stick with it. Because I didn't want to be pregnant and alone. Because

I didn't want to have the life I grew up with anymore, and I didn't want that for my kids. I sure as hell wasn't gonna blow it up just because I wanted to tear some other guy's clothes off."

"I want you," he said. "I want you, and I understand that you don't want me."

She was immobilized by that. "What does that mean?"

"You're attracted to me, but you don't want it. You don't want me to take your clothes off. You don't want me to kiss your lips. You don't want me to taste every inch of you. And you sure as hell don't want me inside you."

She couldn't breathe. His words were tracing erotic shapes through her mind's eye, things she was never going to be able to unseat. To un-imagine.

"I don't understand…"

"Because if you did, you'd be across this room already. Because you know what's holding me back. It's you. I cannot be part of hurting you. And I cannot be part of taking advantage of you, and I sure as hell can't have you thinking you owe me. And it doesn't matter that I know you're attracted to me. I know something is stopping that from becoming want, because if it was *want*, then the want is on both sides. And it would be enough to push us together."

"I have the girls. And I just think that if…"

And she knew that it was a lie. The moment those words passed her lips. Even thinking about whether or not it was smart and all of that, it was just excuses. She didn't want to get hurt. She didn't want to get burned by the intensity of the thing between them. She had discounted common sense once for a man, and ended up married to someone who had never been faithful to her. So this was all about fear. It was one thing to want Boone when she couldn't have him. It was quite another to have him and contend with what that might mean.

With where he might fit into her life, or with where she would want him to fit into her life even if he didn't.

But she knew one thing.

That she had fifteen years' worth of complicated regrets. Like trying to pick broken glass out of a piece of cake. And she just didn't want any more of that. There had been good things about her marriage. Even though she was hurt by it now. Even though it wasn't going to last forever. Even though it was over.

She had her girls. She had some work experience. She would find a way to use the things that her marriage had given her. Even as she moved forward without her husband.

But she didn't want Boone to be a regret. Not anymore. He'd been one, deeply, for fifteen years. And that was what she didn't want. More than anything. More than she wanted to be protected. More than she wanted Boone to be a safe space. And yes, when she had first shown up at the house, she had maybe wanted safety more than she wanted him. For a minute.

Because it was wonderful to have him remove the burden. Wonderful to have him give her a place to stay. Wonderful to have him carry her bags.

But she would leave. She would leave in four weeks, just like she'd said, and she would start fresh on her own. But she would know. She would know what she'd been missing all this time, and he would be resolved. She deserved that. She needed it.

"I do want you," she whispered.

She took a step toward him, her heart pounding. Nothing was stopping her. And she was giddy with that. Giddy with a sense of freedom and wildness.

And it was like years had been lifted off her shoulders. Not just the years of marriage, but the years that had come before it. The years of feeling like she had to be good. Better. To avoid ever stepping into the trap of poverty again. To avoid food insecurity and homelessness and all the things she had grown up so terrified of. The things that had shaped her. And yes, they had made her strong, but sometimes she was just so tired of being that kind of strong. She didn't want to do it anymore. And he made her feel, in that moment, like she could just be. Like there was nothing but now. Because there were three hours until she had to go get the girls from school. Because her wedding rings were gone, and her vows meant nothing. Because he didn't look at her and see somebody who deserved to be treated like less because she had been through something difficult.

Because he had listened.

And all those things combined to make her feel free.

And she knew what she wanted to do with that freedom.

Nothing was holding her back.

And for the first time, she reached out and she touched Boone Carson.

Chapter Five

Wendy's hand on his chest was so much more erotic than anything he ever could've imagined. His heart was pounding so hard he thought it was going to go straight on through his rib cage. And then she would be able to hold it in her delicate hand, and that would seem about right. That would seem like the appropriate fee for this gift. This gift of her delicate hand against his body.

They had been foolish to think it wasn't going to end here.

Maybe they had needed to be that foolish, for a time.

God knew he had.

He had needed to construct a ladder made of lies so they could climb up to this moment.

Because the truth would've sent them both turning away.

Thank God for the lies that had brought them here.

He wanted to savor the moment.

This moment *before*. When it was like storm clouds were all gathered up ahead, swollen with the promise of rain, but not a single drop had fallen. Where the air had changed to something thicker, more meaningful. Thick with promise.

The promise of her mouth on his.

In only a few moments he would taste her. And when he did, he was going to part her lips, slide his tongue in deep.

But he hadn't yet.

And it was the promise that kept him poised on the edge of a knife. That kept him on high alert. The promise of strawberries, the forbidden, and the need that had been building in him for fifteen years.

He was in no rush for the first raindrop to fall.

He could live in this moment forever.

Except then her touch shifted. Except then, she moved her hand up to curve around the back of his neck, the touch erotic, purposeful. Glorious. And the minute her fingertips made contact with bare skin, it was too much. It was electric. And all his control snapped.

The rain began to fall.

He wrapped his arm around her waist and brought her hard against him so she could feel him. Feel his need. Feel the way his heart was beating almost out of his chest, feel how his cock had gotten hard.

For her. His breathing was ragged, pained. And he knew she could hear that, feel that. The way his chest hitched, the way his breath tried to cut his throat on each and every exhale.

She swallowed hard, and brought her hand around just beneath his jaw, traced it, down to the center of his chin.

"Wendy," he whispered.

She licked her lips, and that was it. He lowered his head and brought his mouth down onto hers.

The impact of her mouth under his was shocking. He had kissed any number of women. More than he could count. Innumerable.

But that had never been this.

No woman's mouth had ever been this.

It was Wendy, and she was imprinted into every cell of his body.

Her mouth was so soft. And she didn't taste of strawberries. It was indefinable, wonderful her. It was nothing else. It never could be.

It had been the easy way out to imagine there was another flavor to compare her to. Something he could hang on to on late nights when he was unsatisfied. A lie. And one he had needed. The same as he could lie to himself and say that having sex with a gorgeous blonde might do something for that need.

Of course, it didn't. Of course, it never could. Because that was just sex. And this was something else.

It was something more. Much more.

Sex was as cheap as vows that weren't kept. This was precious. Real. Deep.

It pulled a sound straight from the bottom of his soul like dying, like hope, like pain and glory and wonder, all rolled into one.

He cradled her head with the palm of his hand as he leaned in, took the kiss deeper.

His heart was pounding so hard he thought it might be a heart attack, and if it was, he would accept that this was his moment to go and be happy with it.

He'd ridden on the backs of angry bulls intent on grinding him into the arena dirt beneath their hooves. He'd won competitions and lost them. His sister had died. His brother had left. He'd felt his heart pound with adrenaline, ache with loss, burn with anger.

And this was somehow more, and better and worse, all at once.

It was new.

Boone had given up on ever feeling anything new again in his whole jaded life, but this was bright and shiny and wholly unique.

This was Wendy.

Not a kiss.

An event.

His mouth shifted over hers, and it nearly brought him to his knees. He tasted her, deep and long, and as much as he wanted this to go fast, to see her naked, feel her naked, be inside her, he also wanted this moment to go on forever. Just like that breath before the kiss.

He wanted everything all at once. The anticipation, the glory of need and the thunder of satisfaction.

But he didn't have the control to hold back, so he tasted her deep, though he kept his hand firmly on the back of her head, and the other wrapped hard around her waist, because if he let himself explore her...

It was Wendy who moved her hands over his shoulders, down his back, then his chest.

It was Wendy who let her fingertips skim down his stomach, and then skimmed his denim-covered arousal.

His breath hissed through his teeth, and he felt like she'd lit a match against him.

He lifted her off the ground, holding her heart against his body as he continued to plumb the depths of her mouth.

He knew what it was like to desire somebody. He knew what it was like to be physically aroused. This was past that. It surpassed everything.

This was something new altogether. Something intense and raw and more.

It was the thing he had always both craved and wanted to close the door on forever. Something altering and destructive that he felt far too familiar with.

Because how many times in his life had the landscape of his soul been rearranged? Torn apart?

He hadn't wanted to do it with her.

And yet, there was an inevitability to all of it. Something that couldn't be denied. And he wasn't going to deny it, not now. It was only that he was very, very aware this wouldn't simply be sex. But something more altogether. Something he had never experienced before.

It was Wendy.

And there was no use comparing her to anyone else. No

use comparing the way his need for her tightened his gut, made his body so hard it hurt, made him tremble with the need to be inside of her. Because there was nothing worthy of drawing comparison to. There was nothing like her. And there never could be.

He moved his hands down to her thigh, gripped it and lifted her leg so it was bent over his hip, then he moved her back against the kitchen island so he could press himself against her, let her feel, at the center of her need for him, just how much he wanted her. She gasped into his mouth, and rolled her hips forward. "Yes," he whispered against her lips.

And he knew he could get lost even in this. And moving his body against hers fully clothed, like they were a pair of desperate teenagers. And he would find pleasure in that. Because already, he had found more satisfaction in his mouth on hers than any previous sexual encounter had ever brought.

Maybe this was delayed gratification. Maybe this was just the way it went when you wanted somebody for years and couldn't have them. Maybe this was the release of self-denial followed by action. Or maybe it was simply Wendy.

He couldn't answer the question, or maybe he just wouldn't.

He would leave it a mystery. Intentionally. Wound up in a tangle he could easily undo if he pulled at the right thread. He knew where the right thread was.

But there were some mysteries best left tangled.

And that was the truth.

But there was no need for deeper truths than the one passing between their lips now, and there was no need for honesty any deeper than the raw need that coursed through his veins. It was enough. And anything more was likely to destroy them both, and it would be nice if, at the end of all of this, they could stand on their own two feet.

Because he didn't want to reduce her, and maybe even more

than that, he didn't want to reduce himself. He wasn't a saint, after all, and he had never claimed to be.

He was simply a man. One who was held in the thrall of the desire he felt toward the woman in his arms.

And even though he could've stayed like this forever, he didn't want something juvenile and desperate to mark the first sexual encounter between them. He wanted it to be her, and him, and nothing in between.

So he lifted her up again, and began to propel them both toward the stairs.

She clung to him, lifting her other leg and wrapping them both around his waist, holding fast as he propelled them both up, and then down the hallway toward his bedroom.

And he knew he would have to address the subject of barriers, especially because she'd been with a man she couldn't trust, and it was going to take a deep amount of trust to want to be with someone like that again.

And he would never violate her trust. Not out of desire, not out of selfish need. Not for any reason at all.

And he would never be lost enough in his own arousal to lose sight of her.

Because she was the reason. She was the answer to the question. She was the fuel for the fire raging through him now, so how could he turn his focus inward? He couldn't. Ever.

When they got to his bedroom, he set her down gently on the foot of the bed, and knelt before her, lifting his hand to cup her cheek. "I have condoms," he said.

"I have taken every test known to man recently out of an abundance of caution."

He nodded. "I trust you. But you don't have any reason to trust me."

She looked at him, her blue eyes seeming to go deeper than his skin. "I don't have any reason to trust Daniel. But you've never given me a reason to not trust you. You gave me a place to go, and I know you didn't do it so we would end up here. I trust that. I know nothing you did was to manipulate me. To use me. You've never been anything but honest with me, Boone."

"I want you. Without one. I don't want anything between us. But I will do whatever you need to feel safe."

"Well, I'm protected from pregnancy. So if…"

That did a weird thing to him. To his gut. Because the idea of Wendy being pregnant with his baby didn't make him scared or upset at all.

It made him feel something else altogether, and *that* made him a little bit scared. Made him a little bit upset.

"Good. Then we don't need it."

He moved away from her and stripped his shirt up over his head.

This was happening. And it was everything he wanted.

He just had to make sure he survived it.

Chapter Six

Wendy couldn't keep her eyes off his bare chest. He was the most beautiful man she'd ever seen. He always had been. Even with her doing her best not to examine the fine architecture of his body, she had noticed.

How could she not?

He was so glorious. So utterly perfect. And shirtless, he was… He was a phenomenon. He was the kind of stunning that could only be compared to a mountain range, looming in the distance, glorious and transcending all other natural wonders. Broad and brilliant, the musculature of his shoulders, his chest, his stomach…

She had always known the desire between her and Boone went somewhere beyond mere physical attraction, but for the moment, she just marinated in the absolute masculine perfection present before her. For he was something else altogether than she'd seen in person. That was for sure.

She was almost startled by the visceral reaction she had to him. By the wave of need that washed over her. She wasn't a stranger to sexual desire, or arousal. She enjoyed sex.

But it had never been like this. It had never been all-consuming. It had never been a driving need that washed out everything else, washed out her fear. Because she was the kind of woman who had been raised from a place of fear, because her mother had known she would need it in order to make her way in the world. Because her mother knew that a woman had to suspect everything and everyone. That a woman could never fully place her trust in another human being, because the moment she did that person could take advantage of her.

Yes, she had always been afraid. And so nothing had ever been able to carry her away, not completely. She had left herself fairly unprotected in her marriage, but even now, she'd known exactly how she would get away. And she had already made sure she and her girls didn't end up on the streets. And perhaps she was giving herself a bit too much credit when Boone deserved more of it, but still, she felt confident saying she had never let herself get lost entirely in any sort of passion, anytime, anywhere.

Except now.

There was no logical thought. Nothing rational or reasonable about this. It was just need. Raw and aching and torn from the depths of her soul.

She was empty, and she needed, more than anything, to be filled by him.

She leaned back on the bed, looking up at him.

His grin… That edgy, wicked grin she had always longed to have turned on her.

And nothing was holding her back now. Nothing whatsoever.

It was freedom, the kind of freedom that made tears prick at the backs of her eyes, the kind of freedom that made her feel like she might be on the edge of a cliff.

And normally that would scare her. She was afraid of heights.

But not here. Not now.

Everything about this man said he would catch her.

She could jump. With all the wild abandon she never let herself feel, she could jump.

Because he was more than strong enough to catch her.

Because he was more than strong enough to make good on every promise the arousal he built inside of her created.

Yes. He was the man who had engineered this desire, and he was the man who would answer it.

Because Boone Carson was a man who kept his word.

Even when they were words he didn't speak with his mouth.

He moved his hands to his belt buckle, and everything in her stilled. He began to undo the leather slowly, and her body rejoiced.

He pulled the belt through the loops on his jeans, and methodically set it on the edge of the bed, right next to her. He kicked his boots off, the movements there slow as well, removing his socks and placing them next to the boots. He was doing this on purpose.

Because he didn't hurry to get up here, and now he was taking his time. She couldn't even be angry, because it was the single most erotic thing she'd ever experienced. An echo of the denial they'd been experiencing since they had first met, and yet now with the promise of that desire being satisfied.

His hands went to the button on his jeans, then slowly lowered his zipper. His pants and underwear came off as one, and the extreme pulse of desire that rocked through her core when she saw the full, masculine extent of him made her mouth dry. He was glorious. The most beautiful naked man she'd ever seen, even though she'd only ever seen one other in person.

He was perfection. He was everything.

She couldn't help herself. Or maybe she didn't want to. She licked her lips.

And he laughed. Enticing. Husky. He made her feel like maybe she was wicked too.

And for the first time in a very long time, she didn't feel like somebody's wife or housekeeper or household manager. She didn't feel like somebody's mother. She just felt like her. Her, if she hadn't been raised to fear everything, to hoard good things and be afraid of what might come tomorrow.

Just who she might've been. Who she wanted to be.

A woman. A woman with the capacity to desire perfection. A woman with the capacity to let herself hope.

All because of Boone Carson's gloriously naked body.

And if that wasn't a testament to the wonder of a perfect penis, she didn't know what was.

And she hadn't even touched him yet.

She put her hands on the hem of her T-shirt, fully expecting to undress herself, until his eyes met hers. "No." The command, the denial, was rough and hard.

"That's for me," he said.

"Okay," she said, her voice trembling slightly.

But she loved the command in his voice, and she didn't want it to go away.

He took her hand and encouraged her into a standing position, and then he grabbed hold of the edge of her shirt and pulled it up over her head.

His nostrils flared, his eyes going hot. "You're so beautiful. And I'm gonna tell you right now, I'm not going to have any pretty words for you. Just dirty ones. Rough. I'm not gonna write you poetry, because I just want you so damned bad. And that is the most flowery, beautiful speech I have. Everything else is going to get a lot harder. You okay with that?"

"Yes."

Because it was poetry to her since it was said in his voice. Because the heat in his eyes might as well be a sonnet, and the music he called up within her a symphony.

He could say whatever he wanted. He could do whatever he wanted. It wouldn't be wrong. It couldn't be.

And he made good on his word. As the layers of her clothes came off, he affirmed her with rough, coarse speech that made goose bumps break out on her skin. Her husband was a cowboy. He'd used all manner of rough language. He wasn't delicate when it came to words surrounding sex, but it was different from Boone. Because it was about her.

Because his language spoke to a level of desperation that healed something inside of her she hadn't even realized had hurt.

This idea that she hadn't been enough. That giving a man her body hadn't been enough. That loving that man hadn't been enough. That keeping his house, raising his children, managing his money hadn't been enough. That if doing all that wasn't enough to satisfy him, it meant there was a deep shortcoming within her she was never going to fix.

Boone made that laughable. He made it clear, so very clear, even to her, that the issue was Daniel.

Because if Boone could be reduced to trembling over the sight of her bare breasts, then maybe she was beautiful after all.

Then perhaps she wasn't wrong. Then perhaps her husband was just a bad husband.

And she had been a good wife. It just hadn't mattered to him. And never would, no matter what she did.

And so this weight that had been resting in the pit of her stomach from the moment she had found out about Daniel's infidelities evaporated. And then Boone took her pants off. Her underwear. And she was naked in front of him. This man she had wanted for so long, for whom her desiring had become as natural as breathing, so much so that she had managed to carry it around all these years, some days barely noticing it.

And now she could feel it. The way that it made her want to be wanted.

The cascade of all those years was suddenly pouring down over her, amplifying her desire. Her need.

She wasn't embarrassed to be naked in front of him, because she knew she had been thousands of times in his mind, and she could see from the heat in his eyes he wasn't disappointed. Far from it. And then he began to tell her. Just how satisfied he was.

And he was wrong. It was poetry. A field of dark desire

dotted with bright, explicit daisies. And it was more than beautiful to her.

Because it was real. Because it was nothing held back. Because it was as honest a moment as she'd ever had in her life, and honesty was perhaps the biggest aphrodisiac of all right now.

Truth.

Unfiltered, unabashed.

And then he wrapped his arm around her waist and brought her bare body against his. And they were touching, everywhere. Naked, against each other. He was so hard and hot, and her desire for him was like a living thing. Demanding. Exulting. And she indulged.

She wrapped her arms around his neck and kissed him, gloried in the feel of her sensitized breasts moving against his hair-roughened chest. Loving the way his large, calloused hands moved over her curves, the way one cupped her ass and squeezed her hard.

Then delved between her thighs to tease her slick entrance.

She cried out as he pushed a finger inside of her, and then another.

Boone. She would never not be conscious it was him.

It wasn't about generic desire. It wasn't about that basic sort of human need that everyone experienced. This was singular. It was for him. About him.

And when he lifted her up and laid her down on the bed, he looked at her like a starving man. And he pushed her knees apart, kissing her ankle, that sensitive spot right on the inside of her knee, and up her thigh, slowly. His mouth was hot, and his eyes were full of intent, and even as she felt a vague amount of discomfort and embarrassment wash over her when he drew closer to the most intimate part of her, she couldn't look away.

Because she had to see it. She had to see Boone's mouth on her. And then it was. She gasped, arching up off the bed, her hand going over her own breast as she squeezed herself, greedy now with all the heat inside of her. And he began to lick her, deep and with intent, pushing a finger inside rhythmically as his tongue moved over the most sensitive part of her.

She was lost in it. In this new music inside of her.

He was an artist, and if he would make her his muse, she would consider herself fortunate.

She closed her eyes, finally surrendering to the overwhelming onslaught of pleasure, finally unable to keep them open. But still, she saw him. His face. His body.

Boone. She was overwhelmed by him.

His touch, his scent. And that realization, his name, him— that was what sent her over the edge, more than a touch, more than his skilled mouth. Just him.

And when she shattered, he clung to her tightly, forcing her to take on more and more pleasure. As he pushed her harder, further, through wave after wave, through a second climax that hit before the first had even abated.

And she was spent after. His name the only thing in her mind, the only thing on her lips. Perhaps, the only thing she knew.

"Boone," she whispered, as he moved up her body and claimed her mouth, letting her taste her own desire there, the evidence of what they had done.

His smile was more than wicked now. It was something else. Dark and satisfied, and everything.

He moved his hands up to cup her breasts, skimmed his thumbs over the sensitized buds there, then moved both hands down her waist, her hips, beneath her rear as he lifted her hips up off the bed.

"I want…"

"Later," he said, his voice jagged. "I need to be inside of you."

And then he was, in one hard, smooth stroke, filling her,

almost past the point of pleasure into the gray space where pain met need, and it was wonderful.

He began to move, rough, hard strokes that pushed her further and further toward that shining, glorious peak again. Impossibly. Brilliantly.

There was no way she could come again. She had never in her life come twice during sex, and a third time would just be pushing it, except each and every stroke demanded it.

It was Boone. Inside of her. Tormenting her. Satisfying her. Creating within her an aching need that only he could satisfy.

And she could've wept with the glory of it. With the intensity of the new, building need in her that felt entirely separate from the need she'd had before.

Because this was about them. Being one. His body in hers. Intimate. Too much. Not enough.

She met his every stroke, and then he took hold of her chin and pressed his forehead to hers. "That's right," he whispered. "Come for me. For me, Wendy."

It was the desperation there, the fact that he wasn't talking dirty to her for the sake of a game, but issuing a command that came straight from the very center of who he was, out of the deepest, darkest desire. That was what sent her over. That was what shattered her. And it was nothing like her other two climaxes. This was like something sharp piercing a pane of glass, cracking and shattering it into glorious, glittering pieces. Making it into something almost more beautiful than what it had been before.

And then he followed her. On a rough sound, he found his own release, spilling himself inside of her, his body pulsing deep within. And she watched him. Watched as he was undone.

By her. By them. By this.

And all she could do was hang on to him in the aftermath. Clinging to his sweat-slicked shoulders as she pressed her head to that curve right there at his neck, as she tried to keep herself from weeping.

"Boone," she said.

"It's about damned time," he said.

And she laughed. Impossibly, because nothing felt light or funny.

Except it was just the truth.

It had been so long in coming, that it was nearly a farce.

Had it always been inevitable? She supposed there was no good answer to that question. The decision as to whether or not they would do something to violate her vows had been taken away from them. And they had certainly kept themselves away from any sort of temptation they couldn't handle for long enough that they deserved a medal.

But it had been taken away from them, the need to resist. And so they didn't.

Lying there with him felt inevitable.

But maybe it was Daniel's betrayal that had always been inevitable, considering he had never once seen a need to be faithful to her.

Maybe that was the thing that had always been set in stone: the failure of her marriage. Maybe it had been fate that day that had brought Boone into her path and said, *Here is the better choice.*

For all the good it had done. Because she had been so bound and determined to do the right thing, she hadn't taken the destined thing.

Except now, in the aftermath of what had been fairly spectacular sex, she was left with the reality that sex was hardly destiny.

It had been amazing. Surpassing anything she had even thought could exist.

But she still had all the things in her life to take care of. And kids to pick up from school in… She looked over at the bedside clock. Thirty minutes.

For a moment she had felt free of all her responsibilities, but she wasn't. Not really.

She still carried them all. She still had to be Wendy Stevens. Mother, a woman in the midst of a divorce.

She still had to figure out where she went from here, and what she did next. Not even three soul-shattering orgasms could take that away.

Because bodies meeting wasn't a promise. Not forever, not really anything.

And in the place she was in life, she could hardly ask Boone for promises.

He looked at her, and she wanted to.

But she didn't.

They had known exactly what to do.

It was funny that neither of them seemed to know what to say.

"I have to go get the girls. Soon."

"Yeah."

"I can't… You know I can't be over here at night."

He nodded. "Yes."

"I just can't have them knowing."

"I get that." He cupped her chin. "It's not gonna just be the once, though. You know that."

She could resist. She could tell him it had to be once. She could tell him that, for their own protection, they needed to keep it that way. That they had to be smart. But she would only end up back in his bed the next time they were alone in the house, and it would just make her a liar.

She wasn't going to do that. She wasn't going to insult them.

Because the truth was, she wanted him again even now, and if she wasn't on a time limit, she would probably be climbing on him.

Because she hadn't been able to touch him the way she wanted to, hadn't been able to explore him. Hadn't been able to taste him.

And she was just not in the space to build up a host of regrets. Or even a single new regret.

"I am going to leave," she said.

"You said."

"I'm not even divorced yet."

"You are in every way that counts."

"Except the legal ways. And I have to get through that."

"I get that."

"Thank you. For being here for me. I really appreciate it. I really… This is going to happen again."

"Yes," he said.

And then it was her turn to be bold. Because why get missish now?

"I need to taste you," she said. "I haven't had you in my mouth."

He growled, and she found herself pushed flat on her back, a whole lot of muscled, aroused cowboy over the top of her.

"Careful."

"I don't have time," she said. "Because as wonderful as that was, I can't stop having my life just so I can please you sexually."

"Tease."

"It feels good to tease."

It felt good to be with him.

It was strange how natural it felt, sliding out from beneath the covers and taunting him with her naked body as she went to collect her clothes.

She just wasn't embarrassed.

And she wasn't going to pretend to be. Why take on shame she simply didn't feel? There was no point to that.

Now she just had to get through the rest of the day with her head on straight. She had to pick up her girls like she hadn't just been ravished. She had to get dinner made.

"I'm probably gonna go out tonight," he said. "Don't worry about saving me dinner."

And that felt… It hurt. It felt like he was avoiding her, and maybe he was.

"Oh," she said.

"I'll see you tomorrow, though."

"Okay."

"I can't have you again tonight," he said. "And I get that might sound outrageously selfish to you. But honestly, I'm not sure I have it together enough to be around you in front of the girls, or to… I just need some space."

She was shocked by that. By the honesty. By the blatant truth that had just come out of his mouth, a truth that exposed deeper feelings in him that she had thought he would be comfortable betraying.

"Oh."

She had wanted to be close to him because she felt needy right now. But he had a point. They needed to figure out how they were going to be around each other if the girls were in the middle of them.

And right now, they were on anything but normal footing.

"Okay."

"I don't want you to be hurt."

She shook her head. "I'm not."

"Don't lie to me, Wendy. There have been enough lies all around us, there don't need to be any between us. Not anymore."

"Okay. I was a little bit hurt. I thought you didn't want to be around me if you couldn't have me."

"Yes…but it isn't like that. It's not because I don't have another use for you. It's just because I don't quite know what to do with myself right now."

"Okay. That's fair."

And maybe a little bit more honest than she'd been with herself.

"I will see you tomorrow."

"Okay."

Chapter Seven

Walking away from her had been the hardest thing he'd ever done. But he had work to finish, and she had to get her kids.

Being honest with her about why he needed a little space had been the other hardest thing he'd ever done. Because it came too close to admitting the truth.

This impossible truth that he had no idea what to do with now that they'd slept together.

He had felt like he was in love with her for a very long time.

But that love had been impossible to act on. So it had felt... safe in a way.

Or at least abstract.

The truth was, Boone didn't know how to love somebody actively.

He knew how to do things for them. But he had no idea what being in love entailed.

He looked at the way his brothers had brought women into their lives, the way they'd rearranged themselves to have them. He didn't like the thought of that. Not at all. Because he'd rearranged his life so many times.

And he just couldn't take all that on right now.

Hell, more than that, he knew it was an impossibility. Wendy was going through a divorce. Wendy had kids.

There was something much heavier to the idea of trying to be with a woman who had been through so much, than if it was a woman he didn't know.

He knew her. He knew how difficult all this was.

He knew about her life, about the things that she'd been through. And about the responsibilities she had.

And he took all that shit very seriously.

So he decided to go out. Decided to go to the bar. And wasn't surprised to find his brother Jace there, since Jace's wife was working tonight.

"Hey," he said.

"Hey yourself."

"What brings you out on a weeknight?"

"I need a drink."

He could confide in his brother.

He could. He was still considering it when Jace looked at him just a little too keenly. "Woman trouble?"

"You could say that."

Because he had been considering telling his brother about it unsolicited, so he sure as hell didn't have it in him to lie.

"Wendy?"

"Yeah."

"You know, this just isn't a great time for her, I would imagine."

"It was a fine enough time for her to sleep with me."

"Oh. Well. I guess I shouldn't be too surprised about that."

"It's not a surprise," he said. It really wasn't. They wanted each other too badly for too long for it to be a surprise.

"What's the problem?"

"Life is just really messed up," said Boone. "I don't know how you ever let go of that enough to be with someone. Especially when everything they're going through is as equally messed up as the world around you. It was easy. To carry a torch for her knowing I could never have her. But the rest of it…"

"Yeah. I get that."

"She's in a bad space," he said.

"So you said," Jace commented.

"It's true though. And it's important I remember that. I don't want her to feel obligated to me."

"Bad news," said Jace. "When you have a relationship with somebody you do often feel obligated to them. It's not a bad thing. I think that's somewhere in line with basic human connection and empathy."

"Yeah, but I don't want this to be transactional."

"Fine. I can understand that. But if you do something for her and she wants to do something for you, that's not transactional so much as it is a relationship."

"She doesn't need one of those right now."

"And that's up to you to decide?"

He snorted. "I didn't say that. But I don't…"

"Listen to me, and trust me. I say this as a man who talked himself into thinking he knew better what the woman in his life wanted than she did. That way lies disaster. If you actually care about her, you need to give her some respect. The respect that she knows what's going on in her own mind. At least that."

"I know she does," he said. "But just… You weren't there. You didn't see her marriage. Okay? I did."

"Yeah. You were friends with her husband. If you hate the guy so much then why—"

"I didn't hate him. Not everything about him. When we were hanging out on the rodeo circuit, he was a good guy. The thing is, he kind of taught me how to have a good time. I needed that. You know how things were after…after Buck left. I had to take on a lot. And it was heavy. And I threw myself into the rodeo after that because I knew it was so important to Dad. I found some things there that I didn't expect to. But Daniel is a fun guy. And he kind of gave me something to look forward to. He taught me how to enjoy what had felt like an obligation before. There were good things about him. But when he married Wendy, things did change." And he left out the fact that a huge part of that was the way Boone felt about Wendy. From the moment he'd first seen her. There was no way Daniel could ever have been good enough for her. Even if he'd been perfectly good after all.

It was just that he hadn't been. So that combined with everything else made it kind of an impossible situation.

"Our friendship has had some cracks in it for a while. And in the end, I chose her. I was always going to choose her. I…" He realized what he'd just said.

"How long have you had a thing for her?"

"Too long. But the timing is bad."

"Word of advice. The timing is always bad."

"No, it really is. And I'm… I'm not someone who just hopes because he wants something. Not anymore."

"Boone, listen. I know… I know Sophia—"

"It was a lesson, Jace. When an illness is terminal, hoping for the best is stupid. It's not charming." He took a drink. "It's been a long time. But I changed. I know better. And I can see clearly, without…without being a blind optimist. The timing is bad."

Jace shook his head. "I get where you're coming from. But when it comes to relationships, the timing is always bad."

"What the hell does that mean?"

"Because at some point, caring about somebody means getting over yourself. And that is a really hard thing to do."

He could understand what his brother was saying. But caring about Wendy had always meant denying himself. It had always meant caring more about her than about him. Of course it had.

He'd always been clear on what loving Wendy meant.

He could care, but he couldn't have her.

And if anything, it just reinforced what he had to do. And that was let her go at the end of all this.

Because that was what caring about her meant.

It meant not being like Daniel. Not holding her to him when it wasn't right. When it wasn't the best situation for her. That was what love was.

It was sacrificial.

So there.

"Well, that's the way I feel about her," he said. "Like my feelings can't be first."

"Great. Just make sure you don't decide for her what her feelings are. Okay?"

"Yeah."

Jace raised his hand, and Cara brought over a couple of beer bottles.

"Do you have a designated driver, Boone?" she asked.

"You have my permission to put me in a cab if I have too many."

"Good. I have to look out for you. You're my brother now after all."

It was weird, the way the family kept expanding. Especially after being so conscious of the contractions in their family for all those years.

But Cara was a sister to him. Another person who cared.

That sat a little bit uncomfortably in his chest, and he couldn't quite say why.

"My biggest problem now," he said, lifting his beer bottle and looking at his brother, "is figuring out how to act like what happened earlier today didn't happen, especially when her kids are around."

"Well, not that I know, but I assume kids are a pretty big dampener on the libido."

"Especially teenagers," Boone said. "Little kids you could get that past, but older ones…"

"I don't know, man. Sounds to me like you just stepped your boot into a whole mess of sexual tension snakes."

He laughed. "Yeah." He didn't laugh because it was funny.

He laughed because it was true. He laughed because the mental image that it painted was far too accurate.

He had gone and done it. The nest of sexual tension snakes had been there all along, and he'd known. Full well.

But it was like stepping in it had been the only option. So there he was.

And now he was going to have to get back to the task of taking care of her. And taking care of the girls. All while carrying on a blisteringly hot, temporary affair with her. Because the snakes had been stepped in. So there was no point going back now.

"I'll figure it out."

"Sure you will," said Jace, a little too cheerfully for his liking.

"Why exactly do you seem to be enjoying this?"

"Because a woman completely rearranged my life some years ago, and a few months ago, I was finally able to figure out exactly what that rearranging needed to look like. I'm glad to see you in a similar situation."

Except it wasn't the same. It never would be. But he didn't argue with his brother. He didn't have the energy for it. He had other things to save his energy for. If his time with Wendy was limited, he was going to pour everything into it. Absolutely everything.

She was so distracted. She needed to get her daughters through homework. And then she needed to get herself off to bed.

She managed that, just barely. But then she couldn't sleep.

She was completely consumed by her thoughts of Boone. And what had happened between them that day.

He was gone still, the driveway empty, and she should be completely okay with that. He explained himself after all.

And, anyway, he didn't have an obligation to her.

It wasn't about obligation, though. She just wished he was here. And when she saw headlights pull up into the driveway, she climbed out of bed and, without thinking, went out the side door of the cottage and walked toward his house.

It wasn't a truck; it was a car. And she stopped and stared at the unfamiliar white vehicle, not quite understanding what was going on until she saw the logo on the side.

He'd gotten a taxi.

He got out of the cab, and she saw him stumble into the house.

And without thinking, she went the same way he did.

"Are you drunk?"

He turned. "Tipsy. Not drunk."

"Okay. Why?"

"I was trying to make it a little bit easier to fall asleep, actually."

"Oh, Boone. Come on inside. I'll make you some tea."

"No. That is counter to my objective. Which is to not think about you. And definitely not to fall asleep with you on my mind."

He was a little tipsy. And she didn't usually find that kind of thing sexy. But here she was. She had a feeling she would find Boone's hangnail sexy. And that was a whole other kind of problem she'd never had before.

"In the house."

"I don't take orders."

"Why not?"

He grinned, and she found herself suddenly pressed up against the side of the house. "Because I like to give them."

Arousal crashed through her body. Yeah. She would really like to take orders from him. Though, that wasn't supposed to be what was happening tonight.

"And tomorrow afternoon when you're sober, and you come in for your lunch break, you're welcome to tell me everything your heart desires. But right now, I'm telling you to go in the house so I can make you some tea."

"I think you'd have more fun if you got down on your knees."

"For sure," she said, breathless with the desire that thought infused in her. "But sometimes you can't get what you want."

"I'm well familiar."

"Inside."

And this time, he obeyed her.

So there was that.

She found an electric kettle—which was surprisingly civilized of him, she thought—and plugged it in, flicking on the switch to start up the hot water.

"I appreciate that you got a cab. I feel like sometimes you guys are not so great with the designated-driver thing."

"You guys?"

"You rodeo cowboys," she said.

"Yeah well." He cleared his throat, his expression going stoic. "My older brother was in a drunk driving accident. He wasn't driving. But they were a bunch of boys that had gone out camping and drinking and… Anyway. He was the only one that survived. After something like that you take the whole thing pretty seriously."

"Oh. I'm sorry, Boone, I didn't know."

"Yeah. Nobody knows Buck. Because he took off so long ago. It really screwed him up."

There was something raw and unspoken in his words. A truth buried there she couldn't quite figure out. And he wasn't going to tell her. Not willingly. Not right now.

And that was okay. Because that wasn't supposed to be the point of this. But now she couldn't stop imagining the catastrophe, and the way it must have hurt everyone.

"Was he injured?"

Boone nodded. "Yeah. He was okay, though. I mean physically. But it's a small town. And people will define you by something like that. And everyone will know. You can't out-run it unless you leave. I know that."

"It must've been hard. Having him leave."

"Plenty of families don't live in each other's pockets."

"Yes. That is true. But I expect it feels different when some-body leaves because of something like that."

"I guess. Were you close to your mom?"

"Yes. Until she died. She died when I was eighteen. And then after that, I met Daniel. I expect I was looking for a con-nection."

"Yeah. Probably."

"We don't often do the best things for ourselves when we're feeling desperate." She closed her eyes. "That isn't fair. He was good to me. As far as I knew. I wasn't openly accepting poor treatment."

"I was trying to remember today, when my brother and I were talking at the bar, exactly why I used to like Daniel. It occurred to me that he was one of the most carefree guys I've ever met. And as somebody who was burdened with a host of care by the time I was sixteen, I liked being around him."

"That's what I liked about him too. I was always afraid. Al-ways afraid of losing what little I had. Always afraid of when the other shoe was going to drop. I was always scared. And he never was. Not of tomorrow, not of his success vanishing, not of our relationship imploding, he just lived. And now, I feel a little bit betrayed. Because so much of that is just arro-gance, isn't it? Thinking you're the center of everything, the most important person, and that nothing you do can compro-mise it. And here I thought I was maybe learning some kind of life lesson from him."

"There's still a life lesson there, maybe. He doesn't have to have had everything worked out for some of it to be true."

"I guess."

"Did he ever make you happy?"

"Yes," she said. "And I guess it was real enough. I guess."

"I can understand why it's difficult. To accept that any of it was real when it seems like he was lying all that time."

"Yeah." She poured the hot water into a mug and put a tea bag in it. "But I guess that's the thing. That was part of his arrogance. He didn't think I needed his fidelity as long as he kept it from me. And I think he didn't much see the conflict there. It's insane. It doesn't make any sense. But I think that's what he thought. And so in his way, I think he loved me. I just think he never really loved anybody as much as he loved himself."

"And that may be why he was so happy," Boone said.

That made her laugh. "That's fair. How happy can you be when you're worried constantly about the happiness of somebody else? When you love yourself most, your joy isn't completely tied to the feelings of others. Like it is when you care about others as much as you care about your own. For Daniel, ultimately your own happiness is what matters…"

"I expect that's the easiest way."

"I wouldn't want to live that way, though. Because I wouldn't have my girls. Makes everything hard. Because as difficult as it is to go through this separation, it's so much harder when you're worried about other people's happiness as much as you are your own. Or more. But then I think at least I know what it's like. To feel an intense amount of caring for somebody else. I think that's the depth of it."

"Yeah. I think that's the depth of it. When I was a kid, my sister died. You might know that."

"I didn't," she said.

"Well. Sorry to bum you out with my family history. But it was a long time ago."

"I'm sorry."

"Thanks. Me too. But you know, that was my first introduction to understanding just how badly love could hurt. But what can you do? You love your siblings. No matter what. And I couldn't turn off my love for my family just because we lost our little sister. So I learned how to kind of move on with it. I learned that you could love even though it hurt. The hurt is part of it. And yeah, I think the way Daniel loves, that's kind of something else."

"Narcissism?"

"Possibly."

"I'm very sorry to hear about your sister. And your brother. Do you see him at all?"

"No. And in some ways that feels harder to deal with than Sophia's death. Because he is still alive. He just doesn't speak to us. He is still alive, he just… He won't come to us for help. After everything we went through. As a family. He put my parents through losing another child, effectively. He lived, but he won't live. And I just can't wrap my head around that."

"This one isn't about me," she said slowly. "It's my mother's story. But she isn't here to tell it, so I'd like to. My father abused her. She loved him, she trusted him, and he abused her. Physically. Emotionally. And I know that the woman she was after him was different. No matter how much she wanted to go back. She just couldn't. And sometimes I wondered why she didn't go home. Why did she go out on her own and struggle? When she could have gone back, because she talked about her family like they were all right. But the issue wasn't them, it was her. She survived something she didn't want to explain to anybody. And she didn't feel like she could go back. And I think there was something sad about that. I never got to know my parents. But I also understand there were things that happened that were so traumatizing she just couldn't face people seeing how they had changed her. And I can't judge her for that. Maybe your brother feels the same. Maybe he doesn't want you all to see who he is. Because maybe in some way he does feel like he died. I don't know. And I'm sorry if I'm overstepping. It's just that I love someone very much who did a similar thing."

He was quiet for a long time.

"This is maybe a little bit of a deep conversation to have when I'm partway into my cups," he said.

"I'm sorry. I didn't mean to overstep. But I—"

"You didn't overstep. Hell. We had sex a few hours ago, I think you can give me some advice."

"It's not really advice. It's just you said you didn't understand, and I hope maybe you might feel less mystified. And even if it isn't true, even if that's not why he left, if he didn't tell you, well, then what can you do? But if having an answer, any answer—one that's about him and his pain and not you—helps, then you might as well choose to believe that one."

"Good point. I can't argue with that."

"You could."

Their eyes met. This felt dangerous. Quite dangerous. Because this was another thing they hadn't done these last years. They hadn't gotten to know each other. They knew each other in the sense that they saw each other around. She knew the quality of man Boone was because she saw the way he interacted with other people. Because they chatted in passing at different things when it couldn't be avoided, and they did their very best to never be self-conscious about the sparks between them. To never draw too much attention to all of it.

But they didn't do this. They didn't sit and have heart-to-hearts. They didn't talk about his dead sister or his missing brother. Maybe she had started it, trying to push him away by telling him about her childhood. It hadn't worked. And now she knew about his, and that was close to having a connection. It was close to something she should be avoiding. And definitely something she shouldn't want.

Definitely not.

"Yeah. But, why? I'd rather kiss you."

"That's probably not a great idea." But she was already leaning in, and when he kissed her, it was almost tender. Nearly sweet.

It could never be entirely tender, though, because there was an edge to the meeting of their mouths that she thought not even time would take away.

It was the wanting. And how long they'd lived with it.

But tonight, there was something glorious about it. An ache fueled by how much she wanted him, and by knowing tonight she couldn't have him. Because she needed to get back to the cottage, needed to get back to the girls.

Because one thing she really couldn't afford was for her daughters to discover she wasn't home. For them to wonder where she was.

So he was forbidden again, but only for a few hours. There was something illicit, in a glorious way, about that.

A fun way because it wasn't impossible, it was just delayed.

So she let the kiss get intense, hungry, and she gloried in it.

In the building desire between her thighs, and the reckless heat that threatened to overwhelm her.

His whiskers scratched against her skin, and she liked that too.

Yes. She really did like it.

And when they pulled away, they were breathing hard, and her whole body felt like it was strung out, ready to shatter at the slightest touch.

"Are you going to touch yourself tonight? And think of me?"

It wasn't a question, she knew. It was a command. Because that was who he was.

"Yes."

"Tell me about it."

"Okay."

"Send me a text and let me know exactly what you thought

I might do. Because you know, 'you have not because you ask not.'"

"All right."

He kissed her again, once more, then picked up his mug and stood. "I'll head to bed."

"Me too."

And she did exactly as he ordered, and when her climax hit, she turned her face into her pillow and said his name.

Then she sent off a furtive text letting him know she had completed the task. But when it came to what exactly she thought about? That was a lot more difficult. And in the end, she only wrote one word.

You.

Chapter Eight

You.

He couldn't stop thinking about that. Couldn't stop turning it over and over in his mind. Damn that woman.

Getting up this morning and heading to work felt like a farce because he was living for that afternoon break. He was living for their agreed-upon meetup. He didn't care about anything else. He lost the ability to do it. He just wanted her.

He had waited all this time for her. And then last night she had…

She had managed to stick a ruthlessly sharp knife blade into that wound, and the painful cut had let out some of the poison.

He didn't know how she had done it. How she'd so incisively given him a truth he needed, even if it wasn't what he wanted.

He didn't need for her to understand him in addition to being the hottest sex he'd ever had.

He didn't actually need for her to be anything, and yet, she was doing her best to be everything.

You.

And by the time the afternoon rolled around, his blood was thundering.

He practically tore the door off its hinges when he got into the house, and when he saw her standing in the kitchen, barefoot and wearing a sundress that came up well past her knees he just about wrote poetry. Or perhaps a prayer of thanks to whoever had invented the sundress.

It was a magnificent work of art. The creation he had never fully paused to consider or appreciate until this moment. Until he had beheld the glory of one on Wendy.

And he was done playing. He was done waiting.

They'd set their boundaries, and he'd made it very clear what he was doing, and what he wasn't doing. Because of that, he felt like he didn't need to waste time with pleasantries now.

"You look pretty. I want you on your knees."

"Here?"

"Yeah. Here."

But because he was a gentleman, he went over to the stove and took down a tea towel. Then he put the folded-up fabric onto the floor, cushions for her. Because he didn't want her discomfort. He just wanted a little obedience. He just wanted…

This was a fantasy he hadn't let himself have. And now he wanted it. And he wanted to hold on to it. Tight.

Slowly, she sank down to the floor, her knees coming down to the center of that folded-up towel.

In his kitchen.

Holy hell.

All this trying to stay clear of domesticity, and he was doing a great job twisting and perverting some kind of house-wife fantasy.

But he liked it. He couldn't help it.

What did he want? Just from his life in general. What had he ever wanted? Past the glory of the rodeo. Past being the one who picked up the slack for people who let go of their responsibilities.

What was left for him?

Was he going to live alone forever?

The years, the long lonely years, stretched out before him, and he realized why he never thought past the rodeo. Why he had put off retirement. Why he had put off this—buying a house. Making a life outside the rodeo.

Because he was clear-eyed. Because he wasn't an optimist. Because he didn't do hope, or dreams, and that meant the future was…

He could hardly even see it.

And that was sad.

But *this* wasn't.

So he was going to push all that to the side, and just be here. With her.

Because all she needed was him. And all he needed was her. That was for damned sure.

He moved closer to her and undid the buckle on his jeans.

And he suddenly felt unworthy of the gift she was giving him. It had been a follow-through of the game they were playing last night, and now it felt like something he maybe didn't deserve.

But she was looking up at him with wide, expectant eyes, and he was powerless to turn away.

He shifted the fabric of his pants, his underwear, and exposed himself to her. She wrapped her hand around the base of his cock and slid her elegant fingers along his length. Then she moved in, taking the tip of him into her mouth, before sucking him in deeply. She was confident. And more than that, her enjoyment was clear.

She wasn't shy—her eye contact bold, the sounds of pleasure coming from deep within her throat intense and raw.

He pushed his fingertips through her hair, held her there, held himself steady.

He didn't think he would survive this.

Even in this, he was so very aware it was her. Even in this, it could be no one else. He felt honored. Which was such a weird-ass way to think of a blowjob. But it wasn't just a blowjob. Because nothing with her was ever that simple. And it never could be.

He was close. So close, and he didn't want it. Not like this. He moved away from her, and she looked dazed, confused.

"Didn't you like it?"

"I loved it," he said, taking her hand and lifting her to her feet. And he kissed her, open-mouthed and hot. "A little bit too much. I need you. To be inside of you. Because I've got a month with you, Wendy, and there isn't going to be enough time. I'm not wasting it."

Something that looked like grief danced over her features, and he did his best to ignore that. They stripped each other naked, and made it as far as the living room rug. He pulled her over the top of him, and thrust up inside of her. Let her set the tempo of the lovemaking this time. Let her have control. She flipped her blond hair over her shoulder, planted her hands on his chest and rode him, the view provided by the position making him feel like his heart might explode.

Then she closed her eyes and let her head fall back, small incoherent sounds issued from her lips creating a glorious soundtrack to his need.

Her climax came quick, and he was grateful, because that meant he could give her two.

As she continued to move over him, he pressed his thumb right there, to that sensitized bundle of nerves, and began to stroke her. She shivered, the second wave of her desire cresting as she cried out his name on a shudder and a shout. And then he followed her over the edge. It had been so much faster than he wanted it to be. But it had been perfect.

That woman. Damn that woman.

"Have dinner with me tonight," he said without thinking.

"I have the girls."

"Well, all of you have dinner with me tonight. I missed you last night."

"You left last night on purpose."

"I know I did. But I don't want to be alone in this house tonight, and I don't want to be without you, and I don't care if that makes sense."

"It's the sex talking," she said, throwing her arm over her face and rolling over onto her back.

"Sure it is. But it's great sex, so it can talk as loud as it wants."

"You're impossible, do you know that?"

"Whether I do or don't is sort of immaterial, don't you think?"

"No." She frowned and rolled over onto her stomach, propping herself up on her elbows. "I have a question for you."

"What is that?"

"Does anyone take care of you?"

"What?"

"Your brother left, and you made it sound like you got a lot of responsibility afterward?"

"Not a lot. It's just there were a lot of assumptions about Buck's place in the family. A lot of pressure for him to be great at riding in the rodeo, to help my dad with the ranch. He was the oldest, and then I became the de facto oldest. I had to pick up where he left off. But I already had my own place in the family, and nobody stepped in to fill that. So it was just a matter of doing a little bit of double duty. But I don't resent it."

"You're lying. You do resent it a little."

"Okay. Maybe. But like anything else, what difference does it make if I do or don't? It is what it is."

"Maybe. But if you admit your resentment, it might inspire you to figure out how to live your life a little bit differently, don't you think?"

"There is no different for me."

"Why not?"

"I don't deserve to be upset about Buck," he said, his voice hard.

"Why not?"

"Because I'm the reason he left."

Her eyes went round. "You...you're the reason?"

"I didn't mean to be. But he was...he was a mess after the

accident. Not physically. Mentally. It reminded me too much of other grief. Other times. The thing is, I know life is hard. But you have to be…you have to be realistic. You can't sit around hoping for things to be different, you have to deal with what's in front of you."

"And that's what you told him."

He nodded once. "Yes. It's what I told him. And the next day he was gone."

"Boone…"

"I don't deserve your sympathy, it's misplaced. But I don't feel guilty either. Buck was imploding, and he was going to do what he was going to do. I nudged him, I guess, with some harsh truth. But like I said, I don't wallow. I just deal."

She was silent for a moment. "Except for you dealing means…not even planning your future? Not wanting anything?"

"It's not quite like that. But I take things as they come, knowing there are certain expectations and I'm going to fulfill them."

"You're just going to ride bulls forever?"

"No. I'm retiring."

"Oh. Well. That feels like big news, Boone."

"I'll probably end up being the commissioner. After my dad retires. That's part of the deal. That was kind of supposed to be Buck's thing, but now it's not going to be. Because he's not around."

"What do you want?"

"I'm kind of uninterested in that bit of trivia. I don't care what I want. What I want doesn't really matter. What I want is secondary to what's going to happen. For my family."

"What you want isn't trivial."

He wasn't in the business of being self-indulgent, and there were limits to how deep he wanted to get into a conversation like this. But it was hard to hold back with her, so he didn't.

Because they were here, and she was beside him, naked and soft and the epitome of every desire he'd ever had.

"What I want has been trivial for years. No one asked me if I wanted to lose a sister. No one asked if I wanted my brother to go through what he did. And most of all, since the moment I met you, Wendy, what I wanted hasn't meant a damned thing."

She looked down and then back up, a sheen of tears glimmering there, and he hated that he'd put them there. And he loved it.

Because it mattered, this thing between them. It mattered now and it always would.

"I don't like that, Boone."

"You know it's true. We had to do the right thing."

"We did the right thing," she said. She scooted closer to him and put her hand on his shoulder, then leaned in, her breast pressing against him. "And this is our reward."

She felt hollow and sad after her exchange with Boone earlier.

This is our reward.

Was it? Was this all?

Was this it?

This furtive, intense sex that was trying to compensate for all their years of pent-up desire? Maybe that was all. Boone wasn't offering more. But Boone was also...

He was stoic and strong. He was commanding and he was so damned good.

All things that were beginning to indicate to her he was a champion martyr.

What I want is trivial.

He claimed he didn't blame himself for Buck leaving, but he clearly did. He seemed to almost relish things being hard.

He was good at being uncomfortable.

She would have said a bull rider had to be, but in the grand scheme of things, she didn't think Daniel did discomfort. Ever.

Eight seconds of physical pain, and then alcohol to numb

the aftereffects. Sex when he wanted it with who he wanted it with, while his wife kept house and peace at home.

Not Boone.

He rode bulls, not because he wanted to—though he claimed he'd found passion for it—but because he was fulfilling the destiny of his older brother, who was gone now.

He took care of his parents and worked to fill a space his dad wanted him in because he felt like he had to. Because of their losses, she assumed. It had started with his sister, that much was clear.

Even wanting her was an extension of just how happy Boone was to sit in discomfort.

He seemed happy enough to indulge with her, but there was a ticking clock on that indulgence. Wendy was starting to feel wounded by that. Crushed by it.

She was starting to question it.

Boone seemed to have made his peace with the pain in life.

She wondered if he had any idea how to have joy.

Do you?

Ouch.

That was a dark question from her psyche she didn't really care to answer.

But then she picked the girls up from school and she knew the answer was a definitive yes. She knew how to have joy.

She had it in spades, even while she had something less than joy, and that might be one of the greatest tricks in life.

To be able to feel this immense pure joy while in the middle of such a massive shift. While in the middle of questioning everything she knew about herself and her life, and where she was headed.

"How was school?" she asked, once Sadie was buckled in and Mikey had finished a monologue about art class.

"Great," said Sadie.

Which was what Sadie would say no matter what.

"What was especially great?"

"Oh nothing." She sounded vacant, and guilt made Wendy's heart squeeze.

Had there been something going on at school that she'd missed while she was busy being consumed by thoughts of torrid sex?

"What's wrong?"

"Nothing, Mom."

"I don't believe you."

"Well, I don't want to talk about it."

"Talking will make you feel better," Mikey said from the back.

"Shut up, Mikey, I'm not you!"

"Okay, that's enough. You don't need to tell Mikey to shut up. She's trying to be nice."

"She's being pushy, you both are. If Dad were here, he would know not to push me."

Because your dad doesn't care as much as I do.

Wow. Thank God she'd managed to hold back those words, because that wasn't fair at all. Daniel had been a dick to her, but when he was home, he was a good dad. The girls were mad at him right now, but they wouldn't always be.

Well, Mikey always would be a little. She had a pure soul that was rooted in honesty, and in some ways, Wendy thought her daughter was a little too like her. Like she wanted maybe a little bit too much from a world that was never going to give it. That made her unforgiving and rigid sometimes, and also made her say things to her grumpy older sister like *talking will make you feel better*, because she only ever said what she believed.

Sadie, though, would forgive him. Because Sadie wanted things not to hurt so much, and forgiving her dad would make that relationship hurt less.

Wendy needed her girls to be able to forgive him.

She needed to keep some of the spite to herself.

You have Boone for your spite.

Well, that was almost a worse thought. Boone wasn't her human crutch, and he sure as hell wasn't there to just listen to her endlessly complain about her marriage.

He would say he was happy to do that, she knew.

Because that was Boone entirely.

What did his feelings matter?

What did his desires matter?

She thought of him ordering her down onto her knees. With a cushion firmly in place for her comfort.

She turned her car down the driveway to the ranch, and had the sudden image of one of her first dates with Daniel, at a pizza parlor that had pinball machines. She'd watched him play for a couple of hours, and she'd thought then that she was so dizzy with her infatuation for him she might as well be one of the balls in the machine.

She felt like a pinball now.

Worried about her kids. Worried about their relationship with their dad.

Flashbacks to giving a blowjob to the hottest man she knew.

Ping. Ping.

And right into the hole.

"We're having dinner at Boone's tonight."

"I'm not in the mood!" Sadie wailed. "I don't want to be social. I just want to have a plate of food and go to my room."

Well, this was wonderful.

"You can have a plate of food at Boone's and then leave, no one is asking you to stay and chat all night."

"You can't just dump this on me."

"I can't just dump you eating dinner next door to the house we're staying in, with someone you like a lot, who has generously given us a place to stay?"

"Yes!" She said that as if it was obvious, and also as if Wendy was an actual monster.

"Fine, Sadie, I'll leave you a plate at home, then."

"You're leaving me by myself?"

She said that tremulously and angrily, and if Wendy weren't also overwrought, she might have laughed. "Unsolvable problem, Sadie," she said. She was often reminding her daughter that she loved to present her mother with a problem, then when given solutions, she had a ready spate of reasons they wouldn't work.

Which was fifteen and fair, she guessed, but why did everything have to be a struggle?

"I just don't know why we have to go to Boone's."

"Because he is my friend and I wanted to spend the evening with him, and he wanted to see you both because he hasn't."

"I want to go to Boone's," said Mikey. "I haven't even been inside the house and we've been here for four days."

That earned a growl from Sadie, and Wendy accepted that there would be no consensus. Which was just life and parenting sometimes, but she didn't like it especially.

She knew she could be a hard-ass about Sadie's attitude if she wanted to be. But the thing was, Wendy had an attitude about things a lot of the time too. She'd smashed Daniel's headlights in after all. And yes, it had felt deserved.

But she knew all of this felt real and deserved to Sadie.

Maybe also you feel a lot of guilt over the whole thing.

Maybe.

Which wasn't fair, it wasn't her fault.

Not the divorce...you wanting to spend time with Boone.

Yeah. Okay fine.

They got home and Sadie went straight to her room while Wendy started dinner with Mikey sitting at the kitchen table. She could have cooked at Boone's, but she would rather be here talking to Mikey while she worked, and in close proximity to the melting down teenager.

"I don't know what her deal is," Mikey said.

"She's fifteen."

"I won't act that way when I'm fifteen."

Her heart squeezed tight. *Oh, Mikey. You will.*

"Thanks, honey."

"What are you making?"

"Lasagna."

"Yum."

At least she was doing something right in Mikey's world. Right now, she'd take it.

And after she was done with dinner and it was time to head to Boone's, Sadie appeared in a hoodie, with her hands stuffed in her kangaroo pouch pockets and the hood firmly over her head. But she appeared.

"Lasagna?" she asked.

"Yes. I can dish you a plate and you can go back to your cave, or you can come over for a little while."

She shrugged. "I'll come over."

So they made their way over to Boone's with a big bowl of salad, a pan of lasagna and no small amount of resentment from Sadie, like a parade. If only a very small one.

Boone opened the door and grinned. "Thanks for the dinner party."

And she noticed Sadie was charmed by him, even if reluctantly.

The house was better organized now, even though they'd spent the last two days having sex, which had taken up a good portion of her cleaning time. Apparently when she was motivated she could get a lot done.

But to his credit, Boone had set the table nicely for them, and he had an array of soft drinks in the fridge, which she knew was for the girls.

"Thank you," she said softly, as the girls dished their plates and took their seats.

"How is everything?" Boone asked.

Thankfully Sadie didn't implode and Mikey took the lead, talking about her art classes and her new friends with a lot of enthusiasm.

It made Wendy feel conflicted because Mikey was clearly finding a group she enjoyed here, even after four days, and Wendy was planning on going somewhere else after the month ended.

You were planning on getting away from Boone's charity, it doesn't mean you have to leave.

No, it didn't.

But how could she live near him without…

Why was she so afraid of that? Why couldn't she entertain the idea of a future with him?

She knew why. She knew all the logical reasons why. You shouldn't go from being married to being with someone new, and the stakes were so high. Her daughters had been through enough and she didn't want to drag them through any extra instability. And it was possible she felt pressure to be the most perfect parent so they would always stay on her side.

Well. She wasn't going to win that game. She was the parent most actively parenting, so she was going to be the bad one sometimes and there was nothing she could do about that.

She looked across the table and met Boone's gaze.

And resisted the feeling of rightness that washed through her.

This had been a weird mistake.

A form of torture.

She hadn't thought it through.

Sitting around a family dinner table with him and eating all together. Seeing where he could fit into her life. Into the most important spaces of it.

"And how was your day?" he asked, now looking directly at Wendy.

She blushed. She could feel it. Her whole face went hot and she hoped—she really hoped—her children would continue to be the preteen/teenage narcissists she could generally count on them to be and not notice subtle shifts in their mother.

"It was good, thank you. And yours?" She nearly coughed as she took a bite of her salad.

"Best I've had in a while."

She almost kicked him under the table.

True to her word, Sadie melted away as soon as dinner was over, but Mikey lingered, and Boone and Wendy ended up at the sink doing dishes while she chattered about the drawing techniques she was experimenting with, and how her favorite YouTubers did certain kinds of animation styles.

Wendy looked sideways at Boone, who looked down at her and smiled. Her shoulder touched his, and it was her turn to feel like she was in middle school.

Her stomach fluttered.

And without thinking she leaned in and brushed her arm against his very deliberately, which earned her a grin.

And another stomach flutter for good measure.

"But I really need to get some alcohol markers, because I think it would help with making the lines on my art crisper."

That jolted Wendy back into the moment. "Oh. Okay."

They finished up the dishes and she walked back to the house with Mikey.

"I really like Boone," Mikey said. "He's cool."

"Yeah. He is. I like him too." An understatement, but the most she was going to say to her twelve-year-old, who blessedly hadn't noticed any of the subtext happening all night.

Unfortunately, Wendy felt steeped in subtext.

And in the aching window into another life tonight had given her.

What would it be like if she stopped worrying about what

she thought was smart, or right—in the context of what other people would say—and just went for what she wanted?

If she closed her eyes and thought of her perfect life, Boone was in it.

So why was she fighting that so hard?

To try and protect herself.

But that ship had sailed, along with her inhibitions, right about the time she'd first kissed him.

The only real question was if she was going to keep on letting her childhood, the pain in her past, Daniel, the pain of his betrayal and the years' worth of lies decide what she got to have.

Yes, it was fast. But it also wasn't.

Boone had been there all along, and so had her feelings for him.

She had kept them in the most appropriate place possible. She had been a good wife. She'd honored her vows.

But the feelings had been there all the same. Daniel had been a great reason not to act on them then. He didn't get to be her reason anymore.

She was her reason.

And because of how she loved she could trust everything to flow from there.

Because she loved her girls, and their happiness would feed hers. She could trust herself.

To make the best decisions she was capable of making—not perfect ones, but not wholly selfish ones either.

She just had to hope that in the end, Boone wanted the same things she did.

But if not…

She was strong. And she had a lot of things to live for, and smile for.

She knew how to hold happiness and sadness in her hands at the same time.

So, if she had to, she'd just hold it all, and keep living.

Chapter Nine

When his phone rang, he half expected it to be Daniel because he had heard from the disgruntled asshole more times in the last few days than he would like to. Actually just twice, but that was more than he would like, and he especially didn't want to speak to him after having incredible transformative sex with the guy's soon-to-be ex-wife. Not because Boone was ashamed, and not because he found it weird. It was because, as angry as he had been before, he was even angrier now. Wendy deserved better. She deserved a whole lot better, and he wasn't going to be able to restrain himself from saying that. Because she was everything.

It wasn't Daniel, however, it was Flint.

"Hey. Calling from your private jet?"

"She doesn't travel by private jet. She thinks that's problematic for the environment."

"Wow. Not because you can't afford to."

"She's very famous," said Flint.

"You don't find that threatening to your masculinity?"

His brother laughed. The sound deep and rolling across the phone line. "No. My masculinity is good. Anyway. Tansey and I are coming into town tomorrow, and I was hoping we could get together for a family barbecue."

"Yeah. Sounds good."

That would be time spent away from Wendy, though. He

could bring her, of course, but that would be integrating her into the family in a way that...

Hell.

"I hear your hesitation. I'm wondering if it's because of your houseguest."

"I don't have a houseguest," he said, mentally trying to determine which person might have told Flint what was going on.

"I talked to Jace," he said. "He mentioned you had Wendy Stevens staying with you."

"Not with me. Wendy and her daughters are staying in the cottage on my property, and Wendy is doing some work for me. I'm paying her, and I'm giving her a place to stay while she works on extricating herself from that situation with her cheating husband."

"Got it. And it has no connection whatsoever with your personal feelings for her?"

"Of course it does. I don't just go offering a place to any random woman."

There was no point lying about it.

"Yeah. Well. Maybe you should bring her."

"Yeah, I was thinking..."

"I know you were thinking. I could practically hear you thinking. But you might as well bring her. And the kids."

"That might be weird."

"It's only weird if you make it weird, Boone. Maybe you should figure yourself out."

"There's nothing to figure out. I'm not in any way confused about what's happening right now."

"Well. Good for you. You're the only one of us who's managed to get entangled with somebody and not be confused."

"It's not an entanglement. I've known her for a long time, and she's a friend. She needs somebody right now. And I'm not going to lie and say there's nothing more happening. But, you know, I would never put pressure on her to make it too much. And that's the problem," he said. "Yeah. That's the problem. If I go inviting her to a family thing she might think I'm pushing her for too much too soon."

"Or she might be grateful. You should leave it up to her."

That was the second time he'd had that feedback from one of his brothers. The second time they had pointed out he was making the decisions for Wendy, and maybe he shouldn't do that.

He could understand. And he even agreed. Because he didn't think it was right to make decisions on a woman's behalf. But he was just… He could foresee issues here, and again, he didn't hold out blind hope something wouldn't be awkward when it was clear it would be.

Except not inviting her…

Dammit.

"Fine. I'll invite her. I'm looking forward to seeing you."

"You too."

He got off the phone, and decided to walk straight back to his place. And there she was. In all her glory. He'd already been back to see her today, already made love to her. And she was looking at him with wide eyes. "I have to go get the girls in, like, ten minutes."

"I could get it done in ten minutes."

Her cheeks turned pink. "I'm sure you could…"

"That isn't why I'm here. My brother Flint and his fiancée, Tansey, are coming into town tomorrow. We're having a barbecue and I thought maybe you and the girls might come."

"As in… Tansey Martin."

"Yes. Tansey Martin. I know she and their breakup are very famous. As is their reconciliation, since there are now songs about that, too, and about to be a whole album."

"My girls are going to freak out." She shook her head. "We probably shouldn't go. Because it's a family thing, and they're just going to be starstruck."

"Oh, they are. Not you."

She laughed. "Okay. I will be a little bit, but I'll be able to control it. Because I'm an adult."

"It's okay. She brings that out in people. You can be starstruck. But also if…if it seems weird to you to come to a thing with my whole family…"

She frowned. "It's weird for you, isn't it?"

"I didn't say that."

"Your face said it. You don't want me to go."

"Wendy," he said, regret tugging at his chest. "I do want you to go. I'm honest, right? I'm being honest. I was just a little bit worried about some of the…"

"You're worried about getting too involved."

"Yes. Because everything feels great right now, but it isn't going to last."

"Why not?"

She looked at him, so open and trusting, and it killed him.

"You know why. I've still got some time in the rodeo left. You and Dan aren't even divorced…"

"That sounds like a lot."

"We don't need to get ahead of ourselves," he said.

"Don't pull away from me just because of all that."

He let out a hard breath. "I'm not. You're the one who said you wanted to leave at the end of the month."

"I might not leave town."

"Great. I'd love it if you didn't leave town."

Except that felt like something clawing at his chest, and he couldn't quite say why.

"Maybe we both just settle down a little bit. And I will come to the family thing, as long as you're good with it."

"I'm very good with it. Perfectly happy."

"If the girls found out Tansey Martin was going to be a thing at your parents' house and they weren't allowed to go…"

"You're welcome to be there. I'm sorry."

He looked at her, and he felt… Wounded. It was the strangest thing. He had messed that up. He hadn't handled it well, and he just had to wonder if in the end he was going to do more harm than good to her. It was the last thing he wanted.

Of all the things, he knew that. But she was just asking those questions. Why couldn't they be together? Why not?

There weren't simple words for why not. That was the problem. Maybe he'd been avoiding thinking about whether or not his plan was to end up by himself because he hadn't planned on finding somebody or because that was the way it was going to be.

The fact was, the one woman he'd been able to imagine himself being with was Wendy. And it had been one thing when she was with another man. One thing when she was married. That had been destiny. She was safe from him when they'd met.

And now, everything else was due to Daniel's shortcoming. It didn't count.

It wasn't a thing.

It meant he got to have her now. It didn't mean he had anything different up ahead of him.

He had to keep clearheaded about it.

"I'll see you later."

"Yeah. I… I probably won't make the girls come over and have dinner tonight."

"Hey. Fair."

"But they'll enjoy the family thing on Saturday. So. And I'll see you before then. I…"

"Yeah. I know."

"Okay, I'll see you."

He didn't move. She did, though, headed past him and out to her car. And somehow, he felt like he'd made a mistake. He just didn't know what it was.

Chapter Ten

She had underestimated how awkward it would be to load everyone up into Boone's truck again with the amount of tension she felt just looking at him.

She was sure even her narcissistic teenagers would feel the tension.

Surely.

They didn't seem to, though. It was only Wendy who was sweaty and nervous and far too hot as they drove from Boone's ranch at one end of Lone Rock, to his family ranch all the way on the other end and out the other side of town.

She was never half so grateful for how absorbed teenagers were in their own issues than she had been these last few days. Or maybe that was simply because she was so absorbed in her own issues. Maybe it wasn't a teenage thing. Maybe it had to do with life being exciting. New.

It was always like that for her kids. Bless them. It was like that right now for her. Bless Boone.

She looked at his strong profile as he pulled the car up into the front of his parents' massive home. Yes, things were definitely exciting with him. But somehow, not easy. And you would think that if you had wanted a man for fifteen years, the coming together would be the easy part.

But maybe that was the problem. Something was holding him back. And she could understand there were logical things. There were things that had been holding her back.

But maybe that was the problem. Maybe she had to go all in.
You've done that before.

Yes. She had. She had gone all in with Daniel. But it wasn't the same.

It just wasn't.

Boone…

Maybe calling it love now, this early, was a little bit foolish.

But maybe she felt a little bit foolish.

Maybe she was foolish. Certainly jumping into bed with a man on the rebound was somewhat typical behavior, but falling for the idea that it might be something more? There was almost no chance of anybody making that mistake unless they were doing it willingly.

Willfully even.

But what if it wasn't a mistake? What if it was him? What if it was always supposed to be him? Or maybe, even more beautifully, it was supposed to be him now, and the way she had felt about him up until this point was essential to being brought here to this moment.

Maybe.

But as she stared at his profile, intently, she just knew something.

She wasn't entirely sure what. But it was certain and settled in her soul. And the one thing she couldn't do in response was hold herself back.

She had to be all in. She had to be his.

"Let's go in," she said.

"Yeah," he said, looking at her and forcing a smile.

Wendy felt heavy, but she got out of the truck, and the girls followed suit.

"Is Tansey Martin really going to be here?" Mikey asked her mom, her eyes large.

"Yes. Why would I say that if it wasn't true?"

"To try and beat Sadie out of her room."

"I would never try and beat Sadie with something as basic as a pop-country crossover star. Sadie is not that basic."

"I'm basic," said Mikey.

"Mom," said Sadie. "You make me sound like a snob."

"I'm not making you sound like a snob. You are a snob. But it's okay. You're fifteen. It's your right."

"Tansey is very nearly my sister-in-law. I assume you know about the song," said Boone.

"Yes," said Mikey seriously. "We watched the short film."

"You should make sure to tell Flint that. He loves it. He's a huge fan. It did great things for his life."

Wendy looked at him in warning. "Don't tell teenagers things like that. They'll do it."

"I'm counting on it."

"What are you supposed to do when there's just, like, a famous person there?" Sadie asked.

"You just, like, eat your hamburger," Boone said, grinning at her.

Sadie smiled, which was glorious for Wendy to see.

Boone was so good with them.

They had a dad. But Boone would make a great masculine figure to have in their lives. He was protective. He was fun.

She wanted him.

He would make her happy.

Or at least contribute quite a bit to her happiness. That would help everybody.

Just jump in feetfirst. You're already there.

The Carson family home was massive, and beautiful, with floor-to-ceiling windows overlooking the craggy mountains and rustic decor throughout.

It was filled with all the siblings—even Boone's sister Callie, who Wendy knew vaguely from the rodeo. That was the great thing. It wasn't a room full of strangers. She knew Boone's parents, and she knew all his brothers, even if only in passing.

She had spent enough time at the circuit to feel like they were family in many ways.

"And how are you finding the single life?" This question came from Abe Carson.

"I'm not technically single," she said, grateful her daughters were occupied across the room. Talking to Tansey, who was warm and wonderful and actually not at all intimidating.

"Philosophically," said Abe.

"Thanks, Dad," said Boone.

"I see," said Abe. "Well, hurry up and get that divorce finalized so my son can make an honest woman out of you."

Her scalp prickled. "Well, I am happy to move it quickly."

She didn't see the point in protesting. Because hell, she kind of wanted Boone to make an honest woman out of her. Or a dishonest one. She just wanted to be with him. And her parameters for what that could look like were becoming quite elastic. At first, she had been a bit concerned about her girls knowing she was sleeping with a man she wasn't married to. But if they had a relationship... She was willing to have a serious and grown-up talk about it. Because this was life, and it was messy. She was in a situation she hadn't chosen, but she didn't have to be miserable.

"Actually, Wendy is looking for some new work. You know she managed Daniel."

"She could manage you," said Abe. "And there are some other guys I know who would love to have competent representation."

"I'm not sure I'm going to be anybody's favorite, considering I just kicked their buddy to the curb."

"If they have half a brain then *he's* not their favorite. I've never had patience for a man who would go out for cheap ground beef when he had filet mignon at home."

"Seems to me," Flint said from across the room, "that it's the man with quality issues, not the woman."

"Sorry, son," said Abe. "I know I'm not woke."

"I don't think I'm woke," said Flint. "I just like women."

Wendy couldn't help but smile at the exchange.

They were a good family. Everybody involved was just… They cared about each other. And it didn't matter if they disagreed about things or saw things differently, they cared about each other. It felt different than what she'd imagined family might be. It had just been her and her mother after all.

And now it was her and the girls.

But even though she had a good relationship with Sadie and Mikey, it hadn't quite been this. Or at least, it had never quite been this between herself and Daniel. Because one thing she noticed was the way Abe and his wife interacted with each other.

There was an ease to them. And she didn't think she and Daniel had ever had that ease.

She looked at Boone. She wanted to feel it with him.

But she had a feeling if she put her hand on his, he would pull away, and she didn't want that.

She felt like they could have something easy and wonderful.

If only they were brave enough to take the chance.

So she got up from her position on the couch and moved over to him, sitting next to him. It was a fairly unambiguous move.

No one said anything, but they all looked.

The other reason she couldn't go putting her hand on him just yet was the girls.

She needed to talk to them. At least, it felt like she should.

Not to get their permission, just to give them a warning. A heads-up. Her mother had never dated when Wendy was growing up, because her father had done such a number on her she had never wanted a man in her life again. It made Wendy sad, in hindsight.

And maybe the only way Sadie and Mikey would ever

be able to understand Wendy wanting to be with somebody else was going to be in hindsight. Or maybe that assumption wasn't fair to them.

"We should go shooting," said Jace.

"What in the redneck?" Cara asked.

"It's a Carson family tradition. We love a good target practice."

Callie looked at her husband. "Will you stay with the baby?"

"Sure," he said.

"I'll stay with the baby," said Callie's mother. "You can all go shoot. I don't mind."

"Can I watch?" Mikey asked.

"Sure," said Wendy.

She had a feeling they were all going out for target practice.

"I guess I'll go," said Sadie, keeping an eye on Tansey, obviously curious about whether or not her new best friend was going.

"Sounds great," said Tansey brightly.

And so with that, they all trooped outside.

"We like to shoot up this way near this big gravel pit. It's got good secure backings so the bullets don't go drifting off anywhere they shouldn't."

"Good to know."

"My dad has extra ear protection in the shed."

"Oh good. So as far as adventurous activities go…"

"This one is occurring in a well-controlled fashion. No worries."

"I wasn't actually worried. I know you would never do anything to put yourself or the girls in danger."

He looked down at her, the exchange between them feeling weighty. Significant.

"I wouldn't," he said.

The girls were behind them, and so she didn't take his hand.

But she did bump her shoulder against his, and he looked down, smiling. She smiled back.

"I like you."

He looked a little bit like she had hit him in the side of the head. "I like you too."

It felt pale in comparison to what she was actually feeling, but she didn't know how to say the other things. She didn't know what else to say.

It felt sharp and dangerous still. And this was the problem with never having been good at math. Order of operations was something she struggled with. She wanted to kiss him now. In front of everybody. Because there was a significant part of her that had already realized she had to go all in. That had already realized there was no going back. That had already realized she would never be able to quit him, never be able to forget him.

And there would be no protecting herself from any manner of heartbreak.

She would be heartbroken to lose him. Whether she told him she was in love with him or not. Whether she said she wanted everything or not.

Whether she did the important work of extricating herself from her marriage, and then tried to do some healing on her own, she was always going to come back to him. So she might as well… She just might as well.

Put herself out there. But there were ways that she needed to go about it. She knew that.

So she just smiled, and she kept *like* as the word, even though it wasn't enough. Not even close.

When they got up to the gravel pit, she and the girls put on ear protection and hung back while they took turns shooting things. Targets, yes, some kind of jelly target that healed itself. And also water jugs. Which did not heal themselves, but exploded grandly.

Mikey was very invested in the spectacle, and Sadie pretended to be just a little bit too cool. But ended up enjoying it all the same. Wendy could tell by the small smile on her face.

She felt a rush of euphoria right then. This could be their family.

Don't rush ahead of yourself and start glorifying all of this. They're just people. And they're not going to fix the difficult situation you're in.

No. That was what she had to be extra careful about.

Boone wasn't a crutch. He never would be. He was more than that.

And she felt…scared. It reminded her of old times.

She didn't like it.

But she really did want him and all these things that he came with. That wasn't so bad, was it?

She knew all these things he could do for her. All these things he had done for her.

And yes, she was working for him, but it wasn't the same.

She wanted to think of something she could do for him.

He felt so much responsibility toward everybody in his life.

And she didn't want to be just another responsibility to him. She wanted to be something more.

She watched as he shouldered the rifle, and she squeezed her thighs together, because whether she should or not, she was always going to find that hot.

Or maybe it was just him. And he could breathe and she would experience a pulse of arousal. Entirely possible. The man had an extreme effect on her.

He blew up the water jug with one shot, and she laughed and clapped. She couldn't help herself.

Maybe it was a little juvenile. But she felt juvenile, she'd already admitted that. This felt new. Wonderful. Terrifying.

And she wanted it. All of it.

They had target practice contests, and in the end it was their sister Callie who bested everybody. Afterward, they hoisted her up on their shoulders, while she screeched in protest, and Tansey, Wendy and the girls clapped. Cara pretended to be furious, while Shelby and Juniper made grand shows out of being gracious losers, since they had competed as well.

When they started the walk back, Flint was up with his sister, and Wendy lagged behind with her girls.

"I want to tell you something," said Wendy.

"What?" asked Sadie.

This was dangerous. Because the girls could make a big scene right here. But…she didn't really care.

Mostly because she just wasn't ashamed of any of it. If they had a bad reaction to it, they were going to have to deal with it.

"I just wanted to let you know that I…that I like Boone."

"Of course you do," said Mikey. "He's cool."

"No, Mikey. I…I *like* like Boone."

Both the girls stopped walking. "You're not serious?" Sadie asked.

"I am. And I wanted to tell you before…"

"Before what?" Sadie asked.

"Just before. That's all. Before anyone else."

"You're not even divorced yet," said Sadie.

"I know. I'm just being honest. And maybe it's premature. I don't know what's going to happen, if anything. Entirely possible *nothing*. But I just like him."

It wasn't Sadie who reacted. It wasn't Sadie who had an explosion. To Mikey's credit, it wasn't an explosion. But she put her head down, and she ran ahead. She wasn't quite in a group with anyone, but she held herself with her head down, and walked, and Wendy was too stunned to catch up with her. She felt frozen, and kept walking at the pace she'd been walking at before, uncertain of what to do. She really hated all the uncertainty.

"It's weird," said Sadie.

"I know," said Wendy.

"She'll get over it."

She looked at Sadie. "Are you over it?"

"I don't know. I think it's weird because… Because it hasn't been that long. But he's been really nice to us, and I know he makes you happy. You haven't been happy. And really, you shouldn't be. You left just a few weeks ago, and everything's been crazy, and you were not happy until we got here."

"But you're not especially happy here, are you?"

"I don't know. I do know that I wasn't happy back home either. I'm trying to be. But this is all weird, and it's a change."

"I want you girls to be happy. And I would never do anything to compromise that."

"That's the thing. I'm not sure there's anything you can do one way or the other. Sometimes we're just unhappy."

It was clarity from her oldest daughter that she hadn't really expected. But she could understand the truth there. They were teenagers. And she wasn't going to be able to make them happy. Not all the time.

"Okay. I accept that. But I do want you to know that I love you," she said. "No matter what. And all this stuff… I don't want it to make you afraid."

"What?"

"We haven't talked that much about what it was like for me growing up. But for good reasons, my mom was afraid of some things. And she made me afraid of them too. And I don't want my issues to become yours. I have them. Of course I do. And you can have your own. Like you said, you can't be happy all the time. Because you have your own life. I'm not in charge of that. But I love you, and I'm here for you. And to the best of my ability, I don't want the stuff I'm going through to mess with you. If you're miserable here, I want you to tell me. But I think I want to try to make a life with Boone. I don't know if he's going to want that with me."

"Okay. I guess that's…fair."

She could tell Sadie wasn't exactly overjoyed, but she didn't look upset or outraged either.

"I'll talk to Mikey."

"Maybe you should talk to Boone first," said Sadie.

"Well, what if Mikey can't deal?" She hated all this fear. This fear that made up her life. She'd been so certain that marrying Daniel had gotten rid of it, but it hadn't. She was stitched together by fear, her whole life a patchwork quilt. Hunger, fear, then family, love. But the thread was fear either way.

She'd been so scared of losing Daniel, of losing her stability, and now she had. She was afraid of messing things up with her kids, afraid of losing Boone…

There was just so much to be afraid of. And it was what she'd known from the time she was a kid.

"Mikey is twelve," said Sadie. "I don't think you should go making decisions based on her moods."

"I could apply the same thing to you."

"I know. You shouldn't make decisions because of me. You're the adult."

She *was* the adult. But she was a freaked-out adult.

Still, she had to act like the adult.

And maybe as much as she wanted to be gentle with her kids right now, there was a merit in setting boundaries too. And in that, she supposed Sadie was right. Maybe she had to figure herself out first. She had a little bit of that epiphany earlier. But there was a certain amount of happiness she had to find before she could be the best parent.

This conversation with Sadie was confirming it. Removing barriers and obstacles she had put in her own way.

"Okay. I'll sort it out with Boone."

"He is nice. It'll be weird for you to be with someone that isn't Dad. But…"

"Yeah, life is weird. I guess if you've learned one thing

from me, I don't want this to scar you, but it's not the worst thing to learn, it's that life changes. And sometimes the best thing you can do is just go with it."

So she was going to go with it. Whether it was smart or advised or not anything of the kind. She was going to go with it because it was her life. And it didn't matter what best practices were. She was living. And it was messy. Real. One of her kids understood, and one of them didn't. She wasn't going to get a one hundred percent buy-in here. She was just going to have to love them.

And herself.

And Boone.

And in the end she was going to have to hope it was enough.

Because fate might've put her in his path all those years ago, but fate wasn't going to make the right decisions for her now. Only she could do that.

She had resisted for a while. But what she wanted was going to require some work. So she was going to have to get busy.

Chapter Eleven

When Boone woke up the next morning, coffee was on in the kitchen.

And he could smell bacon.

It was Sunday, but he still had ranch work to do. He wondered if Wendy...

Yesterday with his family had been a whole trip. He had been so close to pulling her into his arms on multiple occasions, and yet he had known he couldn't. Because what was the point of it? But she was here today.

He walked downstairs, and there she was in the kitchen.

"Good morning."

"What are you doing over here?"

"I decided to make you breakfast."

"Thank you."

"You're welcome."

"Do the girls think you're having an early shift?"

"You're hilarious. It's the weekend. The girls aren't going to know anything until sometime after 10 a.m. But, anyway, I'm not worried about it. I told them."

"You told them?"

"Yes."

"What did you tell them?"

"Not that we were banging on every surface in the house, but that I liked you."

"That you liked me."

"Yes. That I *like you* like you."

"And how did that go?"

"Fifty-fifty. But I wasn't asking anybody's permission."

"Okay…"

She held up a hand. "You don't have to say anything."

"I figure I probably should."

"There's not much to say."

"Well. The thing is… I thought you were leaving in a month." He'd reminded himself of it every day. The reality of it. Of the situation.

She was still married.

She had kids.

She was leaving.

"I keep telling you, I'm not necessarily leaving. I appreciate everything you've done for me. What do you need?"

He looked at her dumbfounded. "What?"

"Boone, what do you need? You're retiring, you're starting this ranch. Do you want to take over the commission?"

"I told you, it doesn't really matter what I want—"

"Why not? Why do other people get all the consideration? Your father doesn't need you to take over the rodeo commission. That's about want. His. So why does it outweigh yours? Or why do your wants not even get to be up for consideration? I don't understand that. It doesn't make any sense to me."

"Because what the hell else am I going to do with my life, Wendy?"

"I was thinking about that the other day. And I was thinking about what your dad said. That I could represent the other cowboys. I know we didn't talk about that for very long yesterday, but I could do that. He's right. It's just a matter of going out and making the most of my connections. I'm really good at this. Representing people. I could do you too. But the thing is, opportunities don't just come to you. And I've understood that when it comes to agenting. But I haven't always been great about that in my personal life. And you're great. You're wonderful with the rodeo, you've got this property, all of that. But do you know… Do you understand that you can't just let life carry you down a current? You have to—"

"Yes I know that," he said. "I'm not just drifting. And I resent the hell out of the suggestion that I am."

"That isn't what I meant. I just meant you can't wait for things to fall into place. You have to get them. And you have to care."

"I care. I care so much that I have shoved everything I've ever wanted to the side. For my mother. For my father. For my friendship with your idiot husband."

"Well, Daniel isn't our problem anymore."

"He's the father of your kids. He is still our problem."

She shook her head. "I don't love him. I haven't for a long time. I don't love him, and I don't want that life back. I don't. It costs so much. And I didn't even realize it. It was so expensive to stay in that marriage. I thought it would be too expensive to leave it. But that isn't it at all. The real expense was in staying there. I wasn't happy. I liked being in that house by myself. I didn't like being in it with him. I didn't like *him*. I like being alone more. I convinced myself that I liked him, but what I felt was a holdover from what we used to have. What I liked, I think, was the part-time nature of it. I don't love him. And I was going to just…let duty or honor or the fear of change hold me there.

"I'm not sorry that I didn't do something disreputable. I'm not sorry that we didn't… I'm not sorry that I was faithful to him. I'm not. But I am a little bit sorry that I convinced myself somehow that doing the right thing would be what made me the happiest. When I say the right thing, what I mean was this idea of the right thing, this idea of what marriage vows were, this idea my husband didn't even agree with. I convinced myself it had to be the best thing, it had to be fate. It's not about fate. It was about fear. Fear of change. Fear of finding out if I left him, I'd have nothing, but that's a terrible reason to stay married. We get to make choices. And we get to demand more. We get to demand better. Anyway, I'm just... I'm deciding. And I'm here to have breakfast."

"Breakfast and demands. That's a whole thing."

"Well, *I'm* a whole thing. But I don't actually want to make demands."

"Except you want to know what I want."

"Let me care about that. Please. If you won't."

But he didn't have words. He didn't have anything. Nothing but a weird, pounding sense of panic moving through his chest, so he leaned in and he kissed her. Because it was better than talking. Because it was better than just about anything. Because when she asked what he wanted all he could think of was her, and everything else felt like details. Everything else felt like it might not matter.

He kissed her because she was what he wanted. Because she was everything.

Because she always had been.

He kissed her because it was like breathing.

It didn't much matter if it made sense. It had never made sense. He held her against his body, and growled.

"There's bacon," she said weakly.

"Fuck the bacon."

She blinked. "Okay."

He backed her up against the wall, kissing her, consuming her.

"I want you, Wendy. And none of it matters. None of it matters."

"Yes," she said.

Except that was wrong. It was wrong that he just... It was terrifying. Because it couldn't last. Nothing ever could.

He could already feel himself losing her. He could feel it

in the dissatisfaction she was expressing this morning. In her asking for things he didn't know how to give.

He could feel it in the way his heart pounded when he tried to imagine forever, but could only picture his house empty.

He was losing her.

By inches.

Because that was what happened when someone was close to you. As close as a person could be. They had to start moving away at some point.

It was the natural order of things. An inevitability.

It was inevitable and he knew it.

He *knew* it.

It was just the way of the world. But right now, he was holding her. Firm against his body, and he was holding her so tight he was shaking.

And it would never be enough.

That was the other problem. When you cared about people, no amount of time could ever be enough.

There was no good cut-off point to a relationship. There just wasn't.

But sometimes things were terminal. And you had to accept it.

It would never feel like quite enough. And he was so unbearably, horribly aware of that as he pressed her soft body against the hard wall of his body and poured every ounce of his need into the kiss.

It was somewhere beyond need. It was desperation.

He stripped her shirt up over her head, but it got hung up on the apron because he couldn't think. Because he couldn't do things in the right order.

Hell. That seemed like a metaphor.

He untied the apron and threw it down onto the floor, taking the shirt with it.

She had on a sexy, lacy bra, not the normal kind of thing she wore.

And it was for him. And that mattered more than the bra itself. That she was wearing it for him, and he knew it.

All of this was for him. The coffee, the bacon, the sex. It was his.

And why did that feel terrifying?

Why did this feel like the beginning of the end? He didn't have an answer for that.

All he had was need.

So he kissed her like he was dying, because he thought he might be.

Because the idea of having to answer the question of what he wanted beyond what he'd already said seemed like a gallows.

And when he had her naked against the wall, he freed himself from his jeans and lifted her leg up over his hip and slid deep inside of her.

He watched her face as he began to move, as he moved deep inside of her, he wanted her. Wanted this. He wanted it to go on forever. But nothing ever did. Nothing ever did. His climax came on too hot, too strong, too fast.

He resented it.

And so he held back, bit the inside of his cheek so he could keep on going. Until she cried out, until her internal muscles pulsed around him. Until she was coming apart all over him, because he needed her to be as shattered as he was.

He needed to gain some control.

He put his hand between them, stroked her, brought her to climax again. He withdrew from her body, and sank to his knees, burying his face between her thighs and licking her until she shattered again.

He would do whatever he had to, to keep this going. Until he couldn't bear it anymore. Until he was so hard it hurt. Until the memory of what it had been like to be buried inside of her became too much, and he pulled her down onto the floor and over top of him, down onto his length, letting her ride him for two easy movements until he couldn't stand it anymore. Until he reversed their positions and pounded hard into her. Losing himself in this. In her.

Losing himself entirely.

And that moment felt endless. And over all too quickly.

And when she shattered again, he lost his own control.

He growled, letting go. Of everything. Absolutely everything.

And it felt like a loss when it was done.

And all she'd asked him was what he wanted.

But it had broken something inside of him.

"I love you."

And that was it. That was the beginning of the end.

Because this bright, white light tried to ignite in his chest and it was the one thing he could never accept. Not ever.

"Wendy…"

"No," she said. "Don't."

"Don't what?"

"Don't argue with me. Don't disagree with me. Don't make this harder than it has to be. You don't need to answer me right now, you don't. We can take our time. I'm sorry, I'm jumping ahead. But I don't know how else to let you know that I don't want to have a time limit on this."

"But everything has a time limit," he said. "Nothing lasts forever. It's better this way. If we can just decide on an end-point and—"

"It's been sixteen years. It's been sixteen years and I want you more today than I ever have. It has been sixteen years since you walked into that bar right after I married my husband and ruined my life, Boone. You ruined me. I have not wanted another man since. I haven't even entertained the idea."

"Except the man you were married to."

"That's different. It should have gone away, and it would've gone away. With time. You know, with the fact that I had children with somebody else. That I was supposed to love him and honor and cherish him for the rest of our lives."

"The only reason you didn't is because of him."

"I know that. I know that. You don't need to tell me why my marriage ended. You don't need to tell me what happened. I am well aware."

"I'm just saying, you were with somebody else and now you're not. And I'm an itch."

"Don't do that. Don't cheapen what we have. If you have to run away from this, then at least take it like a man. Don't belittle what we have. It's not fair. I deserve more than that, and so do you. Just be honest. Be honest about the fact that you can't cope, or that something's holding you back, or that you just don't feel the same as I do, but don't make it about me. I spent my whole life afraid, Boone. I'm just tired of it. I'm done. I don't want to leave a legacy of fear for my daughters. I don't want to be small and reduced because of something somebody else did to me. I want to live. I want to live, and I really, preferably would like to live with you. Yes, I came into this thinking there was no way it could be more now. How could it be? How could it be when you and I both know what a stupid idea it is to jump into a relationship at this point in my life? But I actually think it was stupid for us not to be together the whole time. Or maybe it wasn't. Maybe it had to be this. Maybe this is our timing. Whether it makes sense or not, maybe this is what's right for us. We didn't get here by betraying anybody, or by hurting anybody. We got here because it was where the road led us, and maybe that's okay. Maybe it's enough. Maybe that's what fate is. And now we have to grab hold of it."

"I love you," he said. "I do. I have. But it can't look the way that you want it to. It just can't. I'm not the right man to be in your daughters' lives. I don't want the responsibility. I have too much already, you know that. Because the thing is, I could never be Daniel. I could never go halfway. I can never mess up like that. I—"

"No. That's a lie, Boone. I know you. You can't love me and want to walk away."

"But I do. Because there isn't another choice. Not for me."

"Why?"

"Because everything ends. Everything. I can't live that way. If you're out there, and I love you, that doesn't end. But if you're here, if you're with me…you have to be realistic about these things."

She nodded. Slowly.

"I get it. Because I know what it is to be afraid. You're afraid. And you have every right to be. Life is crazy. And hard. You never know what's coming. But you can cling to what you want. You can fight for it. It doesn't have to be…" Suddenly something in her softened, even as she broke. "It's easier to want what other people want. To try and do it for them, because if you want something then you're the one that's going to get hurt. If you want me and you can't have me, you can love me but… You don't want me to love you. Because that's what you can't trust."

"That isn't it."

"It is. You don't trust me. You don't trust the world. Because it took a lot from you. You trusted your brother, and he left you. You were just a kid, and your sister died. Of course you don't trust in things to last. Of course you don't trust in people not to leave. Boone, I married a man because I felt passion for the first time, and then I was pregnant. And I didn't want to be alone. I entered my first relationship out of fear. Now I'm not afraid. And I'm not afraid to be alone."

"I thought she wouldn't die," he gritted out. "My parents told us she would. They said…they said the kind of cancer she had there was no chance. I didn't believe it. They were honest, but I couldn't deal with it. When she was gone I… I fell apart.

I hoped. I hoped and I believed…past reality, and it damned near killed me and I knew I could never do that again."

She wanted to weep. For the boy he'd been. The boy that was still in him now. Who was afraid to hope. Afraid to love.

"Boone, it took bravery to decide to be with you. I wasn't running from something. I was running to it. It's different. And I know it is. And no, I can't promise you that the world won't continue to be harsh and hard. But I can promise you that I am in this forever. Because if my love was so easily destroyed, then I would've gotten rid of it a long time ago. But I can't. I can't. I love you. And it's only right now, standing here, that it feels like a clear sky filled with stars. It was always cloudy until now. My love was there, but it couldn't shine bright. I couldn't see it clearly. But now I can. Now I do. It's been love all along."

She could see in his eyes that he knew it too. It was the thing that terrified him. Knowing he was afraid didn't help this hurt less, but it did make her feel resolved. She wasn't going to be afraid. She wasn't going to flinch, not now. Because she could see the fabric of her whole life, stitched together by this fear. Fear of scarcity. Fear that there just wasn't going to be enough love to go around. That there wasn't going to be enough of anything. It had driven her into her relationship with Daniel, and it had kept her there. It had made her cling to the companionable, the unobjectionable. It had made her ignore any red flags that might've been there, because she didn't think she deserved to see them. Didn't think she could afford to. She wasn't going to do that now.

"We've both been given a lot of bad things," she said. "We have both been given a lot of bullshit. But we have a chance to have each other. We have a chance to have something new, something different, and I'd like to take that chance."

"I want you to be happy," he said, his voice rough. "More than I want anything in the whole world, I want that. But I can't…"

She looked at him, and she felt pity. "I can be happy without you."

Something flashed through his eyes, and she saw the contrary nature, the complexity of it all. He wanted her to leave him be because he was afraid. He wanted her to be happy, but he also didn't. Maybe he wanted them both to be a little bit sad all the time because they couldn't have each other, but they could have the possibility of it. Maybe that was the problem. If she was out there, away from him, he would be able to think about what might've been. Instead of trying and failing and knowing what couldn't be.

But he didn't understand that her love would cover all the failure.

"Sorry," she said. "But it's true. Because I have Mikey and Sadie. And that means I'll be happy. Because I have a life. Because I have skills. Because I am going to move forward in this work that I've enjoyed doing. Because I'm happy enough with myself. That doesn't mean a part of my heart won't be broken. My life would be better for having you in it. But I won't be miserable. I'll never love another man the way that I love you. I don't even have any interest in it. My life is full enough without a man. It will never be full enough without you, though. But life is complicated. In the same way I was able to be committed to my marriage while knowing the possibility of you and I existed in the world, I will be able to be happy if you can't get yourself together. You're not going to hold my heart hostage. Not all of it. A piece of it. Yes. You might hold my body hostage too. I think I'm set for sex. Unless it's you. So yes. Part of me will be crushed. Part of me will be devastated. Part of me will never get over you. But you can rest in the knowledge that I'm out there happy in the world. You can rest in that. And you can love me from a distance. We can have half. We'll be fine. We did it for all these years." She swallowed hard. "But why? Life breaks us enough, why should we break ourselves? Why, when all we need is a little hope?"

"I can't believe in impossible things anymore. I have to believe in reality."

"Why is a sad ending more believable than a happy one?"

He said nothing.

She dressed, slowly and methodically, and she began to prepare to go.

"Wendy…"

"Don't say anything else. Because you can't say anything true. And I'm done with lies. I get that the lies are to yourself. But I just… I can't."

And when she walked out, she did cry. Real tears, falling hard and fast. And she felt like something in her chest was irrevocably cracked.

She stood there for a long moment, examining the difference. Between losing Daniel and losing Boone. Between knowing that it was over with him, and knowing it was over with Daniel.

The problem with Boone was he'd been there, a possibility, a distant fantasy, for fifteen years.

He had been the other part of her marriage. A piece of herself that she held back. Reserved for him. And now she'd given everything.

It was horrendous. And it hurt.

And she wouldn't trade it.

Wouldn't trade going all out. Wouldn't trade taking the risk.

She only hoped that in the end it was a lesson. If not for her, then for Mikey and Sadie.

That even if it was improbable, and even if it would hurt you, even if other people did not understand, you had to try for everything.

Because you were worth it.

Chapter Twelve

He didn't know what to do with himself. He had just done the dumbest thing he'd ever done in his whole life. And he rode bulls for a living.

He let her go.

You had to.

Why?

These were the rules he had set out for himself all these years ago, this embargo on hope, and now what were the rules doing for him? What had they gotten him?

He'd hurt the woman he cared for most.

And he'd devastated himself.

It hadn't protected him.

He felt like that boy, crumpled outside a hospital after being told his little sister was dead. He hadn't tried to hope and he still felt that way.

Because it won't last. It won't last.

And nobody understood that half as well as he did.

Screw Buck. Honestly. And cancer and everything else. Everything that had ever taken something from him.

He couldn't breathe.

He walked out of the main house, and stood there in the middle of the driveway, considering going to the cottage. To what end? Because what the hell was he going to do about any of it?

She was right. He was afraid. But he didn't know how not

to be. And why did somebody like Daniel—heedless, reckless—get to have her? Treat her lightly, hold their love loosely and shatter it almost intentionally?

How are you any different?

Dammit.

And how was he any different than Buck for that matter? Who had run away rather than trying to sort it all out. Who had shut his family out, shut out everyone who cared about him.

How was Boone any different?

He wasn't different.

He'd just built a different wall around himself. He called it responsibility. He let himself believe it made him different than those he didn't respect.

It hit all the ways that he was the same.

He texted his brothers.

Because he had to fix this. He had to fix himself. And one thing he knew was that he couldn't do it alone.

But the biggest difference between himself and those men was that he was going to fix this.

He was going to fix himself.

Because otherwise, it was only hurting other people to protect yourself.

He wouldn't do that to Wendy.

Because he loved her. And if there was one thing he knew, it was that.

She agreed to meet with him. Finally.

This was the last little pocket of fear. The last foothold. She was done with it.

Because what did she have to lose? She went back to the house that night, and she texted Daniel, and told him she wanted to meet in the middle. So the next morning, she took the girls to school, and then got onto the road, headed a few hours west to where he was stationed—not their house, somewhere out on the rodeo circuit—and walked into the diner that he suggested, feeling oddly calm.

There he was. Her husband of all those years. She was still mad at him. It was impossible not to be. He'd lied to her. Nobody felt good about that. Ever. Nobody liked to be tricked.

But she wasn't in love with him, and she was clear on that. She wasn't in love with him, so it felt...it felt not painful in that specific way.

He looked up from the mug of coffee in front of him and half waved.

"Hey, Wendy."

"Hi. Looks like you got your truck fixed."

"I just got a new one. I mean I traded it in."

That sounded like Daniel. Why fix what you had when you could just trade it for something new?

They were different that way. It was sobering to realize. All the ways in which she had ignored this.

"I want to see the girls," he said.

"I'm not keeping them from you. I realize it might feel that way because I left. But you go this long without seeing them all the time."

"I know that. I know I've been a pretty shitty partner and dad. I mean, there's not even anything to say about what kind of husband I was. I don't know how to explain... But it was like I had two lives. And it just felt easy. To go from one to the other."

She almost laughed. "The sad thing is, I understand what you mean. It's just that I had a different life than you. But I pretty much felt like a single mom while you were away, and I kind of enjoyed the time to myself. I didn't think about you much when you were gone. And I thought that was healthy. To not miss you. To not be clingy. I realize now that maybe there was just something missing." She chewed on the next couple of words for a long moment. "I did want to be with someone else. I just didn't do it. I let that make me feel superior to you. But the truth is, my heart wasn't with you the whole time. And I'm not saying that to be hurtful or cruel."

"I know," he said.

"You know what? That I'm not trying to be hurtful?"

"I know you want someone else. I know you and Boone... I know there's something between you. There always has been."

And then she felt ashamed. He'd known that the whole time, and they never talked about it. All the things she and Daniel had never talked about. They hadn't had a marriage. They were roommates with kids.

"I'm not accepting responsibility for your behavior, and I want to make that really clear. But we were not good together. We didn't fight. We weren't ever toxic. The most toxic thing that happened was me breaking your headlights. But we shouldn't have been married. I thought because we didn't fight, because you weren't cruel to me, that there was no reason to leave you. But we weren't in love, Daniel."

"I loved what we had," he said, and he did sound miserable.

"I believe you. I did too. In a lot of ways. But there was something... We can have more. You'll find somebody someday that makes it unthinkable for you to be with anyone else. Someone you feel passion for."

"I guess I don't understand what that means. I wanted you. And that was real. It always has been."

"Just not enough to not want other people."

It didn't hurt her feelings; it didn't make her feel insecure. She had a man who wanted her in that deep, all-consuming, specific way. She didn't need Daniel to want her that way. Not now. It would've been nice if he had when they were married. More than nice. It would've been right. But that ship had sailed. And she'd moved on.

"I'm not with Boone, I would like to make that clear. It's not happening right now."

"You want it to."

"I do. I'm in love with him, Daniel. And I have been. I mean, I guess not really, because I didn't let myself know him well enough to have called it that when you and I were married. I tried very hard to protect our marriage."

"I didn't," said Daniel. "I'm sorry about that."

"You didn't. But I can't be mad, not about that specifically. I'm mad that you tricked me. I'm mad that I had to find out the way I did. But we were never much for honest conversations. So it had to get to a place where it came to that, I guess. I'm sorry. I don't think you were all that smooth. I just let you get away with it, because I wasn't paying attention."

"You were a good wife, though. I just didn't want to be a full-time husband. It's as simple as that, and I convinced myself I didn't have to be because what you didn't know wouldn't hurt you."

"I know you didn't want to hurt me. I actually know you're not a malicious man."

"I don't know if I feel all right about you being with Boone."

"Well, it doesn't matter what you feel. I have slept with him. Just so you know." A part of her, a small, mean part, enjoyed the bit of shock and hurt in his eyes. "He doesn't want to be with me, though. So don't worry about it."

"So you're just going to leave it at that? It's hard for me to believe he doesn't want to be with you after… He cut all ties with me over this."

"Boone has his own issues. And I'm not going to talk about them to you. I'm just letting you know the status of the situation. If it changes, and I hope to God it does, I'll let you know. But you and I need to be very clear with each other. And we have to figure out how to parent the girls. Because if Boone and I do end up together, there doesn't need to be a story from them or from you about how I tried to replace you. Not in their lives. You're their father. I want them to forgive you. I want them to have a relationship with you. Because the one good thing we did was them."

"It was. It is. I promise you, I'm going to do a better job. And I'm going to prove to them they can trust me as a dad."

"Good. For now, I'm staying in Lone Rock. I'm happy there. I need to find another place to live, but the girls are doing well at the school."

"I'm all the way in Bakersfield…"

"Not all year. And maybe you'll see fit to move, I don't know. Houses are cheaper up here anyway. You can get something big."

"I'll think about it."

"Okay. Well, I need to go because I have to drive back, and I have to get the girls from school. But I'm glad we could talk, Daniel."

"Me too."

"Maybe now that we aren't together anymore we'll be able to do that."

She said goodbye to him, and she didn't feel any pull to go back.

She hadn't thought she would, but it felt healing and clarifying to face him.

It was the right thing. She'd done what she needed to do for her daughters.

For herself.

When she got into her car and started back to Lone Rock, she cried. Because she still didn't have Boone, and she wanted him.

This was heartbreak. It was a strange thing. Her marriage had dissolved only a month earlier, and her heart hadn't been broken at all. It was losing the possibility of Boone that had done it. But at least she knew she could survive that.

She didn't have to be afraid of anything. And maybe in that small way, Daniel had done her a favor. He'd set her free from fear. And it was like that thread that had held her together—that thread she *thought* had held her together—all these years had suddenly vanished. And she didn't feel so much like a patchwork quilt now. She just felt whole. And like herself.

She knew that every choice she made from here on out wouldn't be because of fear.

It would be because of love.

That was a gift. And if it was all she took away…it would have to be enough.

Chapter Thirteen

"I need an intervention," Boone said.

He looked at Kit and Jace and Chance and Flint, sitting in chairs in a half circle, and folded his hands.

"Okay. For what?" Kit asked.

"Dumb emotional shit. Go. Fix me. How are you all in love? Tell me."

"Because there was no choice," said Chance.

"None whatsoever," said Kit. "I wanted Shelby for years, and once I could ever—

"I convinced myself that I didn't want Cara," said Jace. "But I was lying to myself."

"Great. How did you not lie to yourself? I'm familiar with wanting somebody for years. And not having them. Shelby was the same as Wendy. She was married to somebody else, so tell me how you fix it. Because you need to help me fix it."

"Wendy?"

"She loves me," he said. "I love her. I love her and I just… I imagine… What if I lose her? What if I mess it up?"

"Yeah. That's scary," said Kit. "It's damned scary. I got Shelby pregnant, so I kind of had to figure it out, didn't I?"

"But now you aren't scared."

"Shit, dude, I have a baby. I'm scared all the time."

"All the time," said Jace. "We don't even have kids."

"What?"

"Why do you think I broke up with Tansey? The first time.

The last time. I'm never breaking up with her again, but it was because I was terrified," said Flint. "We had it hard."

"So hard," said Chance. "You never get over having someone in your family die like we did. Not really."

"Hell, I closed off all my feelings. My hope of anything. I didn't believe in miracles of any kind. Because that belief failed me when Sophia died," said Jace. "Which was why I didn't see that Cara was a miracle. She was another chance to find that kind of hope again."

"Shelby and I have both been through loss," said Kit. "She loved her husband. Chuck was a great guy. I know she would've loved him for the rest of her life. I also know that life is just… It can be merciless sometimes. But she got to love him for the amount of time she had him. Just like I got to love Sophia while she was here. And I will love Shelby, I'll love our son. No matter what. No matter the cost. Because it's worth it. It just is. Loving people has only ever made us better. So even though it hurts, we cling to that."

"But you're not…afraid?"

His brothers laughed. "Hell no. When you care about things life feels high stakes," said Chance. "I love Juniper more than anything else in the world. I'm not worried I'm going to mess it up, because it drives me. No, I can't guarantee anything. But she's the reason I wake up every day. My life changed because of her. And I don't regret a damned thing about it. I never could. I would never live a life where I didn't love her."

"But I just thought that if I loved her, and made her life better…"

"I would never live a life where she didn't love *me*," said Chance. "It's hard. When you've been through the kinds of things we have, it's really hard to accept the fact that you can't protect yourself. Because if you do, you're just living half a life. You gotta let her love you. You could have her, you could have stepkids, and kids. You can have a house full of love."

"It's just…it's so much easier to be a martyr about it." As he said it, he knew it was true. "To just tell myself I have all these responsibilities to people. To call it that is not love. To call it that and not… I don't know what to do about how unfair the world is. I don't know what to do with Buck leaving. With Sophia dying. I used to have hope, and it didn't get me anything so now I do things instead of feel them. I'm just trying not to grieve the losses I've already had. And trying not to ever earn any more grief."

"It's okay to grieve." That came from Flint. "It's another expression of love."

"It just feels risky."

"It is. But you have to ask yourself, what's life without risk? We are bull riders. We're a fucking metaphor. Accept it."

He laughed. "I don't think I'm actually all that brave. I'd rather throw myself on the back of a bull than… Than let myself hope. And have that hope get destroyed."

It was too vivid in his mind even now.

That burning bright certainty he'd had that Sophia would get better because the world couldn't be that cruel.

And then it was.

"But hope is what it's all about. I read that somewhere. Faith, hope and love. Without them, what's the point?"

He couldn't answer that. He didn't know what the point was without Wendy.

He needed her.

He needed her, and that was the truth.

And maybe that was the miracle. Nothing else seemed as terrifying now. Nothing but not having her. After living that way for all these years, he'd thought it was the safe thing. The easy thing.

But he wanted more now.

Looking around at his brothers, he thought more just might be possible. Maybe everything was.

Maybe that was healing. Maybe that was the miracle of love.

To live in a world, a broken, pain-filled world, and be able to want love, no matter the cost.

Suddenly it was like all the walls were gone. Torn down. Suddenly it was like he could see clearly.

This was life.

And it *did* matter what he wanted. What he wanted might hurt him. Might kill them.

But he wanted it all the same. And actually, maybe he would be the rodeo commissioner. Maybe not. He realized that none of it had mattered because all he really wanted this whole time was Wendy.

So he was going to have to win her back.

Wendy was just getting out of the car with the girls when Boone pulled up to the cottage in his truck.

"Wendy," he said, looking wild-eyed. "I love you."

She blinked. "Okay."

"I love you and I want to be with you. Fuck everything else. Sorry. Screw everything else."

The girls exchanged a look.

"Boone…"

"I love you." And then he pulled her into his arms and kissed her. Then she lost herself a little bit, it was impossible not to.

"Boone," she said, looking at Mikey and Sadie, who were staring at them both.

"Sorry," he said. "I'm sorry, and there's another part of this conversation," he said. "And it includes the two of you."

She had just been talking to the girls about how she'd seen Daniel, and how he wanted to see them. This was all very in-convenient timing.

But it was life. And it was happening. A lot of feelings, a lot of un-ideal sorts of moments clashing with each other.

"I'm not trying to take your dad's spot, because he's your

dad. But I've known you since you were born, and I care about you. And I love your mom. And I'd be happy if you were all right with that."

"Everything is changing," Mikey said sadly.

"I know," said Boone. "And I don't like it, either, quite frankly. I just about messed everything up so I could keep some things the same. Because nobody likes change. I can't say that I've been happy all these years by myself. But it seemed pretty safe. And I was happy with that. So when your mom said she wanted to be with me, I said no. But I realized that I'm more afraid of not having her in my life. More afraid of not sharing a house with all three of you. More afraid of what the future looks like if you're not my family. I want you to be." He cleared his throat. "I… I have hope, Mikey. Even if I'm not certain. And I'm tired of living without hope."

And it was like Mikey realized for the first time that adults had feelings. Feelings and fears and all of this scared them too.

"Oh."

"I care about both you girls a lot," he reiterated, his voice hoarse. "I care about whether or not you're happy."

"I want my mom to be happy," Sadie said. "And you should be happy too."

"We should be happy," Boone said, looking at Wendy.

"Boone," she said, wrapping her arms around him and just hugging him. Because the connection between them had been more than sex. And she wanted to show him that now.

And also not make out with him in front of her kids. Because they were asking a whole lot of the girls, and she didn't need to traumatize them on top of it.

"What changed?" she asked.

"I accepted that there was always going to be some level of risk. I accepted that I had to let love be bigger than my fear. And you know what? I just don't feel afraid anymore."

And neither did she. Because the love inside of her was too big for that.

This was fate. Nothing less than waiting, stumbling through the darkness blind, fighting through all the issues they were beset by.

Grabbing hold of each other and refusing to let go.

It was that simple.

"I dreamed that at my brother's wedding, I crossed the room and kissed you," he said, keeping his voice low. "I dreamed it every night for weeks. And it's funny, I thought because you were off-limits there wasn't anything to learn from that except that I wanted you and couldn't have you. But there was. It was up to me to cross the room."

"And now it's up to us to hold on."

"I'm never letting go now. You know…you're the most beautiful woman I've ever seen."

"What's for dinner?" Mikey asked.

"Meatloaf," she said.

And it hadn't even broken the moment. Both girls went in the house and Wendy just stood there in Boone's arms.

Finally.

"I think this is going to work," he said. "I have hope. In you."

She smiled. "Good. Because I love you."

"That's all I need."

Epilogue

Welcome to Lone Rock...

He hadn't seen that sign in years. He wasn't sure if he felt nostalgic, or just plain pissed off.

He supposed it didn't matter. Because he was here.

For the first time in twenty years, Buck Carson was home.

And he aimed to make it a homecoming to remember.

* * * * *

BREAKING
ALL HER RULES

Chapter One

Grace Song tightened her hold on her bag and swore internally as another cab passed her, a passenger in the back.

The bag was heavy, she didn't want to pay surge prices for a rideshare and she was running late after her disastrous lunch meeting. She did not need this right now. Not with her boss breathing down her neck like he had been. Not with the client from hell leering at her boobs and making comments about what she could *do with his financials ifyouknowwhatImean.*

And then had come the wholly unsubtle: *If you want the account, you might want to make this lunch date end in dessert.*

If he wasn't such a valuable potential account she would have kneed him so hard his balls would have gone back up inside his body. Okay, she wouldn't have done that. Because her default position was to freeze up. Because in her mind, inaction was often better than making the wrong move.

Somehow, she'd managed a curt, cold response and extricated herself.

And now she was going to be late for her next appointment because apparently, there were no cabs. She leaned toward the road and signaled again, a little more vigorously. She was just getting irritated now. And she knew if she let herself get too irritated she would get blotchy. And she didn't want to meet a client while blotchy.

Her bag was heavy. It had her laptop, her tablet, her phone and a legal pad, because even though she had about a million electronic devices to help her organize things, she still needed to write things down physically most of the time.

She liked notebooks and shiny electronics. Everyone had their quirks. And she no longer had anyone in her life, taking up space in the apartment, telling her she had too many pens and things. So there was that.

She could have as many pens as she wanted. And framed pen-and-ink drawings of flowers and other frilly things. Independence was hers.

A cab, sadly, was not.

Another bright yellow car whizzed by and she resisted the urge to flip them her middle finger. She was flipping the world the bird on the inside, it was something she would never do on the outside. All vulgarities would be kept to herself.

Apparently, there was still *someone* who told her what to do. The calm, steady voice of her father, still in her head guiding her actions even though she hadn't lived at home in twelve years.

She lifted her hand again when she saw another cab approach, and groaned when she saw the silhouette of someone in the back. Then the cab crossed a lane, cutting through traffic like a demolition-derby driver, before stopping at the sidewalk in front of her.

The driver lowered the window on the passenger side. "Where are you going?"

"The Stanton Building."

He looked over his shoulder at the man in the back. "That's out of your way."

"I don't care."

The voice from the backseat was deep and masculine, kind of rough. And if Grace was into that sort of thing she might have been intrigued. But she didn't have time to be into that kind of thing. She was into career advancement.

So exciting.

And getting a cab. She was seriously into getting a cab even if she had to share it.

She opened the passenger door and got inside, dragging her giant bag with her and closing the door, running her hand over her hair to make sure it was still in place.

"Thank you," she said, barely looking over at her companion. She leaned forward and started digging through the aforementioned giant bag. Her phone was in the top inner pocket, where she always put it. She hadn't checked her email for ten minutes and she was feeling a little twitchy.

It felt all weird in her hand. Too hard and square. Plus, it was just plain black. Not at all to her taste. Since her pretty Kate Spade case had bit the dust in a freak trip-and-fling-the-phone-across-the-room incident a couple of days ago, she hadn't had the time to go and replace it.

She unlocked the phone and punched the email icon, then waited while it connected to the server...and waited...and oh, gosh. Could it be any slower? They were in the middle of Manhattan for heaven's sake. There should not be a black data hole right now.

"Busy?"

She looked to her left, her eyes landing on a denim-clad thigh that was...well, it was muscley. That much was evident even with the jeans. Then she looked up, and saw his hat. Skipped right over his face and to the white cowboy hat on his head.

And then she looked at his face. Blue eyes, dark brows, a square jaw dusted with some rough-looking stubble. Very interesting lips. Again, if she was into that sort of thing.

"Yes," she said, looking back down at her phone.

"I'm sharing a cab with you. You might look at me for more than two seconds."

She bristled, looking over at him again. "Aren't you supposed to be naked in Times Square?"

"I'm not that kind of cowboy."

"Which kind are you?"

"The real kind."

"Oh. Well. Please don't tell me you have cows in the trunk."

"Nope."

"Great. Well." She looked back down at her phone, her pulse doing a strange, fluttery thing at the base of her throat.

"My name is Zack," he said. "Zack Camden. Are introductions not the thing in the big city?"

She rolled her eyes and put her hands flat on the seat, her phone still under her palm. "Grace Song."

He stuck his hand out and she shifted, releasing her hold on the phone and moving to shake his hand. His fingers were rough, his skin hot. She felt a zip of lightning shoot through her, zipping straight to her stomach, making her feel all tight and weird.

Then he pulled away and she wondered, for one, heart-stopping moment, if he'd felt it, too. Then he reached into his pocket and took out his phone. Black, and unadorned, like hers. But hers wasn't caseless by choice. His screen was probably getting all scratched up in his pocket. That…denim and his muscles. It was probably being crushed in there. Poor shiny device.

"Sorry," he said. "Normally I'd consider this rude but it's work-related so…"

"What did you think *my* phone usage was—unicorn-related?" she asked, curling her lip.

"Funny," he said, hitting the accept button. "Yep. Uh-huh. Landed about an hour ago. Going to the hotel. Nope. Nope. Not going. Nope. Hotel. 'Bye." He hung up, then set the phone on the seat between them.

"Business, huh?"

"Yep."

"What sort of business?" she asked, completely unsure as to why she was bothering to play his little let's-be-friends game.

"The business kind," he said. "The kind you don't wanna do, but have to because...business."

She blinked. "I don't understand not wanting to do business."

He looked her over, his dark gaze assessing. "I bet you don't."

"What does that mean?"

"You look like a business type."

She smoothed her plum pencil skirt and charcoal-grey jacket. She did not look business-y. She looked classy, feminine and well put-together. Though, she'd basically just confessed to being a workaholic, so maybe she should cut him some slack. Or not.

"And what does a business type look like?" she asked, crossing her arms beneath her breasts. He looked her over again and his gaze lingered, very obviously, on said breasts.

"It's not a look so much. You seem kinda stiff. Although, also you just admitted you were a business type."

"Fair enough."

"What sort of business do you do?" he asked.

"I'm a financial advisor." She wished she could take it back as soon as she'd said it. Because he hadn't told her, so why was she telling him? Because deep down, she really was trained with manners, good graces and all kinds of things that didn't exactly scream "ice-cold business bitch." She was working on that. Mainly because if something about her demeanor screamed that a little louder she might not be fending off clients at lunch meetings.

The jerk.

"Very interesting. So you help people manage money?"

"People. Gigantic corporations. It's not like I'm helping random citizens balance their checkbooks." Oh, there was ice-cold bitch! Something about Zack the Cowboy seemed to bring it out. Along with an unhealthy bit of churning in her stomach.

"So if someone had investments, et cetera."

"Got investments?" she asked.

"Maybe."

"You don't seem like the type."

"No," he said, leaning in slightly, whiskey-colored eyes clashing with hers, making it hard for her to breathe, "I'm the type who would have cows in the trunk of a cab in the middle of Manhattan."

"You have to admit," she said, her throat tightening, making it impossible for her to speak, "you're a little out of place."

"I feel perfectly comfortable. You're the one who seems uncomfortable with me. What does that mean, do you think?" he asked, the side of his mouth quirking upward into one extremely cocky smile.

"I don't know. I suppose the fox is never uncomfortable in the henhouse?"

His grin broadened. "Are you saying I'm a...predator? Among chickens?"

"Just trying a little animal analogy for your benefit, pardner. We're New Yorkers, even if we are chickens, you come into our henhouse and we'll mess you up."

He laughed and she felt an answering smile tugging at her lips. "See? Isn't this more fun than work email?"

Yes. Dammit.

"I live for work emails."

"Well, I can't compete with that."

Dear Lord, was he flirting with her? She didn't have a lot of experience with non-sketchy flirting. Most of it came in the form of overbearing, threatening comments that had a greasy film coating the words. It always made her feel violent. Of course, her response was typically just to sit there with her hands tightly folded.

This was different. She wanted to respond to this, rather than punch him in the face. Which was stupid. They were just sharing a cab to her office. And after that she wouldn't ever see him again. Much less make good on any of the flirting.

Which was just as well, because hadn't she just been celebrating her freedom from male tyranny in her personal life?

Yes…yes, she had.

Though, a little male tyranny in bed might be nice….

No. No, no, no. Maybe other women did that sort of thing, but she did not. She wasn't a one-night-stand girl. She wasn't a sex-for-the-sake-of-sex sort of girl.

She didn't have time for that kind of stuff, plus, the idea of kissing a stranger, much less getting naked with him, was just a big fat no-go for her. That was for other types of people. Frivolous, irresponsible people. Like her sister, for example, who had left morals, common sense, clothing and all else by the wayside. And Grace had seen where that led.

There would be none of that.

She looked back at Zack and a sizzle of electricity skipped over her skin, making her feel tingly. And…it was a lot like her skin crawling. Just with heat instead of disgust.

Was she really, honestly thinking about sex in connection with a stranger in a cab? There was something wrong with her. Long work hours and a lack of sleep, or something.

It had been six months since Mark moved out, and she honestly hadn't missed him—or his body—much. The split had been as gentle and amicable as the entirety of the relationship.

They'd sort of drifted into a relationship, then back out. And the best thing about drifting out of the relationship was that she hadn't felt obligated to help him move out. Unlike when she'd been trying to impress him.

Lifting giant boxes with her spindly T. rex arms was pretty low on her list of things to do.

As was sex with a stranger. Lower. Lower than box-lifting. Which was low.

"No, nor should you expect to," she said. "We've only just met, while I've had a deep, involved relationship with my work inbox for years."

"That's longer than a lot of things."

"Longer than most marriages."

"Hell yeah. Less painful, too."

"Well, that all depends."

"On?" he asked.

"On which client I'm dealing with. And who one is married to."

"Fair point. How close are we to your office?"

"Five minutes," she said.

"Give me some financial advice."

She arched a brow. "For free?"

"We'll trade. I'll give you a quick taste of my services, too."

"Oh…please tell me you aren't really a stripper going to a theme party."

His dark brows shot up. "I think I'm flattered that you consider it a possibility."

"Don't be. I've been in the company of male strippers." At a bachelorette party she'd basically fled. She'd spent the evening in the bathroom tapping out desperate emails on her phone. And she'd later been called a prude. But whatever. She could not handle random naked guys shaking it in her face. "Some of them are pretty…worse for wear."

"Well, you are a surprise. Now where's my consultation?"

"Pay off your mortgage before retirement. Never get involved in a land war in Asia. Your turn."

He reached into his shirt pocket and took out a pen and a little note card. She arched her brow and watched as he started scratching the pen over the surface, keeping it turned away from her so she couldn't see.

His teeth closed over his lower lip, the expression of concentration sending a shock of lightning straight through her. And for just one moment she allowed herself to think, with uninhibited enthusiasm, that he was one fine specimen of a man.

Not the kind of man she would ever go for. He wasn't clean-cut and clad in a suit. He didn't have glasses and a reedy frame, which seemed to be her type, if two lovers was an indication of type.

He was as far from that type as you could get. He had those untrendy jeans—blue Wranglers—a plain button-up shirt and he was built like a house. Broad and hard-looking. Like his muscles had muscles.

Also, he had that rough-looking ghost of a beard on his face. Like he was just too darn manly to shave or something.

"Here you go," he said, handing her the card, his fingers brushing hers, a spark passing from his body to hers. He smiled, like he'd felt it, too, and it made the blood in her veins turn to warm honey.

Oh…

She looked down at the card and an unexpected laugh broke through her lips. He'd drawn a fox. All sketchy lines, in black ink, sitting in the middle of a street, tall buildings behind him.

"This is your professional offering?" she asked, arching a brow.

"Ouch. I didn't know you were an art critic."

"Maybe I missed my calling."

"Maybe. Though, I think most critics have a little bit of a meaner look about them."

"I don't look mean?" she asked, forcing her eyebrows together, feeling her forehead crinkle. She was risking fine lines for this guy, what the eff was wrong with her? He held out his hand and planted his thumb between her brows, smoothing out her forehead. "Not so mean." She should be annoyed that he'd touched her. He didn't know her. What right did he have to touch her?

"I..."

His gaze dropped to her mouth and all the words got completely sucked out of her head. Every word she knew in English and Mandarin. And the little bit of high school Spanish she remembered, too.

All with his eyes. Those were some very powerful eyes.

And he started leaning in. Oh...no. What was she going to do? This man that she didn't even know was about to press his mouth to hers, and she wanted him to. Oh...oh...shoot.

The cab pulled up to the curb and stopped.

"My stop," she said, jerking back from him, her hand searching for the door handle. She reached into her purse and pulled out a twenty. "Just...keep the change. I...yeah." She started to get out.

"Wait," he said.

She turned, his absolutely perfect face stopping her in her tracks for a moment. "What?"

"Your phone."

She reached in and grabbed the phone off the seat. "Thanks. See you...well, I won't see you."

She closed the door and headed toward her office building, her hands shaking. Her whole body shaking. She'd just been saved by a timely stop.

Saved from making a huge mistake.

She curled her hands around her phone, the picture of the fox pressed up against it. Yes, it would have been a mistake.

And she didn't have time to linger on it. She had work to do.

Chapter Two

Grace whipped her phone out as soon as she hit the elevator. She swiped the slider and the phone opened, without asking for a code or pausing to recognize her face.

Weird.

The email icon at the bottom showed two hundred unread messages. Just the sight made her insides recoil in horror. "What the…"

She scrolled through the icons and saw…an app containing sex facts, and one containing information about beer.

What. The. Hell.

Then she opened the mail client. Mostly, it was junk. A couple of read messages with the subject line *Urgent* from someone named Marsha Colbert.

This was not her phone. It was Zack Camden's phone.

"Argh!" she said to the elevator, her frustration echoing back at her as it came to a stop. The doors slid open and she pasted a smile on and slipped the phone back in her bag.

"Hi, Grace."

Carol, her boss's PA, greeted her brightly. "Hi, Carol," Grace answered, doing her best to keep smiling.

Always appear unruffled. Always.

That was her motto. She never, ever wanted to appear like she was drowning, even if she was paddling like hell beneath the water to keep her head from going under.

You didn't get anywhere in life by complaining. You didn't

get anywhere cutting corners. If you worked harder, better than everyone else, that would win in the end. It always did. She lived by that, always. And she would live it now.

"Doug was looking for you," Carol said.

Grace forced her smile wider. "Wonderful, I just have a client…"

"He said it was urgent," Carol said, looking apologetic.

Oh, frick. Carol was only apologetic if Doug was breathing fire.

Double argh.

She walked down the hall and toward her boss's office, a feeling of impending doom crowding her heart, shoving up against her breastbone. Suddenly, she would give a hell of a lot to be back down in that cab with Zack Camden. And not just so she could check her email.

They sometimes called the walk to Doug's office The Green Mile. And for good reason. It wasn't because the shiny tile was green.

She lifted her hand and knocked. "Come in," she heard him say through the heavy oak.

She pushed the door open and smiled, even wider than she had coming in. "Hi, Doug."

"Grace, have a seat."

Shoot. A seat. He wanted her to sit? Oh, she was screwed. She obeyed, sitting in the chair in front of his desk. It didn't escape her notice that there was a box of tissues within her reach. Not his reach—hers.

For emotional breakdowns after he screamed at people, she imagined. Or worse, if he didn't scream at all, but set about condescending to them until they melted into watery shame.

Luckily, she had tear ducts of steel.

She took a deep breath. *Ice bitch, take me away.*

She would not care. She *would not* care.

"Look, Grace…" Doug leaned back in his chair, his tie riding up. His tie was too short. He looked like he got dressed in the dark. You'd think that one of the more high-powered businessmen in the city would know how to properly dress. But no. Obviously, not. "I had a call from a client just a little bit ago."

She gritted her teeth. "Right."

"He complained about your conduct."

Her mind shot back to the lunch meeting she'd had an hour ago. Yeah, there was no question he was the one who'd filed the complaint.

"What about my conduct?" Grace asked. "Specifically."

"He said you're quite rude and abrupt. Very cold."

Bastard. Bastard jerk-face bastard. She would never say any of that out loud, but it was the truth. Of course she was cold, she hadn't agreed to let him bang her.

"I…apologize that it was perceived that way…."

Doug held his hand up. "It's not perception when it's a client, Grace. It's fact. If a client is alienated, all that matters is their truth."

Grace felt her eyes go wide completely of their own accord. She worked to keep the rest of her face frozen, her hands clasped firmly in her lap. "Of course," she said, her lips barely moving.

"And since you were late meeting the client who was in your office…"

Because of the other client. And the taxi debacle.

Grace bit the inside of her cheek.

"I have moved her to another consultant. Consider this a warning. I like you, Grace." Grace snorted internally. As if liking had anything to do with anything in this office. She hated Doug. If her keeping the job was about liking him, she'd have lit his desk on fire and said adios sometime back when he'd had her play the elf at the company Christmas party for Secret Santa because she was "so cute and petite."

He continued. "I'd hate to let you go. You're a sweet girl."

She was going to blow a blood vessel in her eye. But she wouldn't say anything. She couldn't. The inaction all but reached in and paralyzed her, freezing her. Because if she opened her mouth she could lose this job, this great job she'd worked so hard at. It could be a mistake. A failure. And she couldn't afford either.

"Thank you, Doug," she said, her words coming out quiet, measured. If only because she was choking on her rage. She stood. "I guess I better go organize a new client. Since I probably have two less—" she forced out the most tortured laugh in the history of mankind "—than I did before I walked in here."

"Great job, Grace. Use this to get motivated."

"Ha! Yes. Yeah." She gave him a thumbs-up, since raising her preferred fingers in his direction would likely be grounds for termination. "Go Team Grace! Population me. I'm gonna... my office." She pointed broadly and went back out into the hallway.

What good was perfection doing her now? Getting reamed by her boss for daring to stand up to some self-important door-knob was not...it was not the way things were supposed to go. She'd worked too hard. Had done her best to please everyone and...and...ugh.

Her heart was thundering hard, and she reached into her purse, fumbling for her phone, to check her email. Except then she pulled it out and there were two hundred unread messages and none of them were hers.

She needed a paper bag to breathe into, stat.

No, more than that, she needed her office. And her damn phone.

She opened the door and shut it, then threw ice bitch out the window and did a full-flail scurry to her desk, jiggling her mouse at high speed to wake her computer up before typing her log-in as quickly as possible.

She clicked into her mail client and read the two—only

two—emails she'd gotten since she'd last checked, fired off two speedy replies and then breathed a sigh of relief when it was back at zero.

And now, she needed to get her phone back.

She typed in the web address she used with her tracking app and clicked on Grace's iPhone. The little circle went around for a while before loading a map. And there it was. She zoomed in, and frowned.

It looked like her phone was at the Mandarin Oriental. Which was several shades fancier than she'd given the man in the Stetson credit for.

But whatever, if her phone was there, she was going to be there, too. She had no more appointments, thanks to Doug.

So she was on a mission to retrieve her phone.

Chapter Three

Zack stepped out of the shower and ran a towel over his chest, then down lower, before wrapping it around his hips and walking out into the living area of the hotel room.

He thought it was a little bit stupid that the studio was putting him up in a place like this, considering he was trying to raise money for a charity. But if everything went well, the proceeds would go above and beyond his hotel-room bill.

"The bar tab is another story," he said out loud.

No. He didn't drink like that anymore. Rock bottom had been a few years back.

Still, he eyed the minibar with no small amount of interest. Then his thoughts shot back to his shared cab ride.

Grace Song.

Hell, he hadn't flirted like that in more than a decade. It had been…well, it had been great. She'd been so damn pretty. So uptight. And he'd wanted to uncoil all that glossy black hair and see just how long it was. How it would feel sifting through his fingers.

That was a grade A fantasy considering he'd been too burned out to have one in the past six years. Mainly he'd just let porn supply the visual while his right hand took it from there.

Which was kind of empty and hollow, really. But hey, he had to get off sometimes, and he genuinely lacked the energy to do it another way.

Though tonight, he could easily imagine which image he might…

He cleared his throat. Slightly creepy. That was slightly creepy. But if no one knew…

He pressed his hand against the front of his towel, against his hardening member. Who the hell cared if it was creepy?

His phone rang, the sharp sound making him jump as he pulled his hand away from his dick like a guilty thirteen-year-old.

He walked over to the phone and swore. If it was Marsha again he was going to growl at her. Because he'd left his phone sitting in the other room on the bed for a reason. He didn't want to deal with people until he absolutely had to.

He didn't want to go "take in a show" or have sushi, or get a manicure or whatever the hell else Marsha might think he needed to do to fully enjoy his time in New York. He would deal with that crap when he had to. Tonight, all he wanted to do was stay in his room, order dinner and jack off. It didn't seem like a major ask.

He picked up the handset.

"Hello," he said, growling already.

"Yes, Mr. Camden. There's a visitor here for you. Grace Song. She'd like permission to come up."

It was as if all his penis's hopes and dreams had come true. *Down, boy, she's not here for that.*

Well, why the hell else would she be here? Unless she was looking for *Fox in the City Part Deux* after she'd discovered his identity.

Maybe she'd used Google to find him. Though, he had no idea why she would. He was some random guy she'd shared a cab with, who'd done a rather terrible sketch on a card for her.

"Yeah," Zack said. "Send her up." He paused.

He looked down at where his hand still gripped the towel. Well, that would have to be taken care of.

He dropped it and left a pool of snow-white terry cloth on the floor before going back into his bedroom and opening up his suitcase.

He ought to get his suit out. If it was wrinkled Marsha would probably have his ass on a platter. Apparently "hobo chic" as she had once called it, was not a thing.

He tugged out a pair of jeans and shrugged them on, pulling them up and stuffing all relevant parts down in there carefully before doing the zipper with even more care. He did not need a zipper incident.

He heard a light knock on the door and he went out into the living area. He walked to the door and opened it. It really was her. All five-foot-nothing of her. Dark hair still pulled back in that little bun pinned primly at the nape of her neck. Her cheeks a pale pink, a streak of blush paint over porcelain skin. Her eyes were deep brown, nearly black, framed with lush dark lashes.

She was perfection. And he hadn't even gotten to her figure, which, though petite, packed the kind of punch that… well, that made him lust again.

"To what do I owe the pleasure?" he asked.

She looked him over, from his face down to his bare chest, to his jeans, which were barely hanging onto his hips, and the color in her cheeks deepened.

"Your phone," she said, holding a delicate hand out.

"What?"

"This is your phone," she said.

"Come in." She looked to the left, then the right. "What, are you afraid entering my hotel room is a felony or something?"

"I don't know you," she said.

"We shared a cab."

"An act I don't even commit with the closest of acquaintances.

I guess I don't have to worry about you kidnapping me and making a pair of underwear out of my hair."

"That is completely disgusting. Also, something Pato might do."

"Pato?"

"He's a…modern artist."

She raised her brows. "Okay."

"Coming in?"

"Sure," she said, stepping grandly over the threshold. "Now where is my phone?"

"It's on my bed. I haven't touched it since I got out of the cab. I'm not in the mood to deal with…well, anything. And I can order fried chicken and pornography from the comfort of my own bed so…"

"Charming."

"I'm not trying to be," he said. Except he sort of wished he could be. So that he could…seduce her, maybe. But he was pretty sure he'd forgotten how to seduce a woman.

Like schmoozing at gallery openings, maybe?

Well, that he could do. For very short periods of time. Because Marsha had threatened to get a shock collar for him if he didn't learn to mind his manners.

"Clearly. Phone?"

"On my bed." He started walking back toward the bedroom, then stopped. "How did you know where I was staying?"

"I tracked my phone."

"Damn, I always meant to install that…"

"It's just an app. It's really simple. I can…show you or…or not. I have to… I don't have anywhere to be."

"Why is that?" he asked, crossing his arms across his chest.

"Because my boss the…jerk…relieved me of the only client I had left in the day after tearing me a new one because of a client complaining about me. Never mind said client was only complaining because I did not flutter my lashes at him when he made it clear he wanted to get into my pencil skirt."

"What?"

"The client I was meeting with, right before I got in the cab. He made a pass at me, I politely rebuffed him. He called my boss because I am, apparently, cold and unfriendly. My boss doesn't care about my side of things. He only cares that I pissed off a client and I am now being punished for not offering a side of sex with my financial advice."

"He can't do that," Zack said. "Your boss."

"Sure he can, because it's the client's word against mine. Because all he has to know is that I dissatisfied a client and the what and why don't matter."

"Did you tell him that the guy was being a douche?"

She bit her lip. "Not as such."

"What does that mean?"

"It means no."

"Well, why the hell not?"

"Because!" she said. "It's hard to be a woman in this business. And people treat you like…like you're there for them, and if you dare complain you're humorless and mean. And if you call them on their crap you're shrill. And if you say someone hit on you and it creeped you out they say you're imagining things, and making mountains out of molehills, and I've watched, for the past eight years, people being driven out of the more high-profile offices, because it gets to be too much. So I just figured if I worked harder, if I did the right things, I would be rewarded for it, but now I'm in trouble because some guy… I just…it's not supposed to be like this."

"No. It's not," he said. And all this made him feel like an ass because he'd been…thinking about her. And she'd been objectified enough today.

Naturally, he couldn't just have a simple fantasy. No. That

would have been too damn kind of life. Life just didn't do kind for him.

Kind of a funny thought, up in a suite that overlooked Central Park, but hey, there were more important things in life than a room with a view.

He'd rather go back to living poor, on a ranch in Pine Ridge Falls, with the people he loved most, than be here alone. But that was another lifetime. Another man. He wasn't even going to think about it.

"Then why is it?" she asked.

"Hell if I know. Life never seems to be the way it's supposed to be," he said. "All you can do is enjoy the little things. Which is why I was thinking porn and chicken."

"I have no little things I enjoy," she said. "I enjoy nothing. And I think I hate everything." She was breathing hard, her eyes wide.

"Everything?"

"I don't even have a life. I don't even think I have any friends left. I work at this job, and I go back to my apartment and order takeout and I watch TV shows. I don't date I don't… I don't…" Her eyes clashed with his, a hard sock of heat hitting his gut.

"What else?" he asked.

She looked away. "If I don't date I think it's pretty obvious what else I'm not doing."

Oh, yes, he was well familiar with that problem. He hadn't gotten laid in so long he was afraid his long uprooted virginity was starting to grow back. If such a thing was possible. He hadn't seen sex since his twenties, and sitting where he was at thirty-five that seemed damn sad.

He'd had a lot more than getting some on his mind, though, but now…now it seemed like maybe he needed to do something about it. Maybe it was time to let another person touch him. Not a handshake or anything, but hands on naked skin. On skin that was normally covered by clothes.

He hadn't been tempted to connect in so long. He'd been avoiding it. He'd been too raw. But everything had scarred over now. Had come out tougher than he'd started. It would never heal, but he wasn't vulnerable anymore. He doubted he possessed the ability to be hurt at this point, to feel loss.

He'd maxed out that garbage a while ago.

"Yeah," he said, his voice rough. Affected. "Obvious."

"I guess maybe not because some people just... I can't believe I'm having this conversation with you. You officially know more of my baggage than my best friend, who I haven't talked to in four months because I'm an unhappy, terrible workaholic, and she's just as bad."

"Well, you're in my hotel room, I'm half-dressed.... It seems logical really."

"My phone?" she asked.

"Oh, yeah." That was why she was here. Her phone. The one on his bed. He'd completely forgotten. It hadn't seemed to matter.

"Yeah," she said, her eyes wide. "I kind of forgot. About my phone. Which I never do, because I'm addicted to using my phone. How sad is that? I am addicted to my phone. To keeping plugged into my office when I'm not there. Sometimes I get so caught up in work email during dinner that I forget to pay attention to the show I'm watching. I am a mess."

"You really are."

"I need to relax."

"I agree."

"Do you know what I need?" she asked, her small breasts rising and falling with the sharp pitch of her breathing.

"What?" he asked, his stomach tightening.

"I just need to relax."

"I agree."

"I need…" Her eyes had dropped back down to his chest. "I need to…make a decision instead of just flying under the radar. I think I need to cut loose." Her eyes met his again. "Got any ideas?"

"I do. But I'm a stranger and I'm pretty sure none of the ideas I have are appropriate for strangers."

"We shared a cab," she said, a desperate light in her dark gaze now.

"Well, then, I guess that changes things. Kiss me."

Chapter Four

Grace thought she might pass out. All the blood drained out of her head and pooled in her feet, her lips cold, her brain fuzzy.

Her skin was chilled, but inside she was burning up.

She didn't know what she was doing. She'd led the conversation here, that was undeniable. She'd been baiting him. Baiting this sexy stranger so that she could see just what he might do. So that she could...what, exactly, she didn't know.

Well, now it had culminated in a request—no, a demand—for a kiss.

His eyes were burning, golden fire, and she could feel it streaking through her.

She didn't kiss strangers. Ever.

Especially not shirtless strangers in hotel rooms that were probably more than her month's rent for one night. Especially not big rough, cowboy-type strangers. Who drew foxes and swore and took her phone and freely confessed to the desire to order porn.

Neither of her exes would have ever admitted to such male crassness.

Likely they engaged in it, but they never would have confessed it.

Though, maybe Zack wouldn't have confessed if she wasn't a stranger. Maybe he was feeling freer, too.

Maybe this would be good for both of them.

Sliding down the slippery slope, Grace?

She wanted to punch inner Grace in her smug perfect face. Except, inner Grace had a point. Inner Grace was thinking of Hannah. Of the bad sister. The one who had gone off the rails, into parties and drugs and now, to the point where no one had a clue where she was.

Hannah, the daughter who made her mother cry, and her father sit in a dark room and just stare ahead sadly, at nothing.

The daughter Grace had spent her teenage and adult years trying to make up for.

But no one has to know about this. No one would ever know.

She was fighting against this strange, icy feeling inside of her. The one that had kept her mouth frozen shut and her words carefully chosen while her boss had effectively ripped her a new one. The one that always checked with her parents before she made major decisions, to ensure that her decisions were good ones.

The one that kept her head down and worked hard, her entire life a big demonstration of just how *good* she was so that no one would ever question it.

And after that showdown in her boss's office, she was tired of that. Tired of trying to be the Grace everyone else wanted to see. The problem was she didn't know how to be anything else.

But no one was here to question this. Zack was a stranger. He didn't know anyone at work. He didn't know her parents. He didn't know her.

This room was out of time, this man out of context with everything else in her life.

Why not? Why not do this. Why not take this.

No one will ever know....

"One kiss," she said. And even as she said it, she knew it wouldn't stop at that.

But she was tired of being frozen in indecision. Tired of being scared to act.

So now she was acting. Just for now. Just for her.

"Sure," he said, arching a brow and moving toward her.

He hooked an arm around her waist and pulled her up against him, pinning her arms, his chest hard and hot against her wrists. "If you want to stop at one," he said, his breath fanning across her cheek.

He smelled good. Like skin and soap. No cologne or any other artificial scent. Just man. And she'd never really appreciated the smell of a man before.

"Well, we haven't even gotten to the one yet. You're counting your chickens before they're hatched."

"Am I still the fox in this scenario? Are the chickens in the same henhouse?"

"I don't know. Shut up and kiss me."

He did. His lips were hard on hers, taking, not asking. And there was nothing about that she should find hot. She wasn't into being taken. She wasn't into brute strength and big hands. Traditionally speaking. Right now his brute strength and big hands were really doing something for her.

Like, lots of somethings.

He curved his arms around her, his palms flat on her back, pulling her in, his large frame enveloping her. He curled blunt fingers onto her skin, her mouth rough on hers, his tongue delving deep.

She arched into him, and his hand slid downward, down the dip in her spine, curving over her butt. She should be... shocked. At the very least she should be shocked. She shouldn't be aroused. She shouldn't want to push her hips back so that his grasp on her was even firmer. So that he was holding her harder.

She certainly shouldn't be angling her head so she could kiss him deeper. But she was. She was doing all those things.

His touch was hot and sure, his tongue slick, his lips firm. She could feel his erection hardening against her stomach. And that was something else she should be offended by. But she wasn't.

She moved against his body, relished the feeling of his hard, thick length against her body. It was amazing. To make a man react like this to her.

She couldn't remember the last time it had been like this, if ever. And that was just from the man's end. From her end... well, it had never felt like this. Sex was something she did because if she was in a relationship, it was part of the package.

She'd never been desperate for it. Had never felt like she wanted to—no, needed to—run her whole body against her partner's, just so she could feel every inch of him on every inch of her. But she did now. She ached for it, the surface of her skin hypersensitive, tingling, desperate for his touch.

Suddenly, she was very aware of her nipples. She usually wasn't. They didn't do much, after all. A little tightening when it was cold. But now... Wow.

They ached. Honestly. She pressed herself against his chest in an attempt to get some relief. It sent a shock of heat down between her thighs. But it wasn't enough. She needed more. She needed everything.

She freed her trapped wrists and moved her hands over his chest, rough hair over hard muscle abrading her skin.

He was so very much a man, a stupid observation maybe, since obviously he was a man. But everything about him was like some kind of testosterone-laden candy land, designed for her own personal pleasure. There were men, and there were *men*.

He was a *man*.

He moved his hands lower, to her thighs, and then she was being lifted up off the ground. She wrapped her legs around his waist, scrabbling to get ahold of him, looping her arms around his neck. And they managed not to break the kiss. Technically, they were still on only one kiss.

He walked them both into the bedroom, then turned and pinned her against the wall, his body hard against hers, his whiskers burning her cheeks as he deepened the kiss. She rolled her hips forward, rocking her clit against his hard abs.

This was crazy. She was crazy. Certifiable. And immoral and wicked. And her parents would kill her dead if they knew she was even considering begging him to take her over to the big bed in the center of the room.

But they will never know. That's the beauty of it.

It was still crazy. She didn't know anything about this man beyond his name.

Well, that wasn't true. She knew he kissed like sin incarnate and that, even covered by denim, his erection promised pleasure she'd never known before. Pleasure she hadn't thought possible.

Right now, that was all she needed to know. She'd made a decision, the decision, and the consequences could go to hell.

That was a more exhilarating thought than she'd ever thought it possible to have. To not care, for just a little bit, what people thought, what would happen next.

She needed it. Almost more than she needed his mouth on hers.

He lowered her a bit so that his arousal lined up with where she ached for him the most. He thrust his hips, hard, fast, against her, sending streaks of heat through her veins.

She wrenched her lips from his. She was the first to break. But she couldn't breathe. She couldn't think. She couldn't…

Pleasure tightened down low inside of her, a wire drawn tight, running through her core. So tight, she thought it might break her.

Grace shifted against him, making sure everything lined up just right. He leaned forward, growling, taking her mouth with his, his teeth sinking into her lower lip.

And the wire snapped.

Release flooded her, internal muscles clenching tight as her climax ripped through her. She opened her lips on a silent scream, her body tightening, shaking. She felt wrecked when it was over. Drained, sated and, at the same time, hungry for more. She needed her clothes off. They were too tight, the fabric heavy on her skin, constricting.

Weird because it was a tailored outfit and it had felt fine earlier.

But she didn't feel like the same person. She didn't feel like she was in the same body.

That could have something to do with it.

"I broke the rules," he said, kissing the side of her neck, his teeth scraping the delicate skin there. "Sorry about that."

He didn't sound sorry at all. Fair enough. She wasn't, either.

"No need to apologize," she said.

"Good. Because I'm going to need you to take your clothes off now."

He helped her get her feet back on the ground, and he released his hold on her. "Take your clothes off," he said, his eyes burning into her.

She found herself obeying. Immediately. Because it was what she wanted. To get rid of these clothes. To be pressed up against him. Skin-to-skin.

"You, too," she said, working the buttons on her blouse with shaking fingers.

She'd never been entirely comfortable with her body. She lacked curves. There was no dramatic swooping in at her waist. Her torso was slim, but straight up and down, and her hips were barely bumps. To say nothing of her A-cups.

She felt like he was expecting her to unveil a work of art, and instead of Matisse, he was about to get *Spaghetti Splattered on a Canvas by Monkeys*. Okay, not that bad, but she didn't really consider herself worthy of the level of concentration, the level of excitement, in his eyes.

She undid the top button, then the next and he put his hand over the front of his jeans, squeezing himself. That big masculine hand caressing his own body was a sight that nearly sent her over the edge.

Again. Already.

He was magic, or something. Orgasm was a rare, elusive creature for her. One that she caught glimpses of through the forest, only to have it vanish into nothingness the moment her partner sneezed while still inside of her, or something.

She doubted even a sneeze could scare this one off. It was some kind of super breed of climax. Rarer, it seemed, than the regular ones, but not as skittish.

He wasn't even touching her, and she was close—so close her heart rate was in high gear. With each button opened, he looked more intensely at her.

She shrugged her top off and let it fall to the floor, and he groaned, curling his hands around his length and squeezing. He didn't seem to mind that her cups did not overflow.

Boosted by that, she reached behind her back and unclasped her bra, letting it fall down her arms. Then she shook it loose and let it join her shirt on the floor.

Not the sexiest move, perhaps, but he didn't seem to care. He was looking at her like she was the first woman he'd ever seen naked.

Though, she wasn't naked yet. She pushed her pencil skirt down, wiggling her hips and taking her underwear down along with it.

"Now you," she said, not sure where she found her voice. Her throat felt too tight to force words out, and somehow she had. Maybe because she needed to see him naked. More than she needed air. Like now.

He unsnapped the jeans and shoved them down his thighs. Those thighs. They were every bit as amazing as she'd imagined. People would go broke putting coins in those old peep-show things just to see those thighs.

Hot. Damn.

Then she looked up just a bit and she really couldn't breathe anymore.

Never mind. If all *that* was on offer in the peepshow she would go bankrupt. She would be found on her hands and knees on the sidewalk looking for spare change. Because he had absolutely the most impressive piece of male equipment she'd ever seen in her life.

"What?" he asked.

"What?"

"You're staring."

"Well…yes. I am."

"Why are you staring at my cock?"

The way he said that word, such a dirty word that you didn't hear in polite conversation, made her heart skitter. "I am staring at your…your…because well, because you're the most beautiful man I've ever seen. And also, I'm interested in having sex with you. So that seems a perfectly good reason to stare."

A slow smile spread across his face. "Say it again."

"What?"

"That you want to have sex with me. So direct and prim."

"How is it prim?" she asked, blinking.

"Because if it would have been me… I just would have said I wanted to fuck you."

Heat seared her cheeks. "Oh."

"Did I offend you, darlin'?"

"No." It was just that she'd never before had someone say something like that to her. It was a far cry from Aiden's "Wanna do it?" back in freshman year of college, and it was an even farther cry from David's vague grunting noise before he'd rolled over to give her a kiss and get a little action before they fell asleep at night.

It was direct. And…earthy. And she liked it.

"Is that what you want?" he asked.

"Yes," she said, without even hesitating. "I do. I want it."

Then he pulled her back into his arms, kissing her, bringing them down onto the bed with her on top of him, his...cock sliding against her clit.

She leaned over and kissed him, his hand curving around and cupping her breast, teasing her nipple.

"Yes," she said. "Yes."

"You wanted that?"

"I've been wanting it. I thought you were going to make me ask."

"Hopefully I'll be able to figure out what you want. But if I don't get it right, I expect you to tell me just what you want. I want to blow your mind. I want to give you the best you've ever had, but we don't know each other. We aren't in a relationship. That means you have to tell me what you want. Because I don't know." He squeezed her nipple gently. "I don't know if you like Italian food or Mexican food better. I don't know if you like classical or rock. I don't know if you like it bent over the bed, or if you like to be on top. If you like to give head or get it."

"Yes," she said, her whole body hot now. "Yes to all. And any."

He was making her experience seem woeful. She'd never been bent over anything. She'd been on top a few times, but mainly to speed things along for herself. Or rather, to make the climax creature less elusive.

"Maybe we'll start here," he said. He lifted his head up and circled her nipple with his tongue, then ran the flat of it over the tightened bud before sucking it deep in his mouth.

She closed her eyes, let the pleasure wash over her, through her. There was something about him. Not just what he did, but *him*.

He traced the indent of her spine with the tip of his finger. Such a mundane action in many ways. But when he did it? It left a trail of fire. It left her feeling like she would never be the same.

"Oh…crap." He reached to the nightstand and opened the drawers, his hand pressed against her lower back, holding her to his body while he turned and fished around in the drawer. "Oh…thank you, Marsha."

She wasn't going to question that. Not too closely. Especially not when what he produced turned out to be condoms. There was no happy road for her mind to go down there.

It didn't matter why he had the condoms. Nothing mattered but this moment, because this was the only moment they would have.

He shifted her, handling her like her weight was nothing, the well-defined muscles in his arm and on his chest shifting as he did. Then he opened the condom and positioned it on the head of his member, rolling it on slowly.

He guided her onto his length, his hold firm. She went with him, taking him in slowly, gripping his shoulders tight as he filled her. Stretched her. He felt so good. So much better than anything or anyone had a right to.

It was like the first hit off a potent drug. She imagined. She'd never done drugs. Because drugs were for the other daughter. The bad one. Just like she'd never done a stranger. Because this wasn't something for the good daughter, either.

Because it was wrong. Because there was a chance that the drugs and the men would be addicting, and that she would never get enough.

That she wouldn't be perfect. That she would be ruined.

He flexed his hips and thrust up fully inside of her, and then she knew. She was ruined. For sex. For all other men. Forever.

There had never been anything like this before, and in that blinding moment, with him fully inside her, she knew there never would be again.

She looked down at him, their eyes clashing, and she felt it hit deep inside.

Then she squeezed her eyes tight and started to move. Holding onto his shoulders, starting slow before building up, the taut wire stretching out again, through her whole body.

She rode him harder, sweat beading over her skin, his hands moving over her curves before gripping her hips and holding on tight.

"Oh... Zack," she said.

She wasn't ready for the second climax. It crashed over her like a wave, sudden and shocking, moving through her whole body, taking her over completely.

It was enough to send him over, too. He thrust up into her two more times before freezing, fingers digging hard into her flesh as he gave up control, his head falling back, his expression that of a man in pain, a harsh groan on his lips.

Then he released his hold on her, his arms thrown back above his head, his chest rising and falling sharply with each breath.

"Dammit," he said, short and sharp.

"What?" She got off him, her hand still planted on his chest, her heart beating fast. "Is something wrong?"

"No, I just... I couldn't think of anything else to say because I think you might have killed me."

She could feel his heart pounding beneath her palm. "You're still alive. I can feel it."

"I don't know. I'm pretty sure...yep, pretty sure I'm dead."

"Because it was good? Or are you now an emotionally scarred ghost due to some terrible error in my intercourse technique?"

"Because I didn't remember sex was this damn good," he said, rolling onto his side.

"So the condoms weren't from a recent encounter with Marsha?"

He looked stricken. "What? No. I mean...she probably made sure they were here. Trying to keep me out of trouble. I think she's of the opinion I land on the evolutionary scale several positions below her basset hound. That is an ugly dog. She thinks he's beautiful."

"Who is Marsha?"

"Do you really want to talk about this now?"

"Only if she's your lover or your wife."

"None of the above. She's my manager."

"Oh." She blinked. "Your manager?"

"Oh…artsy shit." He waved his hand. "Not a big deal."

She flashed back to the fox. "What kind of artsy…stuff?"

"I'm an artist, I guess," he said, looking painfully uncomfortable.

"You're an artist?" she asked, feeling completely incredulous that the rather rough, uncultured man who'd just taken her against a wall was an *artist*. "That's how you make your living?"

"Yeah."

"That's…incredibly hard to do."

He lifted a shoulder. "I got lucky. I got some recognition for some things early on. And then I signed on with Marsha and she's…well, she's not a basset hound. She runs more toward pit bull. But that's what you want in a manager, right?"

"I suppose you do."

"I'm here for a gallery thing," he said, lifting a shoulder. "I'm not very comfortable with any of it yet."

It was so weird, sitting on a stranger's bed, naked, talking about work.

But it was interesting. To see him uncomfortable. He was so confident, so unaffected. But there was something to the way he talked about being an artist. A strange dismissiveness.

She had a feeling, for whatever reason, that probably meant he cared about it.

"You're actually doing an exhibition here?"

"Yeah, and schmoozing stuff. It's not my thing. I've done

it before, but I don't get any more comfortable with it, it turns out. Damned inconvenient all things considered."

"I guess it would be."

"Anyway, I don't really want to talk about me. I'd rather talk about you. And your breasts."

She looked down. "These ol' things?"

He threw his head back and laughed, then lifted his thumb and dragged it over her nipple, sending a shiver through her body. "Yeah. I'm pretty impressed."

"At the private school I went to the girls used to ask if I'd gotten bitten by mosquitos on my chest."

"Small is fine," he said. "You're small and perfect. And real. Better that than fake, I think."

"Well, you're in the minority." She stood up. "I guess I should go. It's…well, what is it…seven o'clock?"

"Nearly."

"I should go home and…water my plants."

"Right. I should…order room service."

"I hope you can skip the porn now."

He nodded. "It's safe to say that particular urge is managed."

"I think I'm flattered."

"Then maybe my charm has improved with the orgasm."

"So…should we…should I just go? I've never done this before." And she was starting to shake, the buzz from her orgasm wearing off, leaving reality in its wake.

"Do you want the honest truth?"

She picked her clothes up from the floor by the wall and started tugging them on. "Depends. But…hit me."

"I've never done this before, either."

"I can't believe that."

"It's true."

"I've been in two comfortably friendly relationships. One wherein I lived with the guy until one day he wanted to move out. Neither of us were too sad about it. That was six months ago… I can't even muster up any sadness over it. And…and that's been it for me. No wild one…afternoon stands."

"Well, I'm sort of coming off a…uh…marriage."

She froze. "Oh."

"I'm *not* married," he said. "It's just… I *was*. And that kind of ate up my wild one-night-stand years."

"I bet."

"That was information you didn't need," he said, looking down. She examined his profile, his square jaw, the rough whiskers on his chin. He was embarrassed now. It was sort of adorable. It made her heart do very strange things. "See?" he said, looking up at her, his forehead creasing, the light from the bedside lamp casting shadows over his muscles. "I'm bad at this."

Well, so was she. Because, suddenly, she didn't want to tear herself away from him.

"Well, me, too. But I promise I won't boil your rabbit or anything similarly inappropriate."

"What about my fox?"

She wrinkled her nose as she wiggled back into her skirt. "Think I'll keep him. Maybe he'll be worth something someday."

"Like after I cut my ear off and die?"

She laughed. "Well, I killed you so…the market value on your work will have gone up exponentially in just the past few moments."

"I'll alert the media. Or rather, I'll tell Marsha to."

"Great. Sounds like a…thing. So… I'm going to go."

"Don't forget your phone," he said.

For a full thirty seconds, she had no idea what the man was talking about. Then the memory trickled in slowly. Her phone. What she was there for. The thing she was addicted to. That didn't seem to matter so much now.

"Right. Phone."

He rummaged around the bedsheets. "Here it is."

"The things it must have seen," she said, holding her hand out, her stomach lurching as he placed it in her palm, his fingertips brushing her skin.

"Yeah, true. I feel like maybe it didn't see quite enough."

That made her stomach free fall into her toes. "Oh. Well. I..."

"Just a second." He got up and walked out of the bedroom, totally unconcerned with his nudity, then returned a moment later with his phone, then he handed it to her. "Call yourself. With my phone."

She typed in her number with a shaky thumb and hit the call button. A second later, her phone started playing a piano riff. She hit Ignore.

"Now you have my number," he said. "If you want...something...again, call me." He took his phone back and threw it on the bed. "If not, don't. No pressure."

"Right," she said. "No pressure."

"This was good," he said.

That was the understatement of the century. "Yeah."

"Maybe I'll see you."

"Sure. Maybe we'll grab the same cab." She wouldn't call. She wouldn't be that weak.

"Stranger things have happened," he said.

"They certainly have."

Like her whole day. Her whole crazy day. A day that she had a feeling had changed something in her forever.

Chapter Five

Zack thought he felt his phone buzz. He shoved his hand in the pocket of the ridiculous dress pants he was wearing, but his phone was still.

Another phantom buzz.

She's not gonna call, moron. Tell your downstairs brain to chill out.

Grace Song wasn't going to call for a repeat performance. It had been a one-time thing. An amazing thing. But one time was better for both of them.

Zack had more baggage than he could carry, and he wasn't about to ask someone else to come walk along with him while he tried to complete the impossible task. It was way better to just trudge along, dragging it behind him. Ignoring it all and forging ahead with his…life.

He looked around the room, at the exhibition of art. Great art. Women in black dresses and suits, men in black suits, too. The uniform didn't vary much. It was New York, after all.

This was the kind of thing Marsha said he had to do be-cause…image, inroads, connections, blah blah, he'd stopped listening after that because he'd seen a Sabrett hot-dog cart and he'd immediately wanted that more than a high-powered art career. With relish, thanks.

Of course, eating hot dogs wouldn't pay his bills. Unless he could become a competitive eater. There was merit in that.

Then maybe he could go back to doing art in the barn on his property.

There's nothing to go back to.

His life was depressing as hell. Which was the thing that sucked so much about loss. Even when the knife edge on your grief dulled, you were still missing something.

Almost a decade and his house felt too empty. He had a feeling it was one of those things that just left a hole. Though, in his case, he thought it might have left a lot more. He felt hollowed out, on a good day.

Sex with Grace had filled him with heat, and that had been a whole lot better than the emptiness. So instead of paying attention to the exhibit, he was hoping his phone would ring.

But it wasn't going to. Because she had more sense than he did. Or rather, more sense than his penis.

Not that that was a feat, by any stretch of the imagination. That body part wasn't known for being the most discriminating. And since his had been on sabbatical for six years…well.

His pocket buzzed and he jerked to attention, reaching down inside again and curling his fingers around the phone, tugging it out. Thank God. It was ringing. And it was a New York number.

He answered it.

"Hi."

"Zack?"

It was Grace. It was her. He resisted the urge to drop to his knees and give thanks in the middle of the gallery.

"Yeah," he said, trying to sound casual.

"I know I shouldn't be calling you."

"I didn't think you were going to." Not that he was complaining.

"Well, I wasn't. Then I thought…a one-night-stand is awfully…you know…dicey. Maybe…maybe… You're probably busy."

"Nope," he said, looking around the room, counting all the very important people. There were a lot of them. "Not in the least."

"Good. Good. Um…121 West 72nd Street. My place. It's small but it's…there's a bed."

"That's all we need."

He disconnected the call, gave a halfhearted goodbye to anyone who might be relevant, then slipped out of the party as quickly as possible.

It took way longer to get across town than he wanted. In the end, it probably would have been faster and cheaper to walk, even though there had been a cab right out front, but he didn't like the idea of hoofing it down the streets of Manhattan with a hard-on that probably looked like a crowbar pushing against the front of his jeans.

Not that it was much better to have something like that while in a cab, but at least he could sit down and pretend it wasn't happening.

He drummed his fingers on his thigh, impatience and arousal coursing through him. Why the hell was there traffic at ten at night? If people were out in Pine Ridge Falls at this hour they were just parked in the bar.

He let out an exasperated sigh, and was about a second from getting out and walking, when the cab stopped in front of an older-looking building with an open convenience store on the bottom floor.

He handed a large bill to the driver and got out, shutting the door harder than was strictly necessary. Then he took his phone out of his pocket, and selected her number out of the recent-call list. "How do I get in here?" he asked.

"Oh! Zack?"

"No. Candygram."

"You have to go to the door, it's next to the store."

He looked around and saw what she was talking about. "Okay."

"And I'll buzz you in. I'm in 3B."

"Great." He heard the buzz and tugged the door open.

"The elevator is rickety," she said.

"I'm good with the stairs," he said, hanging up.

He was surprised how old the building was. Surprised that Grace didn't live somewhere with a shiny lobby and more frills. Though, he did know that rent was inflated beyond reason here. Still, he'd never had a reason to look for a place in the area, so he had no idea just what that meant in a practical way.

The stairs were narrow and drafty, dirt pushed deep into the grooves between the steps. It was obviously clean overall, but not scrubbed deep. Another testament to the age of the building. It would never sparkle.

He found himself fascinated by it. The architecture. The lines. It was rooted to the earth in a way other buildings didn't seem to be. Like it was created rather than built.

And that made him think of a potential piece. A collection.

Unusual for him to get any inspiration here. Typically, he needed to be home. Closer to all the past's poison. He had to kind of wallow in it to feel enough to work sometimes.

Dammit. He was some kind of clichéd tortured artist. What the hell was that? He blamed it on eating fricking pâté at all these parties. Back at home that crap came out of a cat-food can.

Which was not what he wanted to be thinking about right now. He wanted to be thinking about Grace. About her soft skin. Her glossy hair. The way it felt to slide deep inside her body.

Yeah, that was better than pâté.

He knocked on the door with the correct number/letter combination, then heard locks jiggling before it opened to reveal Grace, hastily tucking her hair into a bun.

"Are you primping?"

Her eyes rounded. "Yeah."

"Why?"

"Because."

"I'm going to take it down, you know."

She leaned into the door, her posture a poor attempt at casual. "Yeah but… I don't ever wear it down so…so it seemed like I should pin it up."

She was wearing a purple dress that formed to her slight curves, a black ribbon tied around her slender waist. She had stockings on. He had some serious opinions on which kind they should be.

"No need to dress for me, darlin'," he said. "But I do appreciate it."

"You are…in a suit," she said, looking him over slowly.

He looked down. "Oh. Yeah. I was at a thing."

"You said you weren't busy."

"I wasn't. I was bored."

"You were bored."

"Industry stuff."

"So you left an important industry event to come here and witness the lowest low my personal restraint has ever experienced?" she asked, arching a brow.

"Are you going to invite me in or do I have to stay in this incredibly narrow hallway all night. Because I have to admit, that's not exactly what I thought you called me over here for."

"Oh, yeah." She moved away from the door and waved her arm, as if ushering him in. "I actually just needed my garbage disposal fixed, and my super was busy. So-o…"

"If that's a euphemism for your lady parts, it needs work."

She clapped her hands and laughed, bending at the waist, then dropping her head forward and shaking it. "You're ridiculous. We're ridiculous. All of this is ridiculous."

She straightened, running her fingers under her eyes and blinking rapidly. "I wasn't supposed to call you."

"I shouldn't have answered."

He shoved his hands in his pockets and looked around the apartment. It was different than the rest of the building. Fresh, bright white paint on the walls, with matching, immaculate rugs over dark walnut floors. There were floral arrangements all over the damn place. And framed, matted paintings of flowers. Somehow it all managed not to look frilly. Just a little simple beauty in an otherwise clean space.

"I'm glad you did. Because I would have felt like a leper."

He walked toward her, his stomach tightening with each step. Then he put his hand on her cheek, curled his fingers around the back of her neck. "You're certainly not a leper."

"That is…not a great romantic compliment."

He frowned. "It's really not. I'm out of practice. Let me try again?"

She licked her lips and nodded.

He took a deep breath and let it out slowly. "Okay. You're beautiful."

That earned him a blush. "Thank you."

"And you smell nice."

"Also good."

"And I think I've been hard since you left the other day."

Her lips folded in and her smile widened, like she was trying to hold something back. "One too far," she said.

"I sensed it might have been. But then I went with it."

"Your instincts are broken, don't trust them."

"Now that is the damn truth." He leaned in and kissed her then, because he knew that it would be better than anything he could say next.

Because she was right, he didn't know what to say. He sucked at this. But he remembered how to kiss. At least, he seemed to remember how to kiss when she was in kissing range. And more to the point: he *wanted* to kiss her.

She wrapped her arms around his neck, arching into him.

The way she responded…it made him feel more alive than he'd felt in longer than he could remember. Everything, even sex, had been just going through the motions after his daughter died.

And there was a point where he just hadn't bothered.

But this was new. It was like fresh grass. All bright and new. The same as what had come before, but entirely different somehow, too.

All terrible metaphors aside, Grace was the first thing he'd felt with his whole body in way too long.

He wrenched his mouth away from hers and tugged down the zipper on her dress, revealing a black lace bra and matching panties. And the stockings were indeed the kinds with lacy tops, held up onto her slender thighs as if by some blessed sexual magic.

He loved those. And he'd forgotten how much until this moment. Simple pleasures that he hadn't even let himself think of in far too long. Blue skies, birds chirping and stay-up stockings on a woman in a thong.

Life was beautiful. Right now. With Grace's bare skin beneath his hands and her name on his lips.

He kissed the curve of her neck, ran his tongue along the line of her collarbone. She tasted so good. So damn good. And he needed her now.

"So why did you call me?" he asked. He probably shouldn't be asking.

"Like I said. One-night stands seem cheap…sordid." She shifted. "Okay, it didn't seem cheap and sordid. I guess that's the thing. I expected it to. But it didn't. And in the end, I just wanted you again. And… I'm so obsessed with not making mistakes. I'm sure I'm making one right now, but I'm enjoying it. So…so why not?"

The question hung between them, unanswered.

"Tell me you have condoms," he said, "because I wasn't expecting this."

"Oh! Right." Grace jumped away from him and walked to counter. And he watched her butt the whole way. She was still wearing heels. A fantasy that he just didn't deserve. Because he had nothing to give her other than this.

So give it to her good.

Well, that was a solution that appeased his libido anyway.

Grace started rifling through the little plastic bag on the the counter, pulling out a candle, a package of mints, a bottle of hand soap and, finally, condoms.

"Did a little shopping before you called?"

"The condoms started this whole thing. I was not going to call you. I wasn't even tempted. Mostly. I mean, I was, but I sitll wasn't going to. But then I was walking down the aisle for things…nonsexual things. And I saw…well, they're ribbed," she said, her eyebrows arching. "I've never, never tried that before."

"Oh, really?"

"Yes. And then I…sort of thought of the fact that there are a lot of things I haven't tried and maybe I needed more than just once with you."

His gut tightened as he watched her tear into the box. She rummaged inside and produced a strip of condom packets, tearing one off. She looked at him, expectation gleaming in her dark eyes.

"So there are these," she said.

"And?" he asked.

"Go ahead and…take it out."

"Take it out?"

"Your…your…take off your clothes," she said.

"What is it you want to see, baby?" he asked, suddenly desperate to hear something raw from those pretty, polished lips.

"I…"

He wrapped his hands around himself, squeezed his erection through his pants. "What?"

She looked down, red staining her cheeks.

"Say it," he said, "or you don't get it. And I know you want it."

She looked up again, her eyes meeting his. "Your cock," she said, drawing in a sharp breath immediately after.

"I like hearing you talk dirty," he said. "And because you did what I asked..." He worked at the belt on his pants, hoping she didn't notice the trembling in his fingers.

Hard to play it cold and commanding when he wanted her so bad it was a physical ache.

He tugged himself free, shoving his pants halfway down his hips. She licked her lips, like she'd done earlier. A nervous tic, maybe. But it sent a shot of pure heat all the way down his spine.

He reached out and took the packet from her hand. "We don't need this just yet," he said. He pushed his pants down the rest of the way, then looked for a place to leave the condom.

There was a little table by the entry door. Polished wood with spindly legs and small, balled feet at the ends of them. He put the condom there, right next to the white vase. Right on a doily.

"Why don't we need it yet?" she asked, standing there, looking confused and sexier than anyone had a right to.

"Because. Things moved a little bit fast last time and I didn't get to do something. I regret it."

"What?"

He pulled her back into his arms and kissed her, pushing his fingers beneath the waistband of her panties, cupping her butt. Squeezing her. Then he kissed her throat, the valley between her breasts. And as he moved lower, he brought her panties down with him, until they were around her ankles, and he was kneeling in front of her.

He braced his hands on her hips and tugged her forward,

pressing his mouth to the tender skin just above the dark hair at the apex of her thighs.

She shivered and he tightened his hold on her, kissing her again, this time just beneath her hip bone, before moving back.

"This is what I want," he said, sliding his tongue between her slick folds, over her clit, then deep inside her body.

He groaned, moving his hands so that he was holding her ass. It had been too long. Too long since he'd indulged himself this way. Since he'd tasted a woman. Given her pleasure while he took his own.

And even that was simplifying it too much. Because in the moment, how long it had been since he'd been with someone else didn't matter. He could have done this to another woman yesterday and it wouldn't have made Grace—her scent, her flavor—any less intoxicating.

She forked her hands through his hair, tugging, the sharp pain sending another throb of arousal through his body.

"Zack." She said his name like a prayer. Or a curse. He wasn't sure which. And it didn't really matter.

He increased his efforts, licking her, sucking her, and she tugged harder on his hair. He moved his hand, pushing his fingers between her thighs, pushing one deep inside her body.

A sharp, shocked sound escaped her lips. He lifted his head. "Should I stop?"

"No!"

He chuckled and lowered his head, tasting her long and deep, and she shivered beneath his tongue. So perfect. So intense. Her response was enough to make him come then and there. But not yet. No, not yet. He needed to be inside her.

"I could do this all day," he said, sliding the flat of his tongue over her sensitized flesh and blowing lightly on her damp skin.

"I would...die," she said, breathless, her legs starting to wobble.

He braced her, held her up, kissing her deeper, working his tongue inside of her until she cried out, her hands moving to his shoulders, nails digging deep into his skin.

"Can't have that," he said, as out-of-breath as she was. And he hadn't even gotten his. "You're too damn pretty."

"Is that the only reason I'm of…any use to you?" she asked, still panting.

"Hell no." He stood up, keeping his hold tight on her, lifting her off the ground. Then he saw the condom on the table. "I need you for all kinds of things."

He moved her to the table. "Put your hands on the doily, darlin'."

She obeyed, but shot him a look. "You need me for sex," she said.

"Same reason you need me," he said, positioning himself behind her, reaching for the condom. "What else would need some big, rough cowboy for? Certainly not for work events. You just need to use me. For your own personal satisfaction."

"That's true," she said. "I'm using you, too."

"We're using each other. And that doesn't have to be cheap or dirty. It's pretty damn hot really." He rolled the condom onto his length and guided himself to the wet entrance to her body, testing her slowly. "Bend over just a little more," he said.

She obeyed, and he pushed in deeper. He swore. "You're so tight."

"You're just big," she said, her voice shaky.

He put his hand on her hip, then slid his palm over her stomach and down between her legs, running his fingers through her folds. "Okay?"

"So…good. I didn't even know… I didn't…" He thrust his hips forward and she moaned in response. "I didn't know it could be so good."

Then he couldn't say anything else. All he could do was

give in to the desire roaring through his body. All he could do was chase his release, each thrust bringing him closer.

"Harder," she said, the word a near growl.

"Like this?" he asked, pulling her back against him as he pounded into her.

"Yes," she said. "Yes. Don't be careful. Just…you don't need to be careful."

So he wasn't. He stroked her in time with his thrusts, until he couldn't hold on anymore. That he'd had this much control was a damn miracle. And it was all gone now.

He pressed his forehead to her shoulder, bracing himself for the release that was about to hit. But there was no preparing for it.

She let out a hoarse cry, her internal muscles tightening around him, and that was the end of his restraint. He swore, holding onto her so tightly he thought he might leave a bruise. She moaned again, shifting her hands on the table, dragging the doily—and vase—to the side, and tipping it and its contents onto the floor. "I hope that wasn't expensive," he said, eyeing the shards of porcelain on the floor.

She laughed, the sound unsteady. She moved away from him. "Careful, don't have shoes on." She still did. She still had the shoes, her stockings and her bra. "I'll get a broom. Stay back."

She ran a hand over her flushed cheeks and walked back into the kitchen area and he couldn't help but watch her butt.

"I'll be right back," he said. "Bathroom?"

"That way."

She gestured to the hall at the other end of the living room. He found his way and disposed of the condom, returning just in time to see her sweeping up the last of the vase.

"It was my Nai-Nai's. Poor Grandma, she loved this vase."

All the blood drained out of his face. "Grace…"

"I'm kidding!" she said. "Sorry, bad joke. And my grandmother is alive, in one of those really nice assisted-living places. The vase was from Target."

Grace felt like she'd made a huge misstep with Zack just now. Which was great since she was still knocked loopy from having sex in her entryway. Like that. She'd never done it like that before. It was intense. And amazing. And then she'd ruined it with a dead-grandma joke.

"I'm sorry, Zack. I didn't mean to upset you."

He shook his head. "No. It's not...it was a joke."

He still looked stunned. And a little pale. "You don't look okay."

"I understand how much things can mean to you after you lose someone," he said. "If I would have broken your grandmother's vase because I was an impatient jerk who bent you over what is...a damn nice but delicate-looking table, I would have felt like a giant moron."

"It's fine. I've never had anything like this. Where...where it seemed easier to do it like that because walking to the bedroom is too hard. I'm...enjoying it."

"I'm glad you find me enjoyable."

"Specifically I find your...male member enjoyable."

"Oh, back on such formal terms," he said, shaking his head. "You were on a more familiar basis with my...member."

Her face heated. "Well, that was... I was in the moment. Have you eaten?"

"I nibbled on some cold shellfish. And yeah, nibble is all I got for that. Tiny, slippery cold... I haven't eaten."

"Would you like to stay? And build up your strength so that you can do—" she waved her hand "—all that to me again?"

She couldn't believe she was inviting him to stay, but honestly...she'd been consumed with not putting a toe out of line for years. For always. Since high school, and college, and then onto her job, where she'd kept her head down and just tried to be...what she thought she was supposed to be. Which was a lot of hard work. And she'd had relationships, but they'd just been a nice addendum to her work life. Like whipped cream on your latte. Sure, it was good, but without it you still had a latte.

Losing David had been like losing whipped cream. Except by then she'd been kind of tired of him. And she was never tired of whipped cream, so maybe that was a bad example.

Not tired of him in an active way. It's just…when he'd said it was time to end it, it had seemed right to her, too. That wasn't normal.

Maybe she was dysfunctional. Possibly a cyborg. She'd long suspected. She'd even been accused of it a time or two.

But hard work and doing right were important. Those values had been instilled in her early, and success in those things didn't come by accident. She'd wanted to show her parents that they didn't have to worry about her. That she was going to do things…perfectly. That meant good grades, that meant while she was getting established very few things could take a higher priority than her job.

Right now, though, her job was causing her stress. And orgasms were…a form of stress release.

"How long are you here?" she asked.

"Two weeks," he said. "I have the exhibition and before that about a million meetings and cocktail get-together thingies."

"You sound enthused."

"I'm not."

"What do you like to eat?"

"Stuff that is too big for a toothpick." He bent down and picked up his pants, then put them on without putting on any underwear. Oh, my. That would be fun later.

He was so hot. All hard abs and pecs, sprinkled with a light dusting of brown hair. For a moment she forgot what they were discussing.

"Right um…pizza? Thai? Indian?"

"Indian would be good," he said, sinking onto her white,

Victorian-style settee. He looked…almost comical on it. So big and masculine and dark against the floral velvet.

"Great, I'll put in an order." She walked into the kitchen and pulled up her favorite restaurant on her phone and placed a quick order. "Done."

"Nothing better than food delivery through an app. We don't have that living out in the sticks so I live off delivery when I travel."

"Yeah, I try not to talk to people if I don't have to. I have to talk to people all day in my business so…"

"So you avoid them later. Good plan. That's what I do six months out of the year, not in a solid chunk, mind you. Then for the other six months I do things like this. I was in Paris two months ago, and went all through Europe. I have to go again soon."

She laughed. "Oh, wow. You *have* to go?"

"Yeah. London."

"I think that sounds amazing." She rested her elbows on the kitchen counter and looked at him. "You don't seem thrilled."

"I am. I mean… I don't know." He took a deep breath and looked away from her, staring straight out in front of him, at nothing. "Sometimes I think my give-a-damn is busted."

This probably pertained to his ex-wife. And she bet that was off-limits for them, since they were just having sex. And apparently eating takeout.

"How did you get into art?" she asked, a safer question. "You really, really don't seem like the type. You're too…"

"Country?"

"Grounded. I think of artists, particularly of the modern variety who are successful, and I think of…whimsy."

"Whimsy?"

"Yes."

He spread his arms out wide, the muscles in his forearms shifting. "Am I not whimsical?"

"Not so much, cowboy."

"What about the fox I drew for you? Wasn't he whimsical?"

"All right," she said, smiling when she thought of the sketch. "He was kind of whimsical. What medium do you normally work in?"

"I do a lot of metal work. Iron. Welding."

"Oh, that makes sense." It accounted for his physique, that was for sure.

"I'm basically a glorified blacksmith. But I make animals and people rather than armor and shoes for…animals and people."

"I think that's amazing."

"Gives me something to pour a lot of physical frustration into, that's for sure."

"It's more interesting than being a financial advisor."

He tilted his head back, his eyes meeting hers again. "Then why are you a financial advisor?"

"I'm good at it. And I do enjoy it. I want… I want to be successful."

He nodded slowly. "You know what's funny?"

"What?"

"I've never cared if I was."

"And you are," she said. The downstairs buzzer went off. "Bet that's the food." She walked to the door and hit the intercom button. "Yes?"

A voice crackled through the speaker. "Ms. Song, I have your dinner."

She pushed the button to open the door, then looked back at Zack. It was funny. Sometimes he just seemed like a man's man. Steady, not taking much too seriously. Like he was a guy who didn't care about much with any great depth.

And then in a flash she would witness a moment of deep, aching sadness that she didn't think matched anything she'd ever felt in her whole life.

She was seeing it now. And it made her wonder if it was there all the time, kept under everything else, but there.

It was terrifying to her. She wasn't sure why, only that it was.

There was a knock at the door and she jumped. "The food." She turned and went to the door, took the order and paid as quickly as possible. Then she went into the kitchen and started setting the boxes out on the counter. "Oh, good. Paper plates and plastic utensils in here. And…want to open a bottle of wine?"

"That would be good." He got up from the couch and walked into the little kitchen, filling up the space even more alarmingly than he'd filled up the couch.

"Everything for that is in the cupboard by the fridge, including the aerator."

"Aerator. That's pretty fancy considering we have paper plates."

"Yeah, well, we're celebrating," she said, dishing rice, chicken tikka masala and naan onto their plates.

"What are we celebrating?" he asked, turning the corkscrew, then tugging the cork out before pouring the wine. He'd skipped the aerator but she wouldn't be shrewish about it.

"Good sex," she said. "Which is a lot rarer than you might think."

"Yeah?" he asked, tipping the glass of wine up to his lips.

"I've never had it before you."

He snorted into his wineglass and sent several droplets of dark red over the edge of the glass. "Really?" he asked, coughing.

"I've had okay sex. I've had orgasms but…you know I can give those to myself. Have been for six months now. Batteries are cheaper than men, I find."

She didn't know why she was telling him this stuff. Normally she'd be embarrassed. But the guy had just bent her over a table so there wasn't really much to be embarrassed about at this point.

He poured a glass of wine for her, and handed it over. "Where do you eat?" he asked.

"The couch," she said. "That's what the coffee table is for. This place is the size of a goldfish bowl so I find less furniture is better."

They took their plates into the living room and he sat on the couch. She eyeballed it, and the little wedge of space left for her. David hadn't taken up so much space, that was for sure.

She let out a breath and sat down next to him, their thighs touching.

"So tell me about the previous sex, which was bad," he said.

"Uh…not bad. Just…not remarkable. I had a boyfriend in college who was young. You know what I mean by that."

"Fast?"

"Very."

"And after that?"

"Two years of celibacy, followed by David. Who I was with for five years. I lived with him for a while. Which I think was kind of the beginning of the end. He was like a fixture, and so was I. And you stop looking at fixtures, especially when you're busy. And you?"

He took a bite of his rice and looked away. "Before you, I hadn't had sex in six years."

Chapter Six

Well, damn. So, he'd confessed *that*. Something about this little velvet couch must have been reminiscent of a psych office. Not that he'd ever been to one. Though, some, like his manager, would argue he should go. Deal with his issues. His grief.

But he didn't want to. His grief was his blanket and without it...without it he would be exposed.

Though, grief was a damned itchy blanket.

Even so, he was attached.

"You...what?" She blinked rapidly, dark lashes fluttering with the movement.

"Are you asking for me to elaborate or to repeat the statement?"

"Elaborate, please. I was under the impression you just went through a divorce. Though, if you hadn't had sex in six years, I can see why the divorce was necessary."

He shook his head. "I got divorced six years ago. Or rather, my wife left me six years ago, I'm not really sure when the thing was finalized. I just signed papers. Neither of us did much. She didn't want the house. We didn't have any...kids to fight over." That always pulled him up. Saying he didn't have kids.

He didn't. But he still felt like a father. He still loved a little girl with everything in him, even though she wasn't here.

"It was an easy divorce," he said, because that much was true. There hadn't been any glue holding him and Stephanie together in the end.

He didn't blame her for it. She wanted to leave their house, leave the town. He didn't. She wanted to run from the memories, he wanted to live in them. And in the end, it had meant she'd needed to run from him. He couldn't be angry at her for that.

"Oh... I... I'm sorry. I mean...good for an easy divorce, but... I'm sorry."

He looked down at his food, a ball of hard, heavy emotion settling in his chest. The worst thing was, now he felt like he had to talk about it. Because pretending Tally hadn't been a part of everything was...it wasn't fair. He didn't want to act like she didn't exist. But he didn't like talking about her, either.

So he wouldn't. Not now.

He set his plate down on the pretty little side table. "Suddenly, I'm not so hungry for food," he said.

"But we just...not a half hour ago we..."

"Come on, Grace. I just told you. Six years." He picked up his wineglass and knocked back the remaining contents. He needed it. He needed to forget.

He needed *her*.

"Where's your bedroom?" he asked.

"Down the hall."

He stood up and she did, too, then he scooped her up into his arms. She squeaked and wrapped her arms around his neck. She was so small, so light. He kind of liked it. Because it made him feel strong. And because he knew he could lift her up and move her around easily. For sex in interesting ways. He was a simple man. At least, he would prefer to be. Sex and beer. He could deal with that.

Maybe that had been half his problem for the past few years. Beer and sadness. Not beer and sex. He was changing that.

He was changing it now.

He charged down the hall, holding her close to his chest.

"That door!" she said, gesturing to the one near the end of the hall.

He pushed it open with his shoulder and brought them inside, putting her down on the center of the bed. He stripped his clothes off as quickly as possible. "This is becoming a habit when you're around," he said. "Why did I even bother to get dressed?"

"You would have emotionally scarred the delivery guy."

"Is my body that hideous?" he asked.

She laughed. "*Hideous* is not the word I'd use."

"What is?" he asked, arching a brow.

"Jaw-dropping. Sexy. An ode to classic masculinity."

"Stop it, Gracie, you'll make me blush. Now take off your dress."

She obeyed, revealing herself to him slowly. Inch by tantalizing inch. "How about that, cowboy? What do you see?"

"I'm an artist, you know," he said, feeling like a jerk for saying it in even a semiserious manner. "So I'm an expert on art and the like."

"Are you?"

"I am. So I know a little something about fine pieces. About beauty." He got down on the bed beside her, tracing her curves, shaping her body with the palms of his hands like she was clay. "You are a masterpiece."

He pressed a kiss to her stomach, then lower, spreading her thighs and burying his face between them. He would never get enough of this. Of her.

"I don't think I was ready for the likes of you, Grace Song," he said, rolling out of bed. "And now I have condom issues to see to."

"See to them," she said, waving her hand.

She lay on her back on the bed, staring at the ceiling. Not

thinking or moving. Then Zack came back into the room, hovering over her.

"You're blocking my ceiling spot," she said.

He smiled. "Too bad." Then he lay down beside her with the subtlety of an earthquake.

"Gah!" she shrieked, popping up off the mattress.

He chuckled and put his hand on her stomach, tracing a shapeless pattern over her skin. "Something wrong?"

"No."

"I'm tired," he said. "Can I sleep here with you?"

"You have that gigantic suite," she mumbled.

"Yeah, but my suite is empty," he said, pulling her close. "I don't want to go back to an empty suite. I'm so sick of empty rooms."

"I bet," she said, putting her hand over his forearm. She hesitated. She shouldn't ask him about his past. Shouldn't ask him about his wife. But she wanted to know. "What happened with your wife?"

He took a deep breath, his chest pressing into her back. "We ended up in a different life than we were supposed to be in. And…in the end we changed too much. Or the world changed too much and we didn't change enough. Hell, I don't know. But I remember looking at her one day and realizing it was the first time I'd really done that in months. That's some stupid stuff."

"But the divorce was…"

"Very mutual. We were done," he said, shifting against her, his chin resting on her shoulder. "You make vows, you know. And you think you know what they all mean. Richer and poorer, sickness and health. And you think, yeah, sure, if my wife is sick, I'll take care of her. If we're ever broken, we'll stick together. But…they don't cover some things."

He paused, and when he spoke again, his voice was rough. "Do you really want to know about me, Gracie?"

"Yes," she said. "And if you want me to, I'll forget it in the morning."

She felt him nod. "Okay. You can imagine a lot of bumps in the road, but I don't think anyone ever… I don't think anyone imagines what losing a child might do to them. I know we didn't."

Grace's heart stopped, everything she knew about Zack twisting, turning. Changing.

"When Tally was born," he continued, "it changed our family. It brought us closer, you know? Stephanie wasn't just my wife, she was the mother of my daughter. But it became clear quickly that not everything was right. That Tally was sick. Her heart… She had a heart defect. And they missed it on all the ultrasounds. They missed it until she was three months. She wasn't gaining weight, and she was short of breath all the time. It was treatable. They said it was treatable. And she was small but…fine for a while."

"Oh, Zack," she said, not realizing she'd spoken the words out loud until he tightened his hold on her.

He cleared his throat. "When she was three, she got a bacterial infection. The hospital said it was common for kids with her condition. And we knew that. We knew to watch for it. But it…" He took a deep breath. "She died in the hospital three days later."

A tear ran down Grace's cheek, and there was nothing she could do to stop it, her heart crumpling into a tight ball she wasn't sure she'd ever be able to release. "I think we were both wrung out after that," he said.

"I don't think Steph or I had anything left to give. Because she couldn't look at me and see the father of her baby girl anymore. She looked at me and saw everything we weren't. It was just too big for us to fix. And in the end…it was better we tried to fix it alone. Tally died eight years ago, but you know that stuff doesn't go away. Steph got married again, they have two little boys. I'm happy for her, and I really mean it. I'm glad she got away, glad she got…filled up again. But I don't want to do that. I don't want to care like that. I don't even think I could."

Grace held tightly to his arm. not sure what to say. He'd had this whole life, this whole depth of love that she'd never even fathomed. And then he'd lost it.

She shouldn't have asked. It was dangerous to know this. To know him this well. To feel this much.

"I'm sorry," she said. It was a stupid thing to say, maybe, but she didn't really know if there was anything else that could be said.

"Me, too," he said. "More than I am about anything else. But I can't change it. That life is gone, and I'm living this one. That's why suites and galleries and things don't matter sometimes. It's funny, I always did art. But it wasn't until… something in me changed after, and I had to do it, to keep from going crazy. I worked in my studio—which is just a barn really—all the time. It was the only place to put all that grief. It made me famous. I think that's why I hate it sometimes, as much as I need it."

There was nothing to say to that. Nothing at all. So she just held him. All night. And when she woke up the next morning he was gone.

Chapter Seven

Marsha was never thrilled about him using his "social time" to get all "broody artiste" on her. Her words. But his art was her paycheck, so she never said no.

Which was why Zack was in a borrowed studio today, torturing metal until his muscles burned. He'd basically turned the place into a forge, which was another reason Marsha didn't necessarily love accommodating him. Because he essentially took over whatever studio he inhabited.

But whatever. He made a ton of money. More than a lot of other living artists. So everyone could deal with it.

And they did.

Which was one of the best things about the art world. He was eccentric here. Not just a jerk. With great genius came great jackassery, or whatever. It worked out for him because it meant he got to do whatever he wanted.

He needed to work today. Needed to get this piece finished. He'd started it back home, and it had come over with the rest of the pieces for the show, but this one wasn't done. And he wasn't sure exactly what to do with it.

It was a giant iron figure, like the rest of them. The vague shape of a man, faceless, as they all were. He was standing. Just standing. And Zack didn't know why. He didn't know what the hell the thing was supposed to be.

And today he'd taken the thing's arm off, bent it at the elbow and reattached it with what would be its palm facing upward.

He had no idea what in hell he was doing.

But then, that was fitting. He didn't know why the hell he'd told Grace about Steph and Tally. He didn't know why he'd spent the night, only to wake up feeling like his chest was being crushed by an anvil.

He'd left at 5:00 a.m. and wandered around until six, then he'd called Marsha about getting the studio space for the day.

Yeah, there was something about Grace that turned his head to oatmeal. And he just did crap. And said crap. And he had no idea why.

Sex.

Yeah, it was probably the sex. It had been so damn long before her. Longer still since he'd wanted it. Really wanted it. With more of himself than just his erect member.

His body wanted sex a lot, it was the rest of him that didn't care. The rest of him that was still too numb,

But not with Grace. She lit a fire in him that he could feel all the way down.

He was still deciding whether or not he was okay with that.

If he wasn't, it meant no more sex for the remainder of his time in the city. Which was not okay with him.

Not at all.

He was enjoying dipping his toes back in the pool, so to speak.

His phone buzzed and he walked across the studio and looked down at the number. A NY number that he hadn't added to his phone, but one he recognized.

"Gracie," he said, picking the phone up and answering it.

"Zack, you left before I woke up."

He leaned back against the wall and looked at the iron monstrosity he'd just been torturing. "Yeah, I did."

"Why?"

"I had work to do."

"Such as?"

"Sculpting. Welding. Had to fire up the forge and hammer things."

"You were hammering me."

His body immediately stood to attention. "Yeah. But… I have a job. And a piece I need to finish."

"What more does it need to be finished?"

He looked at the lifeless lump of iron. "I don't know. It's dead. I can't figure out how to make it live."

"Lightning storm?"

"Yeah," he said, laughing in spite of himself. "Maybe. Want to come and be my hunchbacked assistant?"

"Can I really come?"

He hesitated. "Sure," he said finally. "Why the hell not?"

"After work. I'll be there after work."

"I'll still be here. Banging my head against a wall."

"Well, I'll see you then. Try not to give yourself a concussion."

"I'll do my best." He hung up and put his hand on his chest. There was a weird feeling there. Originating from around his heart and spreading outward.

Happiness. For heaven's sake. He felt happy. Standing there in front of a crap-ass statue, he felt happy.

The thought of seeing Grace and showing her all this was the cause. He was happy to see her. To show her his garbage work. What the hell?

He shook his head and took a deep breath. Sex was more powerful than he'd given it credit for, that was all.

It certainly wasn't that his heart was thawing out. Hell no. It was just his body.

That was it. That was all it could ever be.

Grace was ready to climb the walls of her office by the time five o'clock rolled around.

Normally she was the last to leave. Such was her level of

commitment. Not just to her job, but to this vague notion that she had to cause no trouble and make no mistakes. But with her boss treating her like he had been, and with the new "projects" that had just come across her desk—which included mundane paperwork that would not advance her or grow her income, and was someone else's flipping job—she wasn't hanging out.

No. She had something to get to. She had life happening. Freaking life. And wasn't hanging around in an office with what smelled like a slowly dying career.

She let out a harsh breath as she exited the building. This was the kind of thing that would make her parents worry, she was sure of it. And they had enough worry. She didn't want to add to their worry. She was supposed to be their success story, her own adding to theirs. She would reach a point, a place, where she didn't have to try so hard. Where they could bask in her accomplishments and so could she.

Success. Success was the gold ring. Not satisfaction. Not vague, positive emotions.

Certainly not burning, quivering lust. Which she didn't just have. She was full-on burning, quivering lust. It was ridiculous.

But she didn't care. She was going on to the art studio, aided by the address he'd texted over. And she was going to screw his brains out, instead of staying at work late. So there.

Yes, she, Grace Song, who had always screwed with her brains firmly in, was about to go shake the brains out of a man. Via her excellent sex skills.

Which, she had, if she said so herself. And Zack seemed to confirm this by his desire to keep...well, having it with her.

She got out of the cab, dodging little puddles on the sidewalk as she went, and scurried into the building.

She sent him a text.

Where R you?

Upstairs.

Where upstairs? she typed, snorting.

Top floor. The whole top floor.

She stepped into the elevator and punched the up arrow, jiggling her knee while she waited for the lift to reach the desired floor.

When the doors opened, she stopped.

The room was massive, a wall of windows on the far side, drop cloths, tables, sculptures, canvases, all throughout the giant space.

"What is this?" she asked, walking inside, her heels clicking on the cement floor.

"It's a space that Marsha has set aside for her clients to use. Though, she hates to let me in because I make a mess."

Her heart stopped when she saw him. He was wearing a white T-shirt, streaked with black, his muscular arms covered in the same dirt. He had sweat tracks on his face and his hair was sticking up at opposing angles, like he'd run his fingers through it several different directions.

"Yeah..." she said, looking around. "You did, kind of."

"And also the fire."

She looked past him, at the wrought-iron stove behind him. "It's warm in here."

"I don't play well with others," he said. "It shouldn't be too surprising."

"You play pretty well with me...."

"When I have to keep my clothes on, people don't like me much."

"I like you," she said, feeling girlish and silly as soon as the words left her mouth. She liked him. What the hell was this, junior high?

"Well, that's only because you mostly don't talk to me," he said, turning to face the big, wrought-iron figure at the center of the room.

She was captivated by it. Completely. There was a heaviness to it, a sadness. She wasn't sure how he'd managed to pour emotion into metal, but he had.

"This is amazing," she said.

"It's junk."

"No, it's not."

"Yes, it is. I don't know what it is except metal. It looks like everything else I've ever made. It has no inspiration." He pushed his hand back over his hair again.

"You're an artist," she said, laughing. "You play it off, but you care about this. And you're temperamental."

"So?" He growled the word. "It's my right."

"You act like you don't care at all. But you're…"

"I'm a wreck over this. Happy? I don't have anything else to care about. So I care about…these," he said, sweeping his hand in the direction of the iron statue. "Not because people will see them, but because…"

Because they were his emotions. Because it was the way he was dealing with his grief. It felt intimate to see this, knowing his past. She wondered if it was what everyone else saw when they looked at his work, even if they didn't realize it.

"Yeah," she said, "I get it."

"Do you?"

"Yes."

"Well, then maybe you can tell me what this is supposed to be."

"I don't think I have an answer for you." But it meant something that he'd asked, even if his words took on an exasperated tone.

"How was your day? Boss from hell poke you with a pitchfork?"

"No, but he gave me busywork to do like I'm an intern and not one of his most valued team members. He's putting me in my place."

"What a jerk. Because you wouldn't screw a client?"

Grace shook her head. "I don't know…maybe it's just because of the way I handled it. I stepped out of line and I… I probably shouldn't have. I should have…"

"Do you really think that, Grace? That you should just be polite when a guy starts talking about your ass in the middle of a business lunch? No. That is ridiculous. You're supposed to feel guilty about dealing with someone else's inappropriateness? No way."

"I know," she said, "I know you're right but…but my parents taught me that you just work hard. They…they tried to instill in us the importance of that. I… I have a sister. Hannah. And she…"

"Let me guess, she's a doctor or something hugely successful?"

"No," Grace said. "She's a junkie. A junkie who's God knows where. We were taught all of the right things but she… she didn't want to work hard. She didn't care about school. Or even our parents enough. But I do. I care. And I want… No one gets anywhere by taking shortcuts, or checking out of life, Zack. Things happen, they aren't always fair, but you have to be able to rise above it. And I've spent my whole life believing that, because I've seen what happens when you don't. Because I won't disappoint my parents the way she did."

"To what end?"

"To not being a loser burnout," she said, frustration rising in her.

"Bull, Gracie. There's so much freaking ground between being so hard on yourself you feel *guilty* for telling some jerk to shove it and being a junkie—the two aren't even in the same hemisphere. So you tell me, really, to what end?"

She took a deep breath, shrugging her shoulders. "Success," she said.

"What about happiness?"

"What about it?" she asked. "It's never mattered. I mean… no one says that, Zack, come on, my sister probably thinks she's happy half the time, but she makes our parents miserable. She's made me miserable. I don't have to do that. I want to aim for…for a certain level of success. My parents worked really hard to give me the life that I have. It wasn't about what made them happy, it was about…making things better. For me and for Hannah. She threw that away, but I won't. Especially not when I've pushed everything else out of the way for it."

"What things have you pushed aside for it?"

She shrugged, then tucked a strand of hair behind her ear. "Everything. Friends. My ex-boyfriend. I just… I ignore people when I get busy because something is going to slip and I know it can't be the job. It can't be my parents. I… I don't know who I would be, to them or to me, if I wasn't the best. I don't know how I would matter."

"Look, Grace, I'm sorry about your sister. I am. I'm sure… I'm sure you feel like you need to make up for the lack of it. I wouldn't know how that is. I'm an only child, and my parents never expected big things from me. Nothing more than taking care of the family ranch, getting married, giving them grandkids. And they were never rushed about it. So… I don't know, the family expectations were always manageable. So I can't speak to disappointing parents, or wanting to make up for what a sibling has done. But what I can tell you is that I've had happiness. True, blinding happiness. Holding your child for the first time? There's nothing deeper than that. It changes you. It grows your world. I've felt that, I've lived it. And I've had success. But only one at a time. Not one with the other. And I think…having had the happiness first? I would choose that, Grace. If you have a hope of that? Screw success. I would trade so much to go back to obscurity, and a small house in Oregon if my daughter could just be asleep in the room down the hall." He lifted his head and looked at her, golden eyes so full of pain it cracked her heart. "The reason I care about all this so much? It's only because I don't have anything else to care about."

"Maybe someday…"

"No," he said, his words harsh, shotgun fire in the stillness of the room. "I had it. And the flip side of that is that I've lost it. There's a limit to what one man can go through and… I don't even think I could feel that again if I wanted to. I think it broke something in me."

"You're not really selling it, Zack."

He laughed. "No, I guess not. But trust me on something, okay?"

"Sure."

"You deserve happiness. You should have that. And you should figure out what it means for you."

"I'll keep that in mind."

"You can go home," he said. "I think I'm going to be here until I figure this out."

She sat down in a chair near where he standing. "Then I guess I'll be a while, too. Should we order food?"

He smiled, and it made her heart do a weird, flippy thing. And she didn't even try to stop it. "Sure," he said. "I could eat."

"Great. Get to work."

She watched him labor over the statue while she sat in the chair and ate noodles from a carton. She took off her jacket, he took off his shirt.

After about an hour she stood up and put the carton under his chin, lifting her chopsticks to his mouth. "Eat."

He opened and took a bite, then glared at her. "Are you force-feeding me?" he asked around a mouthful of food.

"Yes. Because you didn't stop to eat."

"I'm pondering," he said, crossing his arms over his bare chest.

She couldn't help but ponder the drops of sweat running down his skin. She wanted to lick his body. All over. And then she wanted to hold him all night. She'd never felt this way about anyone before. And that was…well, it wasn't what she'd bargained for.

It felt a lot like what she'd been missing in her previous relationships.

It felt a lot like she was falling for him.

Lusty. It's just super extra lusty-pants stuff.

It was all it could be. He'd said himself, it would never be anything else ever.

"Well, chew and ponder at the same time," she said.

"It's good."

"I know. One of my other favorite places. I don't cook, if you were curious about that."

"You don't strike me as the type. I cook," he said. "If you were wondering."

"You cook?"

"Yes, because I also eat. And I'm single. And there isn't much in the way of good takeout in Pine Ridge Falls."

"Oh, seriously, that's a place? It sounds like a hollow in a… made-up story with woodland creatures."

"It's a real place," he said. "On the Oregon coast. And there are expanses of beach with no one there. Trees, mountains and not a single high-rise building."

"Sounds like…a good place to visit."

"That's how I feel about the city."

For some reason, that made her heart sink. Which was silly. Because it wasn't like their relationship had staying power. It wasn't like they had to want to live in the same place.

They just had to want to inhabit the same space, naked, for the next couple of weeks. This wasn't about changing things, or finding deep feelings. It was about letting go, exploring this completely unknown level of chemistry.

That was all.

"Well, fine, but in the city you have takeout."

"And at home I have the farmer's market. And beef from local ranches…"

"We have Whole Foods."

He laughed. "You do. But the traffic."

"Yeah, I know. I know. But this is why you order groceries, and food, and have it come to your house. And then you don't have to leave. Or see people."

"Are you really blaming your job for your lack of a social life? Because it sounds to me like you're kind of a willing hermit."

"What about you? Do you have friends in Mayberry Glen?"

"Pine Ridge Falls. And not many. It's hard. Everyone kind of looks at you with sad eyes all the time. Because in a small town everyone knows you and your business. And you can hardly go out and eat alone without people patting you on the back and asking if you're okay."

"Thus your cooking skills."

"Thus. Plus, like you said, being alone is nice sometimes."

"Boy, aren't we a pair?"

"Yeah," he said, a small smile tugging the corners of his lips. "We are."

She wrapped one arm around his waist and kissed his mouth. He leaned in and deepened it, and she tried to wrap her other arm—still clutching the takeout—around his neck.

"I think we can call this finished," he said. "I'm in the mood for something other than art."

"Me, too."

"Not here, though, because technically it's a shared space and I don't share. Not my studio time, and not you."

And she feared that all her good intentions, her desire to

remain detached, had crumbled in that moment. She did her best to keep it light. To keep it teasing. "Oooh. Possessive."

"I'm old-fashioned that way. No other guys are invited to this party."

"Other women?"

"Nope," he said, "not even then."

"Good. Because while certain extra, vibrating artificial body-parts are welcome… I'm not that adventurous."

"Well, maybe we should see just how adventurous you are."

Chapter Eight

Grace and Zack spent the next week in bed together. Okay, not entirely. There was still the matter of work for Grace and work-related functions for Zack. But they either slept in his suite, or her apartment.

Grace had to admit, she kind of liked staying in his suite. It made her feel like a fancy call girl. Or, you know, something less sordid but kind of naughty.

The thing about spending so much time with Zack was that he was sort of an irresistible son-of-a-gun. She only wished the irresistible factor was limited to his body. Sadly for her, there were other things. Things in her chest that seemed to respond to the things that came from his chest.

Which, she supposed, was a very avoid-y way of admitting she responded to his feelings. That she felt them in her.

Grace watched from her position on the couch as Zack crossed the suite completely naked, and unashamed.

His body was so hot. Muscular thighs, washboard-flat abs. Not to mention his cock. Yeah, she'd thought it. She could even say it now, mostly without blushing. When they were actually in the moment, anyway.

Or when she was in her own private moment, fawning over his gorgeous body. Like now.

"You're sexy," she said, sliding her hand over her stomach as she watched him.

"Really?"

"Yes," she said, shamelessly admiring the lines that ran along his hip bones, pointing downward to that most glorious part of him. "I've never enjoyed just staring at a man the way I enjoy staring at you."

"Oh, yeah?"

"Yeah."

"You like me, huh?"

"I told you," she said.

They'd been all over each other from the moment she'd gotten off work three hours earlier, but that hadn't seemed to dampen her need for him. Far from it.

"I need a shower," she said. "Want to come?"

"I think I did. And that's why you need a shower."

"That was a dirty joke."

"Yes," he said, "yes it was."

He didn't look like he was joking, though. He looked kind of grave. And she wished he wouldn't. Because it made her feel things. Deep, sincere things that were more important than the hierarchy at her company. That were more important than fiscal and professional success.

The happiness he'd talked about. A deep, altering feeling that she was afraid was going to rearrange her entire, well-ordered insides.

This wasn't what she'd wanted. Not at all. But she was afraid it was what she had, whether she was looking for it or not.

"All right," he said, "lead the way."

"No thanks. You can lead the way."

He arched a brow.

"I want to watch your behind while we walk," she said, fluttering her lashes at him.

"I think I'm a bad influence on you," he said.

"I actually like to think I'm being a bad influence on myself, and I'm taking you down with me."

He did smile at that. A genuine one that made her heart squeeze tight.

"Go on now," she said, standing back and waiting for him to start walking toward the bathroom.

She followed him and took in the view, then waited while he turned the shower on and let it warm up. She stepped inside, and he stayed out, watching her as she washed away the evidence of their passion.

"What?" she asked. "Get in here!"

"I like the view."

"Well, I want to touch."

He stepped into the shower and pushed her against the wall, the motion swift and decisive, his kiss hard. She gripped the back of his neck and held him to her, kissing him back with everything in her. All the emotion. All the need. All the everything that she hadn't been wanting or expecting. It didn't matter what she wanted, she realized suddenly.

It was there all the same.

Wanting anything other than sex with Zack Camden was a recipe for disaster. It made no sense. He didn't want anything more than sex, and even if he did, they would still live a broad expanse of country away from each other.

So there was no reason for her to say the words that were pounding through her head. No reason at all for her to feel them or think them. And really, really, really no reason to say them.

But he was so perfect against her, so hot and hard and slick.

She put her hand on his chest, and she could feel his heart beating. And she couldn't hold it back, not anymore.

"I'm in love with you, Zack," she said, the words torn from her on a sob, the force of them shaking her. She hadn't expected them, but she knew the moment they left her mouth that they were true. That this was what the burning, brilliant sensation that had been building inside of her over the past week meant.

Because she loved the person he was making her become.

Because she loved his strength, his talent. Because his pain had broken her and his smile lit something inside her on fire.

Because he made her want something more, when nothing and no one else ever had.

He froze, then pulled away from her. "Grace, don't," he said, his voice hard.

"Sorry. No...you know what? I'm not sorry," she said, pushing away from the wall, the water washing over her body. "Because I didn't say that for you. I said it for me. And it has nothing to do with what you expected, or what I expected, or what makes sense. Or what might be considered good. It's just...true. And it's not for anyone but me. Not to make up for anything or to atone for someone else's sins, this is...this is what I feel. I've fallen in love with you, and I well know what that feels like, Zack."

"How? After a week? Do you know how stupid that sounds?" he asked, shoving the shower door open and getting out, tugging a white towel off the rack.

"I'm never stupid," she said. "I'm a lot of things. I'm a prude—well, maybe not now, but ask my friends, I always have been. I'm cautious. I'm a people pleaser. I work so hard to please my parents, to be everything Hannah isn't and achieve some vague idea of success that I don't even know what I want anymore. So yeah, I'm a lot of things, but stupid isn't one of them."

"I didn't say you were stupid, I said... I said you can't... Grace, you can't possibly love me."

"Why?"

"Because," he said, turning sharply to face her, "I can't love you."

"What you can and can't do has nothing to do with me,"

she said, trying to ignore the stab of pain in her chest. "It has nothing to do with what I feel."

"So I don't have any choice in the matter?"

"No. I'm in love with you. End of discussion. I didn't ask for anything—" she shut the water off and stepped out "—and I won't. But I love you. I've lived with a man, slept with him, shared closet space and a toothbrush cup with him, and it wasn't this. It wasn't like he'd taken up residence in my chest. I know that you can be with someone for a long time and not feel this. That time has nothing to do with it, that... sense has nothing to do with it. If reason had a part to play in love... I would have loved damn David. But I didn't. I love you, you jerk."

"I can't," he said, his words broken. He crossed the room and cupped her face his hold tight, his eyes intense on hers. "I just think... It's like my whole chest is scooped out, Grace. I can't give you more than this. I can't give you what a man should give you when you say things like that to him. I'm like... I'm just like one of my statues. A bad one. One that doesn't feel anything or mean anything."

"Your statue isn't bad," she said. "It's just not finished. What do you need to be finished, Zack? How can I make you whole?"

"I don't know," he said, his hold tightening. "I think I might be dead inside."

She put her hands on his face. "I wish I could figure out how to make you live."

"Just touch me," he said, his voice rough.

"I can do better than that."

"Can you?" he asked, a note of desperation wrapped around his words.

She took a deep, shaking breath, her eyes never leaving his. She felt everything, every change wrought in her body from the moment she'd met him. And she didn't want safe, or prim. She wasn't the woman she'd been when she got in that cab, angry and unable to express it for fear of shocking or making waves.

She wouldn't be silent now. She wouldn't keep it inside.

"What if I fuck you?" she asked, the words hard, unfamiliar on her lips. But wonderful.

He growled low in his throat and gripped her hair, tugging her head back, pain shooting through her scalp, sending lightning bolts of sensation along her skin. His lips crashed down on hers. Taking. Taking everything she'd offered. Selfishly. Angrily. And she didn't care. She took it all. All the rage. All the sadness. All that emptiness he had, she filled. She poured herself into him. Her feelings. Her love.

Because this was her first time. Feeling this. Wanting this. She wasn't drained. She was full to bursting and she could do nothing but give to him.

His kiss was rough, his teeth biting into her lip, his hold tight on her hair, his arm wrapped around her waist, keeping her tugged up against him. She could taste his desperation, his grief. His pain. He shifted and lifted her feet off the ground.

He was so much stronger than she was. So much bigger. Physically, he had every advantage, but emotionally, she could tell he was on the verge of breaking.

That in that way, she was the one with the power to destroy, and the power to survive.

But just like she trusted his strength, trusted he wouldn't use it against her, or hurt her in any way, she had to let him have the ability to trust her, too.

She'd pushed and she needed to let him take what he needed to survive the push.

She fumbled with the towel at his waist and it loosened and fell around their feet. He lifted her, set her on the bathroom counter, stepping between her thighs, pressing hard against her, sending pleasure crackling along her veins.

This was all he could handle. This was what he could take from her. So this was what she would give. Because she loved him. And that meant, for now, for this moment, they didn't need to give and take equally.

It meant she didn't need it all from him now.

She wanted it, desperately. But she had to give him time to get there.

He lowered his head, kissing her collarbone, moving lower and taking her nipple deep into his mouth. She held tightly to his shoulders, gasping as he teased the entrance of her body with the blunt head of his shaft.

"Condom," she said, the word almost impossible to force out.

He swore and lifted her up from the counter, carrying her into the bedroom and depositing her on the bed. He wrenched open the nightstand drawer and produced the box of condoms, which he tore into with shaking fingers.

He was still shaking while he rolled the protection onto his length, something wounded, desperate in his eyes.

It made her heart twist. And it gave her hope. Because he was feeling. Whatever he said about not having the ability... he was feeling.

He joined her on the mattress and hooked her leg up over his hip, driving into her, a harsh sound on his lips as he buried himself to the hilt.

He moved inside of her, broken words pouring out of him. Dirty words. Incoherent words. Words that somehow touched her deep down in her soul.

She clung to his shoulders as he rode her hard, her body trembling, another orgasm rising from deep within, so strong, so overwhelming that she had to look away from him as it overtook her completely.

He followed right behind her, lowering his head and shuddering as his pleasure wracked his body. He lay on her, his skin slicked with sweat, his eyes closed tight, and she held him.

She wanted to tell him that she loved him again, but considering that was the source of his emotional breakdown she doubted it would be helpful.

A lesser woman might take offense to that, but she didn't. If only because the fact that her loving him affected him so much meant that at least it mattered. Even if he didn't want it.

She stroked his hair, moved her hands over his face, his stubble-roughened jaw. She didn't want to live without this man, and that was one hell of a sobering realization.

He'd changed her. He'd changed what she wanted, what she expected.

Which was horrible because she'd been completely fine until she'd met him. She'd been happy with the trajectory of her life. Happy to live on a pass/fail grading scale, where emotion and desire didn't matter.

Now she wanted more. Stupid Zack Camden.

And looking at him, at the blank expression on his face, she felt like he wasn't going to give it to her. Not now that he'd made her want it. Not now that he'd made her see.

"I think we need to stop now, Gracie," he said, the words so loud in the silence of the room.

She closed her eyes, fought against the pain that was ravaging her chest. Like a pack of wild dogs.

"I take you don't just mean we need to stop having sex for the night."

"You know what I mean," he said. "It wasn't supposed to be like this. You weren't supposed to get hurt."

And neither were you.

She left the last part unsaid, but she knew it was true. He was more worried about his own feelings than hers, she would bet a lot on that.

Not that it fixed anything, really. Because the end result

was the same. Except these feelings, love and all that, weren't just pass or fail.

It wasn't all about the end result. It was about all the things that had happened on the way. It was about the fact that she was happier with the person she was now, than the person she'd been the day they met.

Even if right about now everything hurt like a son of a bitch.

There was some clarity and real change in there, too. And later that would matter. Later. Right now everything sucked.

And for the first time she felt embarrassed to be naked in front of him.

She moved away from him, turning her back to him to shield herself. At least her skin. Futile, since he'd seen it, and she'd just revealed everything on the inside. But it made her feel slightly protected, and she needed a little protection right now.

"I know that's not what you intended," she said. "Hell, Zack, it's not what I intended, either. You don't fall in love with a random hookup who lives across the country. There are rules about those things. And I know that. Even though this is the first time I've ever actually done anything like this, I know that. But you and I have never followed the rules. You drew me a picture, and I sleep with you all night. You told me about your past, and I told you about my parents. You broke a vase in my apartment and I didn't even care. You make me swear. You make me…want. And none of that is supposed to happen. None of what's happened between us makes sense. It's not normal. We're too different, you're too screwed up."

She looked over her shoulder, back at Zack, who was lying on his back staring at the ceiling.

"It shouldn't have happened like this," she said. "But it did. So I'm going to say it one more time, Zack. I love you. Like…really and truly. You've changed me in a hundred different ways, and even if we don't end up together, I'll never be able to go back to my life and live it the way I did before. You broke me. Like you broke the damn vase. I can't put it back together and have it be the same."

"I'm sorry," he said, after a lot time. "But I can't, Grace. More than that, I don't want to. I don't want you to love me. I don't want to love you. I... I watched my wife grieve this horrible thing that no one should ever have to go through, and I didn't help her. I couldn't help her. I just locked myself up and lived in my own grief. I'm not meant to be the other half of a couple. For too many reasons to list."

"Is one of them that you're a damn coward? Clinging to the past when what we have is completely different?"

Zack pushed into a sitting position and got off the bed. "You don't know what the hell you're talking about. Sure, I'm a damn coward, because I know what it's like to have your heart ripped out of your chest. I know what it's like to try to keep living when you have nothing but a bloody hole left where it should be. Forgive me for not wanting to try again. Forgive me for feeling done with it. You're right. We're too different and it's not because I'm a cowboy and you own pantsuits. It's because you think love is some wonderful, happy thing that I should want to have."

"You're the one who told me that it was better than success, Zack. Better than perfection."

"If you can keep it. Grace, I hope you have it all someday. A husband and kids or even just a job that makes you delirious with glee. Whatever it is that's going to make you excited to get up every morning. That'd be great. For you. But I got my shot. And it ended in...it's the worst nightmare you have as a husband. As a parent. To watch your wife hurt beyond heal-ing. To lose the child you're supposed to protect. It's a night-mare, Grace. The worst possible way it can all end and that's how it ended for me."

Her heart tightened, her lungs compressing. "Zack... I

won't even pretend to know what you went through. And I'm not trying to belittle it. I'm just..." A tear rolled down her cheek and she didn't bother to wipe it away. She didn't care if she was an ice bitch now. She didn't even want to be one. She wanted him to see how she felt. That for her, this was worth the pain. "I can't understand why a man with so much to offer the world, a man who could have so much, doesn't want anything for himself anymore."

"I can't," he said, his voice raw. "And I can't explain it much better than that. It's just that… I can't do it. I can't risk that pain. I can't even… I can't even imagine it. I don't want to. I don't want this at all."

She nodded slowly and got off the bed, her hands shaking as she walked out into the living area, collecting her clothes. "Okay," she said, shouting into the bedroom. "That's…" She turned and saw him standing naked in the doorway. She lowered her voice. "I don't understand, Zack, and I won't even pretend that I do. But one thing I do want you to know before I go."

"What's that, baby?" he asked, the tone in his voice so sad it nearly killed her.

"That I love you. Still. And even if you can't find it in yourself to give it back, I want you to know that there is still someone who wants to give it to you. Who loves the man who's been through the nightmare. I want you to know that you're not done changing the world, because you changed mine. Because your artwork is amazing, and I know it's changing people. That your success is deeper than you think it is. And that's it."

"That's it, huh?" he asked, his eyes blank.

"Yeah. Except… I love who you made me. I love *you*. Again. Because it should end that way. Not with anger. But with that."

She dressed silently and grabbed her purse off the table by

the couch. And then she walked out of the suite and into the hall. It was as far as she made it before her knees gave out.

She slid down the wall, clutching her purse to her breasts, tears rolling down her cheeks. Damn that stupid cowboy. And her stupid cab dilemma. The stupid phone mix-up. All those little things from that day that had turned into the biggest thing that had ever happened to her.

That had shaken everything in her, changed her irrevocably.

She was sitting in the hallway of a hotel she couldn't afford, having failed at love, with a career that was crumbling. And it didn't feel like the end of the world. It felt like the start of something big.

Something sad, with regard to losing Zack, but something big.

Her life was actually kind of a mess, for the first time in her memory. She stood up, took a deep, shaking breath. Her parents would not be proud of her behavior. Or where she was at in her job. But it wasn't their life. It was her life. Her mess.

And she was going to embrace the heck out of it.

Chapter Nine

If he was hung over at the fundraiser tomorrow, Marsha was going to kill him. He didn't really care. Except it was for charity, so maybe he should not make a total idiot of himself.

He sat down on the cement floor in the studio, whiskey bottle in hand, and tipped it back. Yeah, he was supposed to be showing these pieces for the Broken Hearts Foundation. Auctioning them off for the benefit of families who couldn't afford medical expenses. For Tally. For children like her.

And here he was, drunk off his ass, or…on his ass, staring down a piece of art he couldn't figure out, feeling like he'd been broken inside all over again.

How was that even possible? He was sure he hadn't had a heart left to break. Or at least that the pieces that remained were too small to smash any further.

That was why he'd told her to go. It was why he'd had to have her leave, before he was tempted to reach out and take what she had on offer. When he full knew he had nothing to give back.

And yet, in spite of his best efforts he hadn't escaped un-scathed. And he knew she hadn't.

But he was in hell. And any noise about him not being able to feel? Well, it was a lie, apparently. He hadn't realized.

He pictured Grace as she'd looked when she'd walked out of the hotel room two nights ago. Pale, tears on her cheeks. He hated himself for making her look like that. Because even while he stood there, telling her he could never feel on that level again, he'd broken her.

He was such a bastard. Such a damn bastard.

He leaned back against the wall, his head hitting hard against the drywall. He barely felt it. It was cushioned by his drunkenness and the pain in his heart.

He looked at the iron figure in front of him. The unchanging, unbending, dead, iron figure that was…him.

That realization made him want to throw something across the room. He didn't want self-actualization. He poured his grief into his work, he didn't learn from it. He hardly believed in any of that stuff, it was just that he'd found when he didn't create, he thought he'd explode from the emotion in him.

He'd never considered it therapy, but he could see now that it was.

And he imagined he was supposed to learn something from this dead piece of work that seemed to mean nothing. To give nothing.

He put his head against his knees, and squeezed his eyes shut. And all he saw was Grace. He hadn't wanted for so long, he'd forgotten what it felt like. But right now he ached with it. And he was trapped.

Between gut-wrenching, blinding fear and a need that made his bones ache. Funny how everything in his life came down to the heart.

To a heart that was broken at birth and stopped beating long before it should have. To a heart that had been numb before Grace had come back in this life, and that was stuttering to life now, burning with each beat.

He staggered to his feet and went over to his worktable and dug through old materials. He had an idea. And he had no idea if it would fix his artwork, or fix him. Or if it was all just the alcohol making something dumb seem like something good.

But he had to try. Because there was one thing he did know,

and that was that he couldn't keep living like this. Because he wasn't really living at all. He was existing. And until Grace, he hadn't realized there was a difference.

She'd brought something deep and rich back into his life. Texture, sound and color. All things that scared the hell out of him. Because he'd adjusted to black and white. To cold iron and dead lifeless metal. Daring to want more seemed like a risk that wasn't worth taking.

He should stick to this life. It was safer. He wouldn't get hurt.

But it was dead. And inside, so was he.

"So then what's the point?" he asked the empty room. He didn't get an answer.

He opened his kit that had a bunch of miscellaneous crap in it, and looked at the red tubes of glass sitting in their case. Color was something he never used. And he rarely used glass because it was just so damn fragile.

But maybe it was time he took the risk.

"I quit," Grace said, her voice strong in the empty room. "And it's not entirely your fault. Though…a lot of it is." She stared down her boss and felt a surge of power. "I'm good at what I do, and you get caught up in this petty system where you punish one of your best consultants because you're try-ing to exert your power. It's my fault that I didn't stand up for myself about the client, because frankly, he was sexually harassing me, and I did keep that to myself. I shouldn't have. I don't trust you would have behaved any better, Doug, but I could have at least given you the chance."

Everything that had been bound up inside her, frozen, sus-pended in her need for perfection, her paralyzing fear of mak-ing mistakes, melted now. Released in a flood.

"Grace," Doug said, spreading his arms out. "I'm shocked. I thought we were all friends here."

"We are not friends, Doug," she growled. "You're condescending, sexist and a bit of a racist."

"Oh, come on now, Grace…"

"You made me be the elf last Christmas, because I was cute, and small. And I believe at some point you suggested I be a ninja elf."

"It would have been cool."

"No. No, it wouldn't have been cool. And it had nothing to do with Christmas. Also, asking the attractive female employees to sit on your lap is awful, and someone has to tell you that. But we're all too afraid to tell you because you're our boss. But you're not my boss anymore. You're just a tiny, little…mole man with an office. An office I no longer have to visit on a weekly basis. Goodbye." Grace turned on her heel, her heart pounding, adrenaline pumping through her veins. She couldn't believe she'd just done that.

Holy crap. "Grace."

She turned and looked at Doug, who was still sitting, shocked. "Yes?" she asked.

"What can I do? I can give you some extra accounts. We can work it out. I won't make you be the elf again."

She shook her head. "We can't work anything out because this just isn't where I want to be. I don't know quite what I want, but…it's not this. And it's not here. But…for heaven's sake please try to be less of a jackass. For the sake of everyone that's left in the office."

She walked out of the office and down the hall, past Carol's desk. "'Bye, Carol," she said, "I just quit. And I told Doug to stop being a jackass."

Carol's eyes widened and she gave Grace a low-profile thumbs-up. Grace walked out the door and got into the elevator, tugging her phone out of her bag and dialing her dad.

"Dad, I quit my job," she said when he picked up.

"What?"

"I quit. I just…walked into my boss's office and quit because I hated my job and I don't have another job, but I do still have my savings…but I don't have another job. And I know you're disappointed because now I've thrown everything off and I… I called my boss names so I'm never going to get a reference from him. And I did because… I'm in love with this guy and Dad, he's an artist. And a cowboy. Which is possibly the most random combination ever, and if there was a way for him to seem more unsuitable to you, I don't know what it would be. I don't even think he went to college."

There was a pause on the other end of the phone, and the elevator doors opened to the lobby.

"I'm not sure what you're saying."

She walked out into the lobby and then out onto the street. "I was just very irresponsible and made a bunch of decisions based entirely on my feelings. I…think I'm having a midlife crisis."

"You're thirty, Grace," her father said, his voice soft.

"I know. But I'm going through something."

"You were unhappy at your job?"

"Yes."

"And you think this will make you happy? You think…this man will make you happy?"

She looked up at the sky, at the buildings looming overhead, the sun burning her eyes. "I don't know. But…it doesn't really have anything to do with Zack because we…broke up. But he made me realize some things. Things I want that I didn't know were so important to me. I'm just sad that… I think you're going to be disappointed in me. And Hannah already…she's hurt you and Mom so much and I just don't want to hurt you, too. I want to be the daughter you want to have."

There was a long pause. "I am so sorry that I never told you," he said.

"What?" she asked.

"You are the best daughter I could ask for. You are the daughter I want to have, no matter what you do."

"But...but I just..."

"You don't need to live your life atoning for your sister, Grace. You shouldn't live your life for anyone. Not even me." He took a heavy breath. "I think I've been too rigid, Grace. Success has always been important to me, and to your mother, because we know what it's like to live in a world where opportunity is lacking. But...hearing you speak now, I feel... I feel that success, doing what someone else might think is right, is not so important if you are miserable in it."

"I don't want you to have to worry. The way she made you worry."

"Grace, I'll always worry. I'm your father. But that's my job. And yours is to live."

A tear rolled down Grace's cheek.

"I love you, Dad."

"I love you, too. No matter what you do. No matter where you work. But I'm not sure about an artist. They don't make any money."

She laughed. Her dad was handling all this much better than she could have anticipated, but even he had his limits, apparently. "Well, that's the least of your problems, Dad. Because the artist doesn't want me."

"What an idiot he is."

She swallowed hard. "Thanks, Dad. That means a lot."

Chapter Ten

Grace adjusted the strap on the back of her black stiletto before getting out of the car in front of the gallery.

She didn't know if Zack would be thrilled to see her, but then...he might not see her. It was a crowded event, and Zack was the featured artist.

That show he'd been alluding to for the past couple of weeks was, it turned out, a charity event. And he'd never said. That man and his secrets. He was so closed off. So terrified of everything. And she couldn't blame him.

For her, pain was a vague fear. She'd tested her worst fear, losing her father's approval, and she'd been met with such kindness. Her fear hadn't had teeth in the end.

The fear of a husband and father was the loss of his family. Zack had found that fear to be very real. For him, the worst nightmare could come and get you when you were awake, and she had no idea just how much that might color the rest of your life.

Or rather, now she did, because she'd seen it in him.

He was the strongest man she'd ever known. The most talented. Funny, sexy and genuinely life-changing. And he was locked up inside of himself. She couldn't help him and it killed her.

But she could come to this. She could donate. She could give in the way that she could, and then maybe, after, she would feel a little more able to let him go.

The thought stabbed her in the chest like a knife, deep and deadly. She didn't want to let him go. She wanted to keep him forever.

It just sucked that wasn't an option. Like, big-time sucked.

It was amazing how two weeks in your life could change everything. And she never would have believed it if she hadn't experienced it.

She smoothed down the front of her dress, and did a quick check to make sure the sweetheart neckline wasn't giving away too many secrets, not that she had many to tell, then she walked up the steps and into the gallery, flashing her ticket as she went through.

The lobby area was filled with people glittering and chatting, drinking champagne and eating little canapés that passed on trays.

Zack must hate this. All of this. It was so very not him. The glitz, the tiny food…the lack of beer. But he was here, giving himself. Giving his talent.

This was Zack's love on display. His love for his daughter.

Her heart squeezed tight and she walked through to the gallery. She stopped when she walked through the door, and just stared, a smile tugging at her lips.

The first piece was an iron bull, large bars of metal bent and twisted into impressionistic shapes that managed to look very real, even without minute detail. It was the strength in it, the movement, even as it was motionless on its pedestal.

Then she went through the room and to the next piece. A man. Bent at the waist and tied up in barbed wire, unable to move. She stopped there. Because she recognized that man. She recognized his pain. The grief that kept him there. The fear that made fighting against it impossible, because pushing at the bonds would hurt so badly. Would make it dig in deeper before he was ever free.

The room was filled with Zack's art. With him. And she

was so glad she'd come. So glad she'd been given this window into the man who had her, mind, body and soul.

There were some paintings, too, some sketches. Some work by other artists. And each piece had a box in front of it with bids inside.

She reached into her purse and pulled out the fox. He was still in there, on the note card. The fox in the big city. Too bad her New York chicken self hadn't really been able to protect herself from him in the end.

She took a deep breath and walked through the display area, to a woman who had a name tag on, signifying her as part of the auction staff.

"Hi," Grace said. "I… I have this piece here—" she showed her the fox "—by Zack Camden. Only…there isn't anywhere for me to bid for it."

The woman frowned. "That's strange. It should be on display."

Grace had a sudden vision of being run out by security. "Well, no… I mean…he made it for me. But I want to…bid on it. What I mean is I want to…buy it. For the charity." She was guessing the big metal pieces were being bid on in amounts far above her pay grade.

"I suppose you could…donate," the woman said.

"Great. But…but you can you please make sure it's listed that it was for the fox?" She just wanted him to know she was there. Not to be impressed that she'd given, but to know she cared. That she always would.

The woman nodded slowly. "I can do that." She pulled a card out from behind her name tag. "Put all the information in here."

Grace started to write on the card, her hands shaking as she entered an amount nearly equal to her month's rent. But hell, who needed a savings account?

"You're overpaying for that."

She turned and her heart stopped for a second, then went into overdrive. It was Zack, looking perfect in a black tux, his hair brushed back, a glass of champagne in his hand. He looked…every bit the part of a suave, urban artist. As much as he looked the part of cowboy. But it didn't really matter to her what he wore. In her eyes, Zack was perfect everywhere.

"I probably am," she said, trying to force a smile, "but… I actually think it's a pretty priceless piece. The artist made it for me in the back of a cab. I actually got to watch him draw it."

"Impressive," Zack said.

"Yeah, well, I'm attached to it."

"I'm surprised you didn't set it on fire."

She shook her head. "I wasn't even tempted to. I love it as much now as I did the day you gave it to me." *And you, too, jackass.*

"That's a compliment I'm sure it doesn't deserve."

"Ah, well. Sometimes in life we get things we don't deserve. On both sides of the good and bad spectrum, huh?" He nodded slowly. "You're definitely a spot of good."

"I don't deserve that, Gracie."

"I quit my job," she said.

"Do you still need me?" the woman asked, looking between her and Zack.

"Oh." Grace scribbled out her phone number and handed her the card. "No, sorry."

The woman took the card and slowly sidled away from her and Zack.

"Awkward," Grace said.

"A little. But I don't really care about awkward."

"I should have known."

"You quit your job?" he asked. "Why?"

"Because it didn't make me happy. None of it did. This whole…living inoffensively and just working so that I would succeed and be good…it didn't make me happy at all. I'd forgotten what happy felt like, if I ever knew…and then…you made me want more, Zack. You made me feel more. Even when…you made me leave I felt more, deeper, in that moment than I ever had. Even the pain was better than the okay."

"I don't think I deserve that, either," he said.

"Sure, maybe not. But it's not about deserving. It's just about love. Whether you're worthy of it or not, whether I'm worthy of it… I love you. You changed me. It's the most amazing thing, Zack. And I just wish… I wish I could have done the same for you. I wish like hell I could have set you free," she said, her chest heaving on a sob, "because you did it for me."

"Grace," he said, his voice rough, "I need to show you something."

He held his hand out and she took it, lacing her fingers through his. The rush of heat and relief that filled her was so intense her knees nearly buckled. She held onto him tight, savored the feel of his skin against hers.

It was like being home.

They walked into the next room, where people were congregating around the newest piece.

"That's the one," she said. "The one from the studio that you hated."

"I didn't know what it was supposed to be."

The figure was standing straight. But his hand wasn't empty now. There was a heart there. Glossy and red, the only real color she'd ever seen in his work before.

"Perfect for the Broken Hearts Foundation, I guess," he said, his voice rough.

She tuned to look at him. "It wasn't just because of that, was it?"

He shook his head. "I sort of had an epiphany or some kind of BS like that."

She laughed. "You really hate this feelings stuff, don't you?"

"I really flippin' do."

"It's okay. Tell me your epiphany and we'll never speak of it again." She leaned into him, tightening her hold on him.

"I didn't think I had a heart left, Grace. I thought it was broken into pieces so small…that it was dust. And then you got in my taxi, and in my bed, and under my skin, and it turns out I have all those damn feelings that I was so much happier living without."

"You were happier without them? And you had feelings?"

"I wasn't really happier. It's like you said…it was nothing, and it was comfortable. Because it was better than pain and risk and all that other stuff I just…didn't want to deal with. And hell yeah, I have feelings for you." He turned to face her, his eyes blazing. "I have a lot of fucking feelings for you."

"You're a poet, Zack," she said, a tear running down her cheek.

"No, just an artist. Just a guy. And I love you, Grace. That's really scary to me. Because figuring out I still had a heart to break was one thing, but deciding that I wanted to love something again? I'm shaking."

"It's scary, even for me," she said, her throat tightening, her heart racing. "I can't imagine how it is for you."

"I realized something."

"What's that?"

"That working with glass sucks. And I burned myself."

She laughed and leaned against his shoulder. "Okay, anything else?"

"Yes. I have a choice I have to make. Loving someone when they're gone is one of the most painful things I can even imagine. It's something I live with every day, and even though the sharpness of it has faded, and will keep fading, it will never go away."

"I understand that," she said. "I would never expect it to. I would never ask you to dishonor your past that way."

"I know," he said. "But the biggest thing I realized was

this. I didn't have a choice when I lost Tally. I can't change my thinking, be braver, be different, and have her back. But I chose to lose you, Grace. I chose fear over you and that… that's stupid. Because this is the other thing…"

"You're filled with revelations."

"I am. The other thing is that I have this chance. This chance to feel again. To love again. To have the most beautiful things in life again. And I was just going to choose fear instead. And that was a dumb-ass idea. I had a lot of reasons, a lot of other things I pushed in front of the fear so I could pretend it wasn't just that I was scared. I failed Steph. I didn't protect my family. But deep down I know that's not true. I know Steph and I just didn't want to make our marriage work, to be honest. Not without Tally. And it was pretty damn mutual. We changed too much to come back together in the end. It wasn't all on me, but it was sure convenient when I was staring down another relationship to make it all about me. Because who wants to admit they're just a quivering coward? I sure as hell don't, but it's the truth."

"Zack…"

"I do love you, Grace. With all my heart. That heart," he said, pointing to the shining glass representation, "and this one." He took her hand and put it on his chest. "And I know I'm not the ideal man. I come complete with a whole set of matching baggage. I live mainly in the country. I don't have what you'd call 'manners.' I'm not 'very pleasant' and I don't 'work well with others.' But… I damn well love you with everything I have in me. I even found some more things in me I didn't know I had left just so I could love you more. I don't bring a whole lot to the table. Just me. And I hope that's enough. I hope you still love me, too."

She turned and wrapped her arms around his neck, tilting her head up and kissing him for all she was worth, with everyone around them watching. And she didn't even care. She was bleeding emotion all over the damn place.

Ice bitch could take a seat. She was no longer needed.

"Yes, you idiot," she said when they parted. "I love you. I really, really love you. The kind where…the place we live doesn't matter and the fact that you're borderline charmless is okay."

He laughed. "Borderline charmless? What the hell, woman. I charmed you out of your panties fast enough."

"You know what I mean."

"Yeah, I do. I'm a moody bastard when I have to wear a tie."

"And I don't even care!"

"Dear Lord, you *do* love me."

"I really do. For me. Not because I'm trying to make up for someone else. So what do we do now?"

He tightened his hold on her. "Well, what are you planning on doing for work?"

"I was thinking I would go into business for myself."

"So you're going to work a lot and make no money?"

She laughed. "Basically."

"I'm in," he said. "And you realize that working remotely might be very possible. And that I have a ranch in Pine Ridge Falls. And you have an apartment here…so…"

"Are you suggesting we live in two places?"

"Why not?" he asked. "Though, if you want to live here… I could…"

"No, Zack. That's part of you. An important part. I want to share in all of it. The good, the bad and the ugly. That's how relationships work. Real ones, anyway."

"That's what I want," he said. "With you."

"You have it."

Zack looked down at Grace, his heart ready to burst. There had never been a woman like her. And she loved him. For a moment, all the bad stuff fell away, and he knew that no matter how hard things had been, he was the luckiest man on earth.

Because he had another chance. Because he had her.

Having her here was best of all. Sharing his past, his pain, and his future and hope, with her.

"I'm ready," he said, looking around the room, at all the pieces of his past, pieces that would always be with him. Pieces that felt manageable now.

"For?"

"Life," he said. "Let's go live it together."

Epilogue

Grace Song looked out the kitchen window and at the light that was still on in the barn across the yard. Zack was working late again. He'd been doing that a lot the past couple of weeks.

She didn't mind, because when he went through those phases he inevitably emerged with an incredible piece of art. Which she appreciated both because she loved the artwork, and because her new financial consulting company was just getting off the ground, and was not terribly steady at the moment.

Her father found it incredibly funny that the artist was the one who supported them. When he wasn't worrying about it.

The past year had been the best of her life. She was learning to love the country. Pine Ridge Falls was a unique town with even more unique people, and the quiet was addicting. And she liked to think Zack was learning to love New York during the time they spent there.

She walked out the front door and onto the porch, breathing in the sweet air, heavy with wood and hay, before making her way across the lawn and to the barn. She knocked, because she always felt like she was intruding on his thoughts when she saw artwork he wasn't ready to display.

"Come in."

She did. He was standing in the center of the barn, barefoot and shirtless, next to the work bench. "I'm finished now," he said. "So your timing is perfect."

"Let's see it." There was no giant new statue taking up all the free space, which was unusual.

"Okay," he said, turning to face her, something small and glittering in his hand.

"What did you do?"

"I learned a new trick. And it took a long damn time."

She moved over to him, her breath catching when she saw what he was holding. "Zack…"

"It's what you think it is." He held his hand out flat, the gold, intricately carved band shimmering in the light. Foxes, she noticed. Foxes on a gold band. No one but Zack.

But that wasn't the best part. It was the ruby at the center, cut in the shape of a heart. "That moment I made the heart figure…it was always leading to this moment." He didn't get down on one knee. He stood, offering his heart. Just like his art piece. And that made it even better. "Will you marry me?"

"Yes, Zach," she said, her throat tightening. "Yes, I will."

"I love you," he said. "You know that, right?"

"I do. Because you show me every day."

"And I promise to keep showing you, every day after this one. Forever."

* * * * *